GROUNDED

About the author

Sheena Wilkinson's first novel, *Taking Flight*, was the winner of two Bisto Children's Book of the Year Awards: the Children's Choice Award and the Honour Award for Fiction, as well as a White Raven Award from the International Youth Library and a place on the iBbY Honour List 2012.

Sheena teaches English in Belfast and lives in County Down.

GROUNDED

Sheena Wilkinson

Fitzhenry & Whiteside

Published in Canada by Fitzhenry & Whiteside, 195 Allstate Parkway, Markham, ON, L3R 4T8
www.fitzhenry.ca
Published in the U.S. by Fitzhenry & Whiteside, 311 Washington Street, Brighton, Massachusetts 02135

First published 2012 by Little Island, an imprint of New Island

5 4 3 2 1

We acknowledge with thanks the Canada Council for the Arts, and the Ontario Arts Council for their support of our publishing program. We acknowledge the financial support of the Government of Canada through the Canada Book Fund (CBF) for our publishing activities.

 Canada Council   Conseil des Arts
for the Arts   du Canada

Library and Archives Canada Cataloguing in Publication
ISBN 978-1-55455-329-7
Data available on file

Publisher Cataloging-in-Publication Data (U.S.)
ISBN 978-1-55455-329-7
Data available on file

Cover design by Daniel Choi
Interior design by Someday

Printed in Canada by Friesens

For my sister Rhona, who wanted to know what happened next, and made me find out.

Acknowledgements

More than ever, I have been grateful for the practical and literary support which made the writing of this novel possible.

I am indebted to the Arts Council of Northern Ireland for their generous ACES award, which has given me fantastic opportunities. In 2011 I was lucky enough to make two visits to the Tyrone Guthrie Centre, Annaghmakerrig, where a month's work seems to get done in a day. Lee Weatherly's mentoring support was invaluable as always – she has taught me more than she'll ever know. Other readers also commented on the first draft with honesty and insight – thank you, Susanne, Elaine, Rhona and Julie. Thanks to everyone at Lighthouse Ireland for their openness and generosity.

Talking to readers, especially teen readers, about *Taking Flight* has been one of the greatest joys of becoming a "real" writer: thanks to everybody who took the story and characters to heart – it's safe to say that without their enthusiasm, *Grounded* would never even have been thought of. Special thanks to the reading groups at St. Dominic's High School, Belfast and Trinity Comprehensive School, Ballymun, for sharing their ideas about the characters' futures. Now you can find out what really happened!

A year ago I knew perhaps two or three people in the Irish children's literature world. Now that world, CBI and beyond, has welcomed me and made me feel part of something very friendly and important: thank you all.

Similarly, the UK chapter of SCBWI has introduced me to wonderful writers and enthusiasts; a huge thanks to Keren David for her championing of *Taking Flight* in corners of the internet far too cool for me.

Anne and Patrick Dornan and my wonderful parents, Poppy and John Kerr, freed me from much domestic drudgery. Having a novel to finish is a great excuse never to clean, garden, cook, or iron again. The staff at Bilbo's Bistro in Castlewellan are very patient about me sitting in the corner scribbling, and have always made me and my notebooks welcome. (I do buy copious amounts of tea. And food.) Scott Naismith, my principal at Methodist College, has been unfailingly supportive of my "other" career, and without his generous attitude I would not have been able to say yes to half the fun things I've been invited to take part in. The generous hospitality of Tony and Jennifer Williams and Juliet Bressan on my Dublin trips makes being away from home a pleasure. It's only possible for me to go off and do those things knowing that the staff of Mount Pleasant Trekking Centre are there to look after my pony Songbird in my absence, and I'm extremely grateful, especially to Sharon and Nicole.

A huge thanks to Siobhán Parkinson and Elaina O'Neill for commissioning *Grounded* and being so great to work with, once again; and, last but never least, to my lovely agent Faith O'Grady, without whose "yes" back in 2009 Declan and Seaneen would never have found so many friends.

I. FLYING

I.

At first it looks like a ghost, lurching towards us out of the early-morning grey mist that's hanging over the main road above the estate. Or maybe I just see it that way because I'm nervous anyway, thinking of what a big day this is.

Seaneen's hand tightens in mine. "What the – ?"

It's not a ghost. It's a kid, off his head. He staggers into the road and nearly falls. Seaneen breaks away from me.

"Seaneen! Leave it!"

She ignores me. Goes after the kid and steadies him with her arm. I sigh and set my bag down on the footpath. It's got all my posh riding clothes in it and it's heavy. "Seaneen, we'll miss the bus!"

Seaneen comes back, half-dragging the kid with her. He's about fourteen, eyes huge and bleary in a thin face, his hoodie wet and rumpled. There's puke on his trainers. "Where do you live?" Seaneen asks him, keeping hold of his arm. He can hardly stand.

He makes a visible effort to focus. "T'con Pade," he slurs.

Seaneen turns to me. "Did he say Tirconnell Parade?"

"Dunno." I live in Tirconnell Parade. I've never seen this kid before but then I don't know half the wee hoodlums on the estate.

"We'd better take him home," Seaneen says. "If he falls into the road again he could get knocked down."

"Seaneen! We haven't got time." And this kid's got nothing to do with us. Not my fault he's staggering around off his head at seven o'clock in the morning.

She stares at me. "Declan, it's only a horse show. Some things are more important."

"Point him in the right direction. He'll be OK when he's off the main road." I check the time on my phone. "Look, we have four minutes to get the bus!"

Seaneen shakes her head. "You go ahead," she says. The kid's body jackknifes and he pukes. I step back. Seaneen doesn't flinch. "Come on," she says to him. "Let's get you home."

I turn away and start running towards the bus stop.

2.

"Last to jump, Declan Kelly on Flight of Fancy."

The gate into the arena swings open and we enter at a trot. Flight feels bold and ready for anything, pulling and snorting already, keen to be off around the jumps again. I lean down and run my hand over his sweaty shoulder. "Steady," I whisper. His red ears flick back at my voice.

The bell rings and we're off. I love jumping against the clock. It's not just galloping; it's all control and split-second timing and courage – mine and Flight's. Only Patrick Scott has been clear so far and he played it fast but safe, going the long way around from number five to number six. We *have* to cut the corner and take the risk.

Flight knows what I want. The slightest shift of my weight is all it takes. He turns for me in mid-air so that we hit the ground just right for the short cut.

"Come on, boy." The jump flies at us sooner than I expect, and he gathers himself before launching with a grunt from his powerful back legs. We seem to hover for ages over red and white poles. Like flying.

Seaneen's face materializes in the crowd, eyes wide. My focus wobbles. A pole rattles.

The crowd gasps; I hold my breath, waiting for the thud. Silence. I lean forward and give Flight his head and he stretches out his neck and gallops through the finish so fast that the few people hanging around the gate draw back in alarm. I have to circle to get him back in control, just as the announcer says, "And that's clear in 39.17 seconds for Declan Kelly on Flight of Fancy. And that's the winner here today."

"Yes!" I pat Flight's neck.

Everybody I know seems to be waiting outside the gate. Because it's not just another horse show. This is Balmoral, the biggest show Flight and I have ever done. "Fair play to you, Kelly," Patrick Scott says, holding out his hand. "I'll get you next time."

Everybody from the stables is here: Cam and her girlfriend, Pippa; my cousin Vicky who owns Flight, all jumping up and down and hugging each other. They press forwards. Vicky flings her arms around Flight's neck. "Clever horse." She looks up at me. "I could never have done that."

"I know." I lean forward to stroke Flight's neck and to hide my ridiculous ear-splitting grin. I look around for Seaneen.

"Declan!" She appears at Flight's shoulder, conspicuous among the horsey crowd in her denim shorts and black tights. "I made it." She grins, her green eyes sparkling. I want to reach down and hug her but

Flight's too skittery. He tries to rub his sweaty head on Seaneen's chest and she steps sideways in alarm. He shakes flecks of foamy slobber over her and she grimaces but then stretches out her hand to pet his neck, which is so wet the chestnut hairs are dark brown.

"I was scared you'd get wrecked," she says. "Those jumps were the size of houses."

I laugh. I feel like I could do anything. Jump a house. Fly.

There's a lot of standing around getting our prizes – a trophy and a fancy rug for Flight – and then posing for photos, which makes me feel weird. Me in the *Ulster Tatler*!

Then the lap of honour, Flight leading, the red winner's sash clashing with his coat, his hooves pounding the turf even though he must be exhausted. As we pass the gate for the second time I see Vicky and Cam talking to a tall, grey-haired man in a faded Barbour over white trousers. It's Fintan Brady, one of the best jumpers in Ireland. And he's looking at *me*. I wonder what they're saying.

When we ride out of the ring for the last time I dismount. Flight shakes himself like a dog and biffs me with his nose. "Come on," I say, pulling the reins over his head. It's the first thing Cam ever taught me – you look after your horse first. And anyway, I want to be on my own with Flight for a bit. I walk him around to the car park. It's full of trailers and trucks with registrations from all over the country. I dismount and tie him to Cam's truck. Nobody's around. I go through the usual routine: untacking, washing, rubbing down, all the time thrilling inside.

We won.

We're the champions.

We *belong*.

Because I've always felt like an outsider in this world. Starting late, coming from a dodgy estate, having the wrong accent, not having my own horse. Even getting my National Diploma in horse care at college hasn't made me feel I belonged as much as winning at Balmoral.

I pour cool water over Flight's hot body and start to walk him around in the sun. "You *are* mine, really," I tell him, scratching behind his ear in the place he likes. Vicky hasn't ridden him for months. She broke her leg last summer and never got her nerve back. In my mind, in my dreams, in every way that counts, Flight's mine. And when Vicky goes to university maybe he'll be even more mine. I buckle on his cooler rug and lead him up the ramp into the cool quiet truck. He blows down through his nostrils and noses at his hay net. "You're the best horse in the world," I tell him.

Flight stretches his head around and bites at an itch on his belly through the fine fleece of his rug, then settles down to pulling strands of hay from the net. I pull his long red ears and he twitches them away.

Around us the show is still going on. An ice-cream truck jingles. I should go and talk to people but I want to stay here with Flight. I climb through into the tiny living area in front of the horses' bit of the truck, open the wee fridge and take out a cold can of Coke. I press it against my burning cheek.

"Dec? Hiya."

I swing around. Scaneen stands outside peering up through the small door, the sun glinting on her honey-coloured curls. She has her hands dug into the pockets of her tight shorts and her black top shows off her lovely tits and her freckly white cleavage. She swings herself up the steep steps. I reach out for her hand and pull her in. The door slams behind her.

Seaneen takes the Coke from my hand and takes a slug. She grins and looks around the tiny space. "Cozy," she says. "Like a wee trailer."

The air in the truck fizzes. Flight shifts and sighs behind the barrier. Further away the sounds of the show drift by – announcements, horses neighing and, beyond that, the traffic rumbling past on the Lisburn Road.

Seaneen sets down the Coke and puts her hand on my leg. "I'm so proud of you," she says. She leans over and nuzzles at me with her lips. Her curls tickle my face. She runs her hand up inside my white shirt. My flesh tingles at her touch. "Hmm," she says. "Those clothes."

"I'm all sweaty."

"I know. It's dead sexy." She giggles and moves across on top of me, straddling me, her leg brushing against my crotch.

"I'm glad you came," I say. "You brought me luck."

"I nearly didn't make it," she says. She blows a stray curl off her face. "That boy, he's called Cian, and guess what? He lives in Gran's old house. His –"

"Don't talk about him." I pull her towards me, and kiss her properly. Her warm body against me is nearly as lovely as the feeling of winning.

Until the knock on the truck door.

Seaneen pulls away.

"Coming!" I yell. I jump up, pull my clothes into some kind of order, and flick the door open. It's probably Cam, wanting to get on the road back to the stables.

But it's Vicky and Fintan Brady. Oh my God. Fintan Brady has a big yard in Wexford. Sometimes he takes on a talented young rider to work for him, help bring on his novice horses. As soon as I see him I know what he's here for. He's going to offer me a job. Behind me I can feel Seaneen, all warm and laughing. I love her, but I know I'd leave her to go to Wexford.

"Declan," Vicky says. "This is Fintan Brady."

"I know." I give Brady a quick smile. I hope I don't look too dishevelled.

"He wants to buy Flight."

II. LEAVING

I.

Flight hasn't got a clue. Vicky leads him out of his stable and up the ramp into the white truck and he swings up, all bizz, ears pricked, big eyes shining as he looks around the yard. He doesn't know it's for the last time. He probably thinks he's going to a show.

I stand at the door of the barn and pick at a loose thread on some random headcollar I'm holding.

Vicky doesn't come out for ages. I suppose she's taking her time saying goodbye, probably crying into his neck. Or not. 'Cause she's the one selling him.

"Declan." Cam stops beside me, leading one of her young Welsh ponies, who sniffs hopefully at my pocket. "It's a good home. You'll probably see him jumping in Dublin someday."

I shrug like I'm not bothered.

But Cam knows me too well. "She couldn't keep him, Declan. You know that."

"Hmm." I rub the pony's tiny black velvet nose.

I do kind of know. The part of me that's eighteen,

finished college, that's ridden and worked with dozens of horses over the last two years knows. It's just that inside there's this other me, jumping up and down and screaming *not fair*.

Cam scratches the black pony's neck and he stretches out his head and neighs. From inside the truck comes an answering call.

"There'll be other horses," Cam says. "There's always other horses."

Vicky comes out of the groom's door, landing carefully on her bad leg, and then she and Brady go around the back and start closing up the ramp.

I don't want to see the truck driving away, its Wexford number plates reminding me how far away he's going, and I don't want to talk to Vicky or any of the Saturday pupils hanging around gawking, so I say, "Right, I'd better get on with some work," and turn and walk into the barn, dumping the headcollar over a hook on the back of the door.

It's dark and cool in here, empty like it always is in summer when the horses are mostly out in the fields. Only bad-tempered Willow, a fourteen-two palomino grade A showjumper is standing in, because Lara, his owner, is jumping him tonight and doesn't want him all blown up with grass. He puts his ears back as usual as I pass his door.

The door of Flight's stable is open. His bed's dirty, even though he was only standing in for a couple of hours waiting for the truck. Might as well muck it out. In fact, I might as well clear the bed out completely. Then I can wash it down and it'll all be ready for whatever horse uses it next.

I take a fork and the biggest wheelbarrow and get started. It's a hard job, but years of working with horses have made me quick and strong. Other lads around the estate take the piss and say horses are gay, but they shut up when they feel the strength in my arms. Not that I've had to hit anybody for a long time. I yank the fork hard into the bottom of the bed and it breaks open into a damp dark blur. The ammonia smell of old piss catches my eyes. I fill two wheelbarrows, getting into a rhythm that stops me thinking. Spick and Span, the Jack Russell pups Pippa bought Cam for her thirtieth birthday, dash in and out, fighting over clumps of dried-out dung.

A shadow falls across the doorway.

"I can't believe you're doing that *already*," Vicky's voice says.

I straighten up, wipe my hand across my sweaty face and look at her. She's playing with her car keys. "It needs done," I say and brush some shavings into a pile.

Vicky leans against the door and sighs. Why's she still hanging around? Flight's gone. She's got her own car parked outside, eighteenth birthday present from Darling Daddy, so it's not like she has to hang around waiting for a lift. She picks at the brass nameplate – *Flight of Fancy*. "I should unscrew this and take it home," she says.

I go back to my brushing but she hovers, if the very solid Vickyish way she hangs around could be called hovering.

"As a memento. Not just of Flight. My whole *child-hood's* been at this yard."

Crap. Even before the fall that smashed up her leg and her nerve, Vicky never hung out at the yard much. The last few months she's hardly been here at all. First her leg, then her A levels, so that Flight became more and more my horse.

Until she and Darling Daddy sold him for £6,000.

"And people don't *understand*," she natters. "About horses. It's like saying goodbye to a really good friend."

I bend over my brush and wonder if I can fit another few forkfuls of shavings into this load. "Can I get past?"

Vicky pouts and shudders away from the teetering smelly wheelbarrow, then follows me all the way to the muck heap, going over and over all the reasons why her dad "made" her sell Flight.

I tip the wheelbarrow up and watch the soft damp landslide of shavings. Vicky stands at a safe distance, keeping her expensive trainers well away from the muck. I don't think she even knew there was a muck heap before today. I spend ages shaking the upside-down wheelbarrow to get all the loose shavings out.

"Well," she says at last. "I suppose I should go. Last exam on Monday." She grinds her toe into the ground. "Thanks. And ... well ... thanks for your help with Flight. We wouldn't have got such a good price if you hadn't done so well on him."

I concentrate on wheeling the barrow back down the slope of the muck heap.

"Oh," she says before she gets into her wee white Fiat, "you can have the name plate. I mean – I thought you'd like it."

Back at the empty stable I unscrew the name plate. But I don't know if I'll bother bringing it home. I want Flight, not a bit of brass.

* * *

"Declan?" Cam looks around the door of the tack room where I'm hanging up the bridles from the lesson she's just taken. "Do you want a lift home?"

"I've got the bike," I say.

"Throw it in the back of the jeep if you like."

"Nah, it's OK."

She picks at a grassy slobber I've missed on Magic's bit. "Declan, people change, lose interest; it's not a crime. Not everybody's as obsessed as you."

Interest. Like horses are just a *hobby.*

"And it's a fantastic home. Fintan Brady's got one of the best –"

"I *know.*"

I wish she'd go but she starts fussing around a pile of saddlecloths that have fallen onto the ground.

"Would you rather Lara'd bought him?"

"God, no." When there'd been talk of Lara buying Flight I'd thought I'd have to steal him and run away with him. Flight hundreds of miles away is terrible but Flight here, owned by that bitch, would be a million times worse. Thank God when she tried him out Flight tanked around the school and then bucked her off.

"Heard about any of those jobs yet?" Cam spits on her hand and rubs it over one of the saddlecloths to wipe the hairs off.

I shake my head. In the last two weeks I've applied for seventeen jobs with horses. Three down south, the rest in England. Sometimes they don't even email you back. Those that did said they were looking for more experience.

"You know there's always your job here," Cam says. "Jim's not fit for the heavy work now. And he's too big to help me back the Welsh ponies next spring."

Two years ago the height of my ambition would have been to work here. It's a great wee yard and I've learned as much from Cam as I did at college. But I want to be a groom in a proper jumping yard where we drive off to competitions in a big silver truck with our logo on the side, where I have the chance to ride wonderful horses, like Flight. To bring on talented young horses. To recapture that last amazing jump-off. To be part of that world all the time, even just as a groom. I can't stay here without Flight.

"It's just … I think I should get away. Get more experience." The best bit of my course was the ten weeks I spent in a jumping yard in Wicklow. Not just the work, which was so hard I used to fall into bed about nine o'clock every night, but the hanging out with the other lads and being away from home. I missed Seaneen and Flight but nothing else.

"Yes," she says. "You're right. Go while you have the chance." Her voice is a bit sad. Cam was working abroad when her parents were killed in a car crash and she came home to take over the farm, turning it into a livery yard, doing a few lessons. I don't think she's had more than a day away from it ever since except for the odd three-day show. Though she takes a bit more time off now Pippa's on the scene.

"What does Seaneen think about you going away?"

"I haven't said much." I wish Seaneen wanted to go away too but she's a homebody and she's got a good job in a daycare nursery on the Falls Road. "I should head on," I say to change the subject. "See you tomorrow."

"Sure you don't want a lift?"

"No. Thanks." Most of the time I'd jump at the

chance, especially as my bike – a cast-off from my old teacher Mr. Dermott – is a rattly heap, but tonight I welcome the ride. Nobody can get to you when you're on a bike, or make you talk. It's just you and the wind and the leg-killing, mind-numbing slog.

But all the way home, though I try not to think, my thoughts swoop and dive with the bike. Whooshing downhill, the air still warm and the fields glowing, I can push the ache of never seeing Flight again to the edges of my mind. I convince myself he's just a horse. If I'm going to work with horses I'll have to get used to seeing them go. And it's daft to get hung up on other people's horses that are bought and sold on a whim. The next horse I get to care about will be *mine*. He'll be so talented that people will be begging me to sell, saying I can name my price, but I'll just smile and say he's not for sale; he'll never be for sale. And he'll know me the way Flight knew me, only even better.

And when I get home, maybe there'll be a letter – from the big yard in Kildare, or the small but successful one in Galway. And I'll be miles away from that empty stable.

It's only when I'm urging the stupid heap of junk up the hill to the estate, cars up my arse and fumes up my nose, that reality crashes back in to taunt me. That I'm never going to get a horse of my own. That being one of the best horse-care students at college hasn't led to a single job offer. Vicky's driving home in her brand-new car and I'm dragging myself up the Stewartstown Road on a second-hand pushbike with a stupid lump of brass digging into my back through my backpack.

2.

The estate's quiet, a few kids hanging around Fat Frankie's fish-and-chips shop.

"Oi!" shouts one. "Go into the liquor store for us?"

It's that wee toerag from the other day. Cian or something. He doesn't recognize me. I say no and he calls out, "Be like that, douche!" and gives me the middle finger.

Cycling past Seaneen's house, I keep my head down, but not before noticing that her bedroom light's on. The instinct to be with her, to lick my wounds, is fierce, but I'm trying to wean myself off her. It's going to be hard enough leaving her.

At least Saturday night TV should have Mum safely pinned to the sofa. If I time it right and land in in the middle of one of her shows, then with any luck she'll just give me a quick wave and carry on watching and I won't have to talk.

I go around the back and wheel the bike up the path to the door. She won't let me bring it into the house.

We haven't got a shed so I usually fling an old blanket over it and lean it against the fence, only tonight I can't be bothered.

The kitchen light's on, and two teabags slump on the speckly surface of the countertop. I touch the kettle. Still warm. *Two* teabags? Mum's always bringing whiny women home since she started going to all these support groups.

Sure enough when I open the kitchen door voices come out to meet me. *Boys ... aye, you're right there ... two wee girls ... no bother ... och lovely ...*

I have to go through the living room to get upstairs so I brace myself. I hope it's not Mairéad, Seaneen's mum, who always wants to know far too much about me.

But the woman sitting on the sofa opposite Mum is somebody I've never seen before. Younger than Mum, skinny with big dark eyes in a thin, prettyish face. Blonde hair with reddish roots.

"*There* he is," says Mum, proving that she's been talking about me to this stranger. "Declan, this is Stacey. From across the road."

There's a plate of funsize Twirls between them on the coffee table. I grab this week's *Horse and Hound* out from under it. I've already checked the jobs pages but I can have another look in case I missed anything.

"Irene's house," Mum goes on like I'm interested enough to want details. She turns to Stacey. "Declan's been dating Irene's granddaughter. Over two years."

"Two years,'" says Stacey. She turns to Mum. "Och, at their age." She must think I'm about twelve.

"Seaneen's a lovely girl. She fairly settled you down, didn't she, love?" Mum says, as if I'm a badly trained dog.

This is a load of crap. If I did *settle down* two years ago, while Mum was away drying out, it was mostly because of the horses. And living with my aunt Colette, Vicky's mum. Not that it wasn't brilliant with Seaneen. The two of us would sneak away from school at lunchtimes to "check the house". It was amazing what you could get up to in an empty house in three quarters of an hour. Always in my bedroom, at the back, so Seaneen's nosy old cow of a granny across the street wouldn't catch on to anything.

"Maybe that's what your Cian needs, a nice girl," Mum says.

Cian. So that's who she is.

Stacey sighs and pulls her ponytail tighter. "God, Theresa, it'd take more than that. He's going to end up in Bankside, I swear."

I need to get out before Mum tells this stranger about my two months in Bankside for joyriding. They're getting on like they've been best friends for years instead of minutes. It's a female thing. They do it with words. My mum can say more in a day than I would in a month, especially now she's had all this addiction counselling and she's in touch with her feelings and that.

"I'm going upstairs," I say. "See you." I reach down and snatch a couple of Twirls.

"Not seeing Seaneen tonight?"

I grit my teeth. "No."

Pushing open my bedroom door, it feels like days since I left it this morning. I pull the curtains shut, even though it'll be light for a couple of hours yet, and fling myself on the bed, not bothering to take off my dirty fleece. Usually I love the way the horsey smell travels home with me – sweat and haylage and leather – and works its way into the house. That sweet, dirty smell on my duvet cover is proof that it's not all going to evaporate, that horses are the most real part of my life and I'm only back here for a short time until I get a job and go …

Anywhere. Anywhere that's too far for me to cycle home every night.

I open the magazine and go straight to the jobs pages. But there's nothing I've missed. At the start I was only interested in showjumping yards, but now I'd take pretty much anything. There's one in Scotland that sounds so brilliant – *trailer provided, lots of travelling to shows, own horse welcome* – that I wonder why I didn't circle it last night, until I see the bottom line – *Must have HGV licence.*

I haven't even got my normal driving licence. Seaneen passed her theory last week and has put in for her test. She gets paid more than me.

Usually when I'm fed up, reading *Horse and Hound* cheers me up. Looking at the pages of beautiful horses for sale; imagining buying one of the houses with stables out the back and acres of land. Mum complains about the horsey magazines piling up beside my bed. I say at least it's not porn. But tonight the fantasy doesn't work. The words *HORSES FOR SALE* across the tops of pages just conjure up the white truck driving off with Flight inside. All the pages of events and competitions, the photos of brave, lovely horses stretching themselves over banks and fences and walls jab at the angry bruise inside me. I hate every person in this magazine. All the ones who won't give me a job. All those rich bastards who can do what they want with their horses. Flight was more mine than he was ever Vicky's. He went brilliantly for me. Mine was the voice he'd calm down for if he was in one of his moods. I was the one he'd jumped his heart out for, launching at every obstacle as if he was going to jump out of his skin. The feel of him under me at that last jump-off, faster than flames, responsive, clever and brave, trusting me ...

It's all meaningless now. Because the owner's name on his passport wasn't Declan Kelly. Was never going to be Declan Kelly. *Owner.* Strange word to think of in connection with a living creature. He'll still be on the road now. Wexford's so far away. I hope Brady stops and gives him a drink and lets him stretch his legs. What if he won't go back into the truck for a stranger? He's not the best traveller.

I fling the magazine away. As a distraction it's useless. I almost wish I did have some porn.

It's too early for sleep. I lie on my bed with my hands crossed under my head and though my body's aching from my marathon muck-out, my head's buzzing.

I half-feel like going out and having a few drinks. Only I'm not on drinking terms with anybody around here these days, except Seaneen. Plus I'm working in the morning and I know from experience, mainly in Wicklow, that horses and hangovers don't mix.

To hell with weaning myself off Seaneen. I've had enough goodbyes for one day. I text her: *Are you in? Will I come around?* Without waiting for a reply, I go and have a long, lovely shower with loads of the shower gel

Colette got Mum for Christmas. I wash the smell of horses and my own sweat away, closing my eyes and forgetting everything but the hot needles pricking and soothing my skin. I shave for the first time in a few days and smile at myself in the steamed-up mirror. Working outside so much has made me tanned already, and I don't seem to get spots these days.

Back in my room I find some cleanish clothes. Seaneen's texted back: *Yes Yes xxx*.

★ ★ ★

Seaneen nuzzles into my neck. As always her springy curls make my skin tingle. I smooth them back. The distraction worked. Even tonight, with her mum downstairs screaming at her wee sisters to shut up and go to bed and let her watch *Casualty* in peace, it was lovely.

I don't mean it was *just* a distraction. I sigh and trace the freckles on her bare shoulder with my fingertip.

"You OK?" she says, her lips fluttering against my skin.

"Just Flight going."

Seaneen hasn't a clue about horses but she knows a lot about me. She hugs me – awkwardly, since she's lying half on top of me. "I know," she says. "Missed you."

"I haven't been anywhere. Just work. It's been mad." That's a lie. The yard's been so quiet that I spent most of last week painting fence posts and watching Cam working with her new horse, a gorgeous grey called Spirit. And making the most of the dwindling time with Flight.

She kisses my cheek. "I wasn't complaining. I just missed you."

Seaneen never nags. She doesn't complain that I'm hardly ever home and that, when I am, I'm exhausted and sometimes stink of horses. She doesn't point out that other guys my age are either on welfare, and so have plenty of time for their girlfriends, or else have jobs that pay a hell of a lot more than I get. I look at her, half asleep in her white bed with the pink duvet pulled up over us both. Opposite the bed a shelf full of old teddies grins down at us. Half of them are battered, with eyes missing and ears hanging off, but Seaneen won't get rid of them. Our clothes are all over the floor, my jeans tangled up in Seaneen's yellow spotty bra.

"Seaneen?"

"Hmm?" She sounds half asleep.

"Nothing." I pull her closer to me. Breathe in her warmth and her biscuity, perfumey, slightly sweaty smell. "Just ... you're the nicest person I know."

She giggles. "Ah, Declan, that's so sweet."

It's true though, and right now, looking down at her curls spread out over my chest, her freckled arm lying across me, I know that I want to stay here with her nearly as much as I want to go away. But only nearly.

I wish I wasn't going to break her heart.

3.

It's horrible at the yard without Flight looking over his stable door or lifting his head from grazing when I call his name. Last night, after I left Seaneen's, I lay awake for hours, my mind zooming all over the place, and today my eyes are gritty. And I have to go out after work to Seaneen's friend Bronagh's eighteenth.

I swill out Flight's old stable and leave the door open for it to dry. Cam sees me but doesn't say anything. But later she lets me ride Spirit. He's huge, a beautiful dappled grey, and she's never let me on him before. The power and lift and bounce of him, the strength and willingness of a good horse, are fantastic. He's as good a horse as Flight, but like Flight he belongs to somebody else so I'm not going to let myself like him too much. When I turn him out into his field behind the yard I don't wait and watch him roll and drink and graze like I always did with Flight. I close the gate and walk away and don't look back.

As I'm throwing my leg over my bike my phone rings. I check the display but it's an unfamiliar number. I press the green button, still straddling the bike.

"Hello?"

"Declan Kelly?" A man's voice, posh, semi-familiar. "Terry Mullan here."

"Oh." Terry was in charge of my horse-care course. A teacher's never phoned me before.

"Bit of news for you," he goes on, and I get off the bike properly and lean against the fence of the sand-school. "Are you sorted out yet?"

"Sorted?"

"With a job?"

"Oh!" I look around the yard that's as familiar as my own street. The whitewashed buildings and the red doors Jim and I repainted last week. "Well, I've applied for loads but –"

"Excellent, excellent. Now, how would you feel about Germany?"

"*Germany*?"

"Hans Peter Hilgenberg's yard. You know him?"

"I saw him at the Dublin Show last year."

"He's looking for a groom. We've sent students to him before, and his yard manager, Anneliese, has emailed to ask if I would recommend someone. They like Irish grooms. Wasn't sure you'd want to go so far from home but –"

"Yes."

Mullan laughs. "I haven't given you any details yet."

It's a job. It's in another country. And Hans-Peter Hilgenberg is an international showjumper. What more do I need to know? An image of Seaneen flashes into my head but I blot it out.

"When can I start?"

"Now look, before you get too excited – there's not a lot of money involved. You'll be starting at the bottom. But you'll learn a lot and it could lead on to something else."

"No, it's perfect. But why me?"

He laughs again. "Well, it wasn't hard. No point sending anyone who isn't going to make the most of it."

Mullan goes on a bit about emailing me the details and getting me to phone this Anneliese but all I can think is a great big YES that fills the sky. By the time I slip my phone back in my pocket I'm halfway to Germany in my mind. Early July, Mullan said. One month from now.

I cycle out of the yard, passing Cam's jeep on her way back in from giving Jim a lift home because his car's off the road. She rolls down the window.

"You've cheered up! Spirit go well?"

Spirit? "Oh – yes. Fantastic." I can't tell her yet. I want to hold it inside me for a bit, until I see it in writing or speak to what's her name, Anneliese. I can't speak German. Will they speak English?

I tell Cam I'll see her in the morning but not too early because I'm going to a party tonight, and start pedalling again. I hardly see the drumlins and hedges and the shorn straggles of sheep clinging to hillsides. I see horses in neat paddocks and me travelling all around Europe. Riding all kinds of brilliant German horses. Horses like Spirit and Flight. Better.

I won't stay in Germany forever. But when I want to move on, I'll have experience in a top yard; I won't be just some eighteen-year-old. I can apply for any of those jobs in *Horse and Hound*.

A couple of miles from home my phone rings in my back pocket. Normally I'd ignore it but a sudden fear that it could be Mullan again, to say he's sorry but it was a mistake, makes me jump off the bike in a muddy gateway and throw it down while I pull the phone out. Just as I press the green button I see it's Seaneen. And I realize that for the first time in two and a half years something fantastic has happened that I can't tell her. Not yet. It's a weird feeling that makes me have to lean against the gate. "Hiya. What's up?"

A sigh at the other end. "I can't go to Bronagh's party. I'm sick."

"You were OK last night."

She groans. "I *know*. But I woke up feeling bleurgghhh."

"Must be a bug." Working with wee kids she does pick things up. I hope I haven't caught it off her. All that kissing we were doing last night ... "Poor old you. Is your mum looking after you?"

"Hmm. I'm just going to bed."

"OK, babe. Hope you feel better soon." I look down at the churned-up mud beneath me, tracing what looks like a hoofprint with the toe of my boot.

"You can still go to the party," she says.

"No. Sure it wouldn't be the same without you."

Her voice brightens up a bit. "I'll probably be OK tomorrow. I'll text you."

"OK. Take care."

I stuff the phone back in my pocket and stand in the gateway, looking across the fields, enjoying the feeling of not having to hurry. This is the last stretch of road before you hit the suburbs and estates and the fields have a grubby halfway look about them. This one has an old bed lying against the saggy fence, McDonald's wrappers clinging to the barbs of wire, and the gate's half off its hinges and tied up with three different colours of baler twine. At the far end of the field is a derelict barn, a few tin sheds, mostly without roofs, and a grey farmhouse with broken windows catching the light. Something about it makes me shiver – maybe it's the contrast with the perfect German yard in my mind. As I pick up my bike from my gate I think I hear a horse neigh, but when I look back the field is definitely empty. Ghost horse, I think, or more likely I'm just thinking too much about German showjumpers.

Back in my own streets, wishing I had a computer so I could Google Hans-Peter Hilgenberg, I wonder how much it'll cost to fly to Germany and how quickly I can get a passport – I've never had one.

Cian is hanging around the liquor store again, playing with his phone. He looks up when I cycle past but stares at me without recognition, cross-eyed with drink or something else.

* * *

Next evening I take a detour past the library. Haven't been in here since Gran used to take me when I was a wee kid. The librarian gives me a funny look when I ask if I can use a computer, and makes me fill in a form and pay a pound. Then I have to wait for one to be free, even though the girl on it is only wasting time on

Facebook. But at last I can go on to my email and, right enough, there's the info from Mullan, the forwarded email from Anneliese – who writes better English than I do – and a link to the yard's website.

It's even better than I imagined. I lean forwards towards the screen. Lists of competitions and prizes. Pictures of shining champion horses jumping impossible fences. The same horses at home grazing under huge trees. Young horses in an indoor school. An outdoor arena with the kind of jumps I've only ever seen at shows. Hans-Peter Hilgenberg has eight people working for him. For a moment that scares me – eight strangers. Always harder than horses. But if they speak German maybe it'll be easier, in a weird way – they might not expect me to say much.

My phone vibrates in my back pocket and I slip it out cautiously, because there's signs up everywhere saying you aren't allowed phones in the library. I check it under the desk. Seaneen: *Where are you?* I text back: *Library*, which she'll think very strange. But her reply is more huffy than curious: *Thanks for asking, I'm still sick.*

Shit. I haven't texted her all day. I've had a pretty easy day at work; it's never busy on a Monday. I took Spirit out on the farm trail, cleaned a load of tack, fixed a couple of dodgy fence poles and went to the saddler's with Cam. I could easily have texted her.

But sure I'm going away. She'll be better off without me and at least she knows I'm a selfish pig. Because part of me's been kind of glad she's been sick. It's easy to think about Germany when I'm away from her.

Sorry. Thought you'd be at work.

How could I be at work, I've been throwing up all

day!!!!!!!!

Sorry, I text back, scrolling through the list of Hans-Peter Hilgenberg's Grand Prix horses, looking for the one I saw at Dublin last year, a jet-black stallion called Oskar. I calculate that I haven't seen Seaneen for forty-eight hours – which hopefully means *I'm* not going to catch the bug. I feel fine. Better than fine. The only weird feeling inside me is the lovely secret I've been carrying about all day. In one month I'll be flying to Germany. I open a new tab and bring up the passport office to see what I have to do. Seaneen doesn't text back.

4.

Cam hugs me for the first time ever. I can see she doesn't want me to leave even though I know she'll never ever say so. She calls Jim into the barn to tell him.

Jim snorts. "We'll miss you, son." He looks at Cam. "You'll need to get somebody in now. I won't last another winter."

"Jim, you're hardly sixty!" Cam says.

"Ach, I'm not fit to break ponies."

For a crazy moment I don't want to leave at all. Things will happen and change here and I won't be part of it any more.

Wise up, I tell myself; you'll be part of something better.

★ ★ ★

I put off telling Mum until Friday evening. There's never any knowing how she's going to take things. When I first went away to college she wasn't long back from rehab and was still getting over the guilt of letting

her boyfriend Barry McCann throw me down a stair-
case while she was lying drunk in his bed. So if she was
sad about me leaving she didn't dare let on. She knew
how close she was to me walking out on her forever.
And I came back most weekends. Even if I spent all day
at Cam's and the evenings with Seaneen, I still slept in
my own bed; this was still my home. And once Mum
started going out and about a bit more on the estate
and making new friends, she liked being able to say,
"Our Declan's at college." Better than saying, "Our
Declan's in Bankside." So maybe she'll be proud of me
now. "Our Declan's away in Germany working in a big
showjumping yard. He was picked out of all the ones in
his course because he was the best." I put the words into
her mouth but I'm not sure how well they fit. I know
she'd rather I stayed at home. When I got back from
college she'd got me some horsey channels on Sky as a
surprise and she'd had my bedroom painted.

"*Germany?*" She says it like it's another planet, and
shakes her head so her earrings swing. I've waited until
after tea. I even did the dishes and made her a cup of tea.
Two years ago news like this would have sent her to the
vodka cupboard, but there is no vodka cupboard now.
Still, she lights a cigarette from the one she's just finished.

"Sure you have a job with Cam." She inhales deeply
and frowns.

"Cam's is great, but – och, Mum! Are you not
pleased for me? I got picked out of everybody. All those
farmers' daughters and Pony Clubbers. People who've
been riding since they could walk. But they wanted
me."

"Och, son, I am proud! 'Course I am." She looks

up at the photo on the wall – me in a suit getting my certificate, with her and Seaneen grinning beside me. "But it's awful far. You've never been out of Ireland."

"I went on a day trip to Scotland with Gran," I say, remembering getting up at five o'clock and feeling sick on the boat. How long will it take to get to Germany? Will I be able to come back for Christmas? Horses don't get Christmas off.

"I'll have to tell Stacey." For a moment I think, who the hell's Stacey? Until I remember it's her new best friend.

"*She*'s hardly going to be interested. She met me for, like, two seconds."

"No, but you don't understand,' Mum says. She lowers her voice as if Stacey's in the next room instead of over the street. "You see her Cian – he's got a few *issues*. That's why they were put out of Portadown. He annoyed the wrong people." She flicks her ash into the ashtray.

"So?"

"Well, I've told her you used to be a bit – you know, wild when you were his age."

"Thanks, Mum."

"Och, son, it's just to make her feel better. You know – seeing how well you turned out might give her a bit of hope. She's at her wit's end with him."

"So what's he done?" I don't give a shit about Cian but letting Mum blather on about him's better than her talking about how far away Germany is.

"Oh," – she waves her cigarette in the air – "drinking, drugs, skipping school."

"*I* never did drugs."

She could say, no, you were too busy stealing cars,

but to be fair to her she doesn't. She lights another cigarette and says, "Stacey had him when she was fifteen. She's two wee girls now and they're no bother, but that Cian … he was in care for a bit when he was younger 'cause she couldn't cope with him."

"Look, Mum, I have to go and tell Seaneen." I try to say her name like it's no big deal but my stomach contracts.

"Oh?" Mum manages to make it sound like a question.

On the way to Seaneen's I text Colette and Vicky, a few people from college and the lads in Wicklow. People who'll be glad for me. I don't know Mr. Dermott's number but I could email him at the school. Maybe it's a bit sappy, telling a teacher, but if it hadn't been for Dermie shoving his oar in and helping me to get to college I'd be on welfare now. Or worse.

The Brogans' crappy red Proton isn't parked outside, which makes me hope Seaneen's on her own, but Mairéad answers the door. She gives me a funny look. She calls over her shoulder, "Seaneen!" and leaves me standing on the doorstep.

Seaneen appears at the door in her nursery uniform of lilac sweatshirt and black trousers. Not the most attractive outfit.

"What's up with your mum?"

Seaneen shakes her head. "She's just … well, she thinks you could have been a bit more concerned."

"About what?" Then I remember she's been sick. "Sorry. You do look a bit rough." Even her curls look lank and her eyes are kind of puffy. But if she's back at work she must be OK.

"Thanks."

"Look – can I come in? I've got" – may as well get this over, and maybe the fact that she's a bit pissed off with me anyway will make it easier – "something I have to tell you."

"Yeah, me too." She turns and leads the way up the stairs.

My insides flip over as I follow her. Is Seaneen about to dump *me*? So much for me worrying about breaking her heart!

Seaneen's room doesn't feel as friendly as it did last Saturday night. She sits on the bed and picks up a cushion. She hugs it. She looks young and worried and fragile. But Seaneen's never fragile.

I sit down opposite her and put my hands on her shoulders. They're rigid. "Seaneen, just tell me. It's OK." I'm scared now. Is she really sick or something?

She chews her lip and doesn't look up.

"Come on, babe."

She takes a deep breath and looks up at me and her big green eyes are sparkly with tears. "Declan, I'm pregnant."

III. RUNNING

I.

For a long time I can't speak. When I do manage to drag some words out they actually hurt, like they're scraping my throat. "Are you sure?"

She nods. "I missed two periods. I thought it was stress – the exams and Gran dying and all. But then on Sunday morning I was sick. And the next day. Every day." She makes a face. "And I feel … I dunno … dead weird. Tired. Everything tastes funny. So I did a test. And I was. Am."

She doesn't say the word again.

I get up and walk to the window. It's a gorgeous evening. Seaneen's wee sisters are out on their trampoline in the front garden. *Mummy, Saoirse hit me! Mummy, I never!*

I lean my head against the cold glass. If I don't turn around, it won't be true. Seaneen will say it's a joke.

"Declan?"

I sense her getting up and coming over. Feel her press herself against my back. The firm softness of her. The tickle of her curls. Her tears hot on the back of my neck. I know I have to turn around and hug her, tell her it'll be OK.

But I can't.

I'm frozen to the glass. And the moment I unfreeze is the moment it becomes true. Germany hovers in the air outside the window and fades away like the mirage it always was.

Seaneen's hand on my shoulder. "For God's sake, Declan, *say* something! You're scaring me here."

"*I'm* scaring *you*?" I remember Mairéad being such a cow at the door. "Have you told your mum?"

"She guessed when I was sick. She was the same way with the twins."

I swing around with a sudden twist of hope. "Is it definitely mine?"

Seaneen's eyes widen. "You –" She steps back, lifts her hand and slaps my face.

Which gives me the excuse I need to get out of that room with its stupid one-eyed teddies, down the stairs and out into the street. And to start running.

At the end of Seaneen's street I stop and catch my breath. I can either turn into my own street or keep going.

I keep going. Slower now. It's not like anybody's chasing me. I can't imagine Seaneen running down the street after me, though I wouldn't put it past that Mairéad.

Pregnant. A baby. A bloody *baby*. If I keep on walking it won't be true. And I could keep on. Walk down the main road, into town. Go to the docks. Get on a boat. Where do they go – Liverpool? Scotland? Who cares. I can hide out until it's time to go to Germany.

Aye right. I check in my back pocket. Two twenty pound notes and a bit of change. That won't get me far.

But I can't go home.

When I get to the main road I slow down. My throat's raw and aching even though there's nothing to make it like that. Might as well get a couple of cans to wash that feeling away. I push open the convenience store door.

In the fridge in front of the counter there's a display of four-packs of Harp on offer. I grab one and pay for it out of one of the twenties, and I have the top off the first one as I elbow open the door to the street again.

"Oi. Mate. Give us one?"

I swing around, nearly choking on the first cool slurp of beer. It's that bloody Cian, eyes glittering like he's already on something. What kind of kid hangs around a backstreet liquor store on his own on a Friday night, hoping somebody's going to be daft enough to give him a drink? I know I had my moments but …

"You live over the road from me," I tell him.

"So?"

"*So* if you're going to go around scrounging off your neighbours, you need to be nice to them. Here." I don't know why but I peel one of the cans out of the plastic rings that hold them together. "Now get lost."

He doesn't. He tears the top off the can and starts dogging my steps down the main road. Probably got his eye on another can. The sun's still shining even though it's about eight o'clock and if it wasn't for the fact that the wee twerp's only fifteen or something we could nearly be two lads walking down the road enjoying a nice cold beer. But every footstep beats out the word. Pregnant. Pregnant. Pregnant. It's a wonder Cian can't hear it.

I cross the road just before the park and he stays

beside me.

"So where's the party around here then?"

"What? Look, get lost. Go and annoy somebody your own age."

"Aren't you Declan Kelly?" He doesn't wait for an answer but his eyes slide towards the other two cans in my left hand. "Ah, go on."

"You can't have finished that already."

He turns the can upside down and shakes it. A few drops fly out, spraying my jeans.

What the hell. "Here you go then."

Cian grins again. "Cheers." When he smiles his face changes more than most people's do. It's a narrow, watchful face, the reddish hair giving him that foxy look, or maybe it's the way he sneaks around scrounging. A sketchy little urban fox.

And something tells me this kid would do anything with anybody for a free drink. And I shouldn't have given it to him. I haven't forgotten the first time I saw him, even if he has. A voice I don't want to hear – Seaneen's? – whispers in my ear. "Yeah, Declan, not very responsible, is it? For somebody who's going to be a *dad*?"

"Look, wee lad," I say. "Get lost and get a life. You're not getting any more. I haven't *got* any more." I open my own second can and start downing it. The beer hits my stomach with a lovely cold wet slap.

"OK, mate." Cian shrugs. "The night's young." He swaggers back across the road, and leaps the park fence where it's broken down. He holds the can up at arm's length and I'm too far away to see if he spills any when he lands awkwardly. He sits down on a swing and starts drinking, his trainers scuffing at the ground as he makes the swing move.

And for a horrible second it's like looking at myself a couple of years ago. I shiver and finish what's left in my can.

* * *

Some pub in town. Too hot, too noisy with bloody Wimbledon on the big screen, too many people bumping into me, but nobody knows me. I perch on my bar stool and try to catch the barman's eye because my glass is empty. He's running around like a headless chicken, sweat running down his plump pink face. Why would a headless chicken run around anyway?

My phone vibrates in my jeans pocket. Should have turned it off. I suppose it'll be Seaneen. I don't know why she hasn't tried before. I reach around to pry my phone out and wobble on the stool. The barman frowns at me. I give him a dirty look. Don't even know what I'm doing here; the place is full of student douchebags in rugby shirts. I check the phone but it's only a message from Colette. *Well done! So proud of you!!!! xxx*

She taking the piss or what? I hit the button to turn the phone off and slide it back into my pocket, only it slips and hits the floor and I have to go scrabbling around under the bar stool among all the feet to get it. The sticky floor tilts like that time Gran took me on the boat to Scotland and there was a storm. I stay down, breathing out slowly, letting the floor and the beer inside me settle before I risk standing up.

What was I …? Something about a boat? No.

Colette. The phone. What does she mean *proud*? Then

I get it. Oh God. I texted her before. She means Germany.

So much for drinking to forget. It's all swishing around inside my brain, melting it.

I order another pint and a whiskey chaser. An old man's drink, but the beer's not really doing its job. Anyway, I feel like an old man in here with all these students celebrating their exams. An old man whose girlfriend's knocked up.

★ ★ ★

Plenty of people staggering about drunk, not just me. A girl in high-heeled sandals giggles beside me. She has curly hair like Seaneen's. "Hiya," she says. A bottle of something neon-yellow sways in her hands. "Oops," she says. "Have to go to the little ladies'..." She points and wobbles.

A minute or an hour later she's in front of me again. "Wanna come to a party?"

"Nah, that's all right."

"Ah, come on." She leans in close. Her breath smells of curry. She rubs her hand over my hair and kisses me on the mouth. Her mate pulls her away.

★ ★ ★

Cold air on my face; cold bricks at my back. Going to wait here for a bit, leaning against the wall. Should have had a piss before I left the bar. Don't fancy the walk home yet. Crowd of kids jostle past, laughing. Their chips smell lovely.

★ ★ ★

I got myself here so I must know the way home. But I don't think this is it. Lots of taxis. But no money left. If I keep on walking I'll sober up. But I don't want to sober up.

Force my feet forwards. They're trying to go sideways. Cars blare at me.

★ ★ ★

Different road. Quieter. Shops instead of bars. Plenty of places for a wee rest. I piss in an alley. The relief.

★ ★ ★

I lean on the doorbell. Colette pulls the door open and her mouth goes all stretched with shock.

"Declan! What on earth are you …?"

I stare at her. Don't know why I'm here, only that I am here. My legs are rubbery. I sway against the doorframe. It catches my shoulder. "Ouch."

"For God's sake, Declan!" She pulls me in, not gently. My legs remember the way to her kitchen but don't seem able to get any further than the table. Chair. Table. Holding me up between them. I smile at Colette. I love Colette.

But she's cross. "Where have you been to get in that state? Overdoing the celebrating?" she asks. She hugs her nightie around her.

"No no no. No *celebrating*."

Colette shakes her head, goes to the sink and pours out a big glass of cold water. She hands it to me. I hate water but I better drink it, she's that cross. It feels too heavy and cold inside me. Makes me burp.

Oh God. I yank myself up from the table, clamp hand over mouth, sink too far, not going to make it. Fall back into the chair, bend over, the puke bursts out. Manage not to splash the table. The floor, my jeans – not so lucky.

I can't look up and meet Colette's eyes. Oh God, let me die now.

2.

Light splits my head in two. I flick my eyes shut again. Revolting sand-mouthed swallow. I shift my head on the pillow and my stomach reels. If don't move a single muscle, maybe I'll sleep it all off. Wake up feeling OK.

But I can't sleep away Seaneen being pregnant.

"Declan!"

I groan. *Go away, Mum.* I don't have the energy to say it out loud.

"Declan!" Louder. "You can't lie there all day."

Not Mum's voice. Oh God. I remember now. I chance opening one eye. Can you die of embarrassment?

"Colette," I say. "I'm so sorry."

"Hmm. I texted your mum last night so at least she won't be worried. I didn't give details."

I close the eye again. "Thanks."

"I have things to do if you haven't," she says. "So if you want a lift home you need to give yourself a shake."

"I can't. I'm dying."

"It's a hangover. You'll live." I feel something land on the bed and open my eyes to see a pile of clothes – my clothes. Washed and dried. Colette shakes her head at me. "I must say, I never thought you'd be so stupid. That kind of behaviour's not going to do you any good in Germany." She half turns to go out.

"Colette, Seaneen's pregnant."

Colette stops dead and swings around. "Are you sure?"

Funny – that's what I said. I nod and wince.

She comes over and sits on the bed. "Declan," she says. "Could you not have been more careful?"

"We *were*. Well, most of the time."

"What does your mum say?"

"She doesn't know."

"Declan." She sounds really sad. "What about Germany, then?"

I chew my lip.

"Go and have a shower. I've left you out a tooth-brush. I'll go and make some breakfast."

I swallow. "No breakfast."

I drag myself to the bathroom and revive a bit under the shower, though when I bend down to grab the soap I get a head rush and a bit of dry heaving. But I get dressed, trying not to think about how my clothes got off me and into the washing machine. Some things it's as well not to remember. I switch my phone on and as soon as the wee clock icon appears I realize I'm meant to be at work. Shit. I've never missed a day. I ring Cam and tell her I'm sick.

"You must have caught that bug from Seaneen," she says.

"Sorry to let you down. I'll be in tomorrow."

"Don't rush back. I don't want to catch it. Might as well get used to you not being around, eh?"

In the kitchen Colette's squeezing oranges beside the sink and the sweet tang hits me as soon as I walk in. Sitting at the kitchen table brings back snatches of last night that I wish it wouldn't. I can hardly look at Colette. When I lived with her that time she didn't always see me at my best, but nothing on last night's scale. At least Brian, her boyfriend, doesn't seem to be around.

"Colette, I'm sorry about last night. I don't even know why I ended up here."

"Well, I'm glad you did." She can't mean that but the niceness of her saying it makes me suddenly want to cry. I must still be a bit drunk. She passes me over a glass of orange juice. "Here."

"Have you any paracetamol?"

Being Colette, she has a neat selection of painkillers in a plastic box with flowers on it, instead of a mad jumble of boxes and bottles all tumbling out of a cupboard like me and Mum. I remember that box from when I stayed here. I swallow two and take tiny cautious sips of the orange. Why do I do this to myself? I've never been able to drink without suffering. Down in Wicklow some of the lads could drink half the night and be up mucking out at seven, but I found out the hard way that I couldn't.

Colette sets a pot of tea down on the table, and then two mugs, and sits down opposite me. "OK," she says. "Are you going to talk to me about this?"

"You said you had things to do."

"I lied to get you out of bed." She pours out two

mugs of tea.

"What is there to say?"

Colette widens her eyes. "I'd have thought quite a lot. For a start, how's Seaneen?"

I shrug, then have a sudden memory of her saying she's been sick every morning. Imagine feeling like this every day. "She slapped me."

"Slapped you? For violating her honour? Sorry – that's not funny."

"'Cause I asked her was it mine." I take a slow sip of tea. "I know it's mine. Seaneen wouldn't – she's not like that."

"I know. And I'm sure she's just as devastated as you."

I remember her white face and her tears soaking into my neck. "I don't know." I reach out for the mug again and notice with disgust that my hand shakes. How much alcohol did I poison myself with last night? "She likes wee kids."

"Liking them's not the same as having one when you're eighteen."

"What would you say if it was Vicky?" I ask, pouring some more tea.

I can see her thinking, *Vicky* wouldn't be that stupid. But fair play to her, she doesn't say it. "I don't know," she admits. "I mean, she's off to Cambridge – hopefully. So I suppose … well, I hope she'd have an abortion."

I stir my tea even though I don't take sugar.

"It's against everything I was brought up to believe in, but" – Colette shrugs – "I think in some cases it's the best option."

"Seaneen won't even *think* of an abortion. Even when there's something wrong with the baby she doesn't believe in it."

"Pity."

"Colette!" But I know if Seaneen phoned me now and said she was going to England to get an abortion I'd be ecstatic.

Would you though? Your kid?

But I can't think of it as *my kid*. It's just something that's going to stop me doing what I want. And it's not *fair*.

"People don't have abortions around our way."

Colette defends herself. "I know. But I think a lot of these girls would be better off at least considering their options."

I don't like Seaneen being called *these girls*.

"What age were you when you got pregnant?"

She gives one of those laughs that people give when something isn't exactly funny. "OK, yes, I was nine-teen."

"Are you saying you should have got rid of Vicky?"

It only feels safe to say this because Vicky's away travelling in India or Mexico or wherever with her boyfriend.

"No," she says slowly. "I can't say that." She gets up and carries the teapot over to the worktop and refills the kettle so I know she's going to keep me here longer, making me talk. But in a way I don't mind. Talking to Colette's always been easier than talking to Mum. She waits for the kettle to boil. "I've often thought about it," she said. "What it would have been like if I hadn't had her. It felt like the end of the world. I was so scared of what everybody would say. Especially with me being at Queen's and all. I mean, people did get pregnant – it was the nineties, not the dark ages – but nobody thought *I* would. All those A levels just to push a stroller. And Peter's family ..." She shakes her head. "It wasn't exactly part of their plans for him. I knew what they thought – that I was just this working-class tart from West Belfast who'd trapped him."

Trapped. Like I feel.

"But you got married."

The kettle clicks and she refills the teapot. "I know. I was twenty." She shakes her head, as if remembering, and carries the teapot back to the table. "It was awful. Peter was doing his finals, and coming home to a baby crying and a wife going out of her mind." She gives another of those funny laughs. "Vicky was a very demanding baby."

I can believe that.

"His friends would come around, and their girlfriends, and I'd feel so ... so left out and frumpy. They'd all be talking about their exams or the gossip and all I'd done all day was look after the baby. My life was just diapers and Teletubbies. I thought my brain would turn to mush."

"But you were smart! Gran always said you had brains to burn."

"Not smart enough."

"Was it *all* awful?"

"Oh, I don't know. I remember the bad bits, I suppose. And don't go telling Vicky all this. It wasn't her fault." She drinks her tea in silence for a minute then looks at me and says, "Do you want some toast?"

I shake my head. I look around her kitchen, which was always my favourite room when I lived here – warm and cheerful and bright, usually with nice smells – and try to imagine her in a cramped flat with a squalling brat.

"No," she says, as if she's still turning my last question around in her head. "It wasn't all bad. Peter's family helped a lot so we hadn't really any money worries. And we moved into this house when Vicky was two. And we loved each other. At least we did at first. But it wasn't enough." She gives me a straight look. "Do you love Seaneen?"

I hesitate. There's a wee rough edge on the china handle of my mug and I pick at it with my nail. "Yes," I say. I couldn't talk to Mum like this. "I mean ... I don't know. I went around to tell her I was going away and then ..."

The cup, the checked tablecloth and the bright walls blur.

"Oh, Declan, love. What a mess. But could you not still go? For a bit? Six months, say? Come back before the baby's born? At least you'd get some experience."

I shake my head. If I went, how could I force myself to come back?

"I wish I could give you some good advice," she says. "All I can say is – it didn't work for me and Peter, but he's a good dad. Always was. Just because he doesn't live with us doesn't mean he isn't part of Vicky's life."

"I know but ..." I groan and push my hands up my face.

"Declan, one thing's for sure. You need to talk to Seaneen. And your mum."

"She'll freak."

"Your mum's stronger than you think."

Mum. Seaneen. Seaneen's mum. Oh God, Seaneen's *dad*.

"OK." I push my chair away from the table. "Can you take me now?"

3.

Colette turns her blue Golf into the entrance of the estate.

"Just leave me off here," I say.

"Sure?"

I nod. Mum knows I've been at Colette's, but I'm not going to make too big a deal out of it.

I should go to Seaneen's first. But I don't turn down her street, even though my feet aren't exactly rushing down Tirconnell Parade to my own front door. My hangover's receded into a manageable tiredness and the sun warms my shoulders under my T-shirt. The street smells of dog shit and exhaust fumes. Stupid to be wasting a summer Saturday here in the city. If I hadn't made such a dick of myself last night, I could have been pounding around the farm trail on Spirit, letting his speed and power carry me far away from this street and this baby.

But I would still have had to come home.

As soon as I push open the living room door I can tell Mum's waiting for me, rather than just sitting on the sofa. The TV's on as usual in the corner, but it's nearly hidden behind the curtain of thick smoke that hangs in the air, and the ashtray on the coffee table in front of her is toppling over with butts. Now she isn't drinking she does smoke more, but she keeps this full-on chain-smoking for special occasions. She's in her dressing gown, and she hardly ever does that during the day now. My heart wasn't dancing for joy anyway and now it plunges right down to my feet.

"So," Mum says, not looking around. "You remembered where you live."

"Sorry." I try not to cough 'cause it'll annoy her but it's impossible not to in this smoke. "I'd no money for a taxi and I just sort of ended up … Colette's was nearer." I shrug. "I was a bit drunk."

"Oh aye," she says. "I bet you were." Her voice is hoarse with smoke and tight with bad mood. I don't bother telling her she'd be a lot more annoyed with me if I *had* come home last night. I look at the hunch of her shoulders, the determined grip of her fingers around her cigarette. Is this about more than Colette? Is it Germany? Has she been sitting here smoking herself into a state about me leaving?

No.

She suddenly stretches out the remote with her left hand and the TV dings off. Not just the sound but everything. Mum never turns the TV off.

"I had some visitors last night," she says. She turns and stabs her cigarette at me. "When were you going to tell me? That's a nice thing to find out from somebody

57

else. How do you think I felt, sitting here like a bloody idiot without a clue what was going on?"

"Whoa!" I say, as if she's a runaway horse. "I don't even know what you're on about."

"You know rightly! You and that wee tramp."

"Don't call Seaneen a tramp!" I plonk myself down on the arm of the sofa. My hangover twists at me again.

"Why couldn't *you* tell me?" Her mouth has that flubbery look that means she's going to cry.

I look down at my arm and scratch at a small scab I don't remember getting. "Mum. Calm down."

"Calm down? I'd Mairéad and Gary Brogan around here till all hours calling you everything. And I didn't even *know*."

"*I* didn't even know!" I make myself look at her. Mum, smoking herself hoarse; me, drinking myself sick. What's the difference? And I wonder what my dad was like, if he'd have reacted any better. Except he crashed a stolen car and died at twenty-two so odds are he wouldn't have. And he was already a father by then.

"You know what, Declan," Mum says, bending forward to stub out her cigarette. "It's not even the fact that you got her pregnant. It's the fact that you never told *me*." Her hand hovers over the packet but then returns to her lap. She twists it around the other one.

"I only found out last night. I didn't get time to –"

"Did you tell Colette?"

I hesitate. "Only 'cause I was there. And," – I shrug – "well, she got pregnant, too. Like, by mistake."

Mum purses her lips, and changes the subject away from Colette. "You young fellas," she says, "you think it's nothing. But you won't get away with it, not these days. You might think you can piss off to Germany but they'll be after you. Stacey gets it off two different fellas, you know. Child support."

For a moment I imagine going to Germany and sending Seaneen money every week. I could do that. I don't care about money, apart from saving for a horse. And Seaneen'd maybe meet some nice fella that didn't care that she had a baby with somebody else. Sure it happens all the time. Look how many boyfriends Mum's had.

Yeah, exactly. Sitting outside on the wall because *Mummy's busy, love,* waiting for it to feel safe to go home.

And the thought of Seaneen with somebody else ...

"I'm not going to Germany," I mutter.

She takes the last cigarette out of the packet. "Well," she says, lighting up. "That's something I suppose." She suddenly gets all cozy. "Och, you and Seaneen – sure you two were bound to end up together. And she's a great wee girl."

"A minute ago she was a wee tramp."

"Och, I didn't mean it. Oh God, I'm going to be a granny and I'm not even forty!"

"Don't."

She goes on as if I haven't spoken. "You'll need to put your names down for a flat around here. That wee girl'll need to be close to her family. There'll be a waiting list. But sure there's no rush. You could even move in here," she says. "That's what me and your dad did – moved in with your gran." She smiles and brushes ash off her dressing gown as if she's about to leap up and start painting the nursery.

"Mum – stop it." I rub my eyes. Every word about flats and waiting lists and Seaneen's family is twisting the hangover deeper in my guts. "I haven't even talked to Seaneen yet. Stop acting like anything's been decided."

Her mood shifts again. "Oh aye – I hear you ran out on her last night." She sniffs. "Mairéad says you were out of there like a bat out of hell."

"For God's sake, Mum!" I shout. "I panicked, OK? I go around there to tell Seaneen I'm leaving the country. And she tells me she's bloody pregnant! How am I meant to react?" My head throbs, and again I have that awful feeling that I could cry. Christ, I need to get a hold of myself. But the thought of going around to the Brogans' now – I can't help a groan escaping. "Mum – don't ever tell Seaneen about Germany. There's no point now."

Mum smiles for the first time. "Och, son, you've had your fun," she says. "You'll just have to pay for it." Then she says, "Could you two not have been more careful, though? I never fell for you until I had this ring on my finger." She wiggles her wedding ring. "Were you not using something?"

"Mu-um!" I've plumbed the depths of mortification already this weekend, but even puking over Colette's kitchen floor doesn't come close to discussing my sex life with my mum. "I'm not stupid. We were careful – just not enough."

I suppose I would have liked Seaneen to go on the pill. We were both virgins when we started having sex so there was no need to worry about catching anything without a condom. But we only saw each other at weekends, and she said she wasn't going to mess her body up with hormones for no reason, and it was going on the pill that made her mate Bronagh get so fat. So we stuck to condoms – only we had the odd slip.

I rub my hand over my face. Mum's smoke is pricking at my eyes and catching my throat. And she wants us to live here with a *baby*.

"OK," I say, and my voice is as thick as the smoke. "I'm going around there now."

4.

There's no red Proton at Seaneen's curb. Let them all be out, I pray. Gary and Mairéad anyway.

Seaneen answers the door. As soon as I see her I blurt out, "I'm sorry. I know it's mine. I should never have –"

"Well, I'm sorry I hit you. I think." She frowns, screwing up her eyes in the sunlight. Her hair's pulled back into a high curly ponytail, leaving her face looking white and exposed. I glance at her belly. It looks the same as usual, though she's wearing a long T-shirty dress thing over her jeans so it's hard to tell.

"Seaneen, can we go somewhere – and talk?"

"I have the twins," she says. "Mum and Dad are at Tesco's."

"Ah, come on, a walk or something. It's a lovely day."

"Declan, stop talking about the weather. Did you not hear me? I said I have to mind the twins." The atmosphere of the house creeps out to me. Not smoky like my house, but frying and children and air freshener.

"Well, sure they can come. We can go to the park. Come on, Seaneen. It's too hot to stay in."

"They're watching CBeebies."

"They'll be better in the park." They can go on the swings and we can ignore them.

She sighs and leans against the doorpost, one hand on her hip. "I don't want them overhearing anything. They're four going on forty."

"It'll be fine."

Saoirse – or Tiarna, they look the same – hears the conversation and comes grumbling out. She hangs around Seaneen's waist and looks at me with suspicious green eyes. "Are we going to the park?"

"No, Tiarna, we –"

"Ah, we are! C'mon, Saoirse!" And she goes running off to get her twin.

I look at Seaneen and shrug.

"Oh, OK," she says. "I've hardly been out all week."

Walking along the street with two wee kids is so annoying. They stop and look at everything – a whitening dog poo, a McDonald's wrapper, a cat under a car with its paws tucked in. They walk too slowly or dash ahead without looking. "Are we going to the shop?" one of them asks. "I want a lolly!" cries the other.

"Shut up. We're going to the park." Seaneen turns to me. "You got any money?"

"Nope." I don't tell her I drank it.

Where Seaneen's street joins Tirconnell Parade one of the twins grabs Seaneen's arm and shrieks, "Can we go and call for Courtney and Madison?" The other one starts running without waiting for an answer.

"It's your woman who moved into Gran's house," Seaneen explains in a tired voice. "That's her two wee ones."

"I'm not taking the whole street to the park. And if they're anything like their brother –"

"You were the one wanted to come out." But she calls after the twins, "Not now. You can call for them on the way home if you're good."

When we get to the main road, the twins stop messing about and, without being told to, take up position on each side of Seaneen, holding her hands. "Good girls," she says. She's still not saying much to me. A silver jeep slows beside us and Seaneen grips the twins harder. "Bloody Emmet McCann," she says as it roars away. "It's people like him give this place a bad name."

"He's a dwug dealer," one of the twins says in a know-it-all voice.

"Don't say bloody, Seaneen," says the other one.

We walk the same route I walked last night with Cian. Even though it's warm and sunny, the park's pretty empty, just a few wee lads climbing up the slidey bit of the slide and two grandads sitting on a bench.

The twins break free and run for the swings, curls flying, and clamber up, clutching the chains in their pudgy hands. They're too small to swing themselves so we're lumbered with one each. I soon realize Seaneen was right: we won't get much talking done. In a way it's a relief because I don't know what to say, and if it's anything like the talk Mum just had with me I'm in no rush for it, but in another it's annoying to have got myself all psyched up for nothing.

But there's something I need to say and it doesn't matter if the twins hear. They're shrieking and laughing and calling out to each other anyway and my one's going higher than the other one because I can push far harder than Seaneen.

"Look," I say, "I won't just leave you."

Seaneen nods. "I know," she says. "I never thought you would."

"Some people do. Natalie Doyle's one did."

"Declan, Natalie shagged half of Ibiza. All she knows about whose that brat is is that it's not Kevin's."

"Well, I just thought I'd say. Your mum seemed to think I was going to do a runner."

"You did last night." She squints at me through the sunlight.

I open my mouth to remind her she hit me, then close it again. "I had to get my head around it."

"And have you?"

"Higher, Seaneen!" Her twin kicks her fat legs up and down. "Look, Tiarna's way more higher'n me. That's not fair."

"Swap." I step aside and take over Saoirse's swing and Tiarna starts wailing.

"Stop squealing," I say, "or we won't push you at all."

"Have you got your head around it?" Seaneen asks again. She seems to be able to concentrate through the yelling and whining.

"Jesus, Seaneen, no. Not yet. I mean – it's a shock." I look at her, pushing, smiling, not as pale now we're out in the air. "Nobody wants this to happen."

"Not *want* to. Not yet. But it's not the end of the world, is it? It's not as if it was a one-night stand like

Natalie." She steps away from the swing and takes my hand. "Like, we've been together over two years, Declan. You must have thought about it."

I pull my hand away. "Of course I never thought about it." I grab the chains of the swing and pull it back further than I have before. When I let it go it swoops way higher than the other one and Saoirse screams, "Not that high! Let me down! I'm going to fall. Seane-e-e-en! Tell him." And she starts blubbing.

"Now look what you've done."

I let the swing go and leave them to it. I go over and sit on the wee bench. The paint's hot against the back of my T-shirt. I close my eyes and feel the hangover nag me again. Why did I tell her I wasn't going to leave her? I can't do this. What if our kid – ah Jesus, *our kid*, how can that be possible? – turns out to be a brat like these?

I rub my hands over my face and try to block out the screeches and the wails. Then I feel someone sitting down beside me. I open my eyes. It's Seaneen. The brats are at the slide. One of them turns around and beckons Seaneen.

"Seane-e-e-en! Come here and catch us. Tiarna won't go on her own."

"You're big girls now!" she shouts back. "You don't need me to catch you. Away and play." She settles herself against the back of the bench with a sigh. "Sorry," she says. "They're a bit of a handful."

"Yeah. I'm not used to …" I don't finish the sentence.

Seaneen puts her hand on my leg. Her hand's warm. "Look," she says. "I know I've had longer to get used to it. But it'll be OK. We'll get our own wee flat. And it's not like I'm a kid. By the time it's born I'll be nearly nineteen and a half."

By the time it's born.

"So when's it …?"

"January. Ah, Declan, wouldn't it be lovely if it was born on New Year's Day?"

"So when did we …"

She raises her voice. "Saoirse! Tiarna! Stay over there and play nice or I won't let you call for Courtney and Madison. Um … well, I was working it out. Must have been at Easter."

I spent a lot of time with Seaneen at Easter. She was upset because her granny was dying. One night she came around late and nobody was in, and I didn't have anything and we thought it would be OK.

A blob of pink chewing gum shines in the sun.

"Must have been then," Seaneen says. "'Cause there was that time – and the dates add up."

I nod. Can't speak.

Seaneen's hand creeps along the bench and her fingers search for mine, less sure than usual. But after a tiny hesitation I close mine around them because what else is there?

5.

I cycle into the yard on Sunday morning in a determined mood. While I'm here I'm going to concentrate on horses and work and not think about anything else.

"Didn't expect you back so soon," Cam says, humping Kizzy's saddle higher on her arm and keeping her distance. "Are you sure you should be here? I don't want to catch anything."

"You won't." I jump off and wheel the bike towards the barn where the ponies are waiting to be tacked up.

"Well, there's plenty to do. Missed you yesterday." She gives me a sudden half-smile. "I did wonder – the way things are – if I could manage without somebody when you go. With Jim doing the odd shift."

"What do you mean, the way things are?" I say, because she's leaning against the barn door like she wants to chat, and I can't risk saying, "It's OK, I'm not going; I'm going to be a dad instead."

"Well, you may not have noticed, Declan, but there's an annoying little thing called a recession going on?"

I shrug. "How does that affect you?"

"Horses are a luxury," Cam says. "First thing to go when times get hard. Remember Libby?"

Libby's owners didn't pay their livery for months. Owed Cam hundreds. Disappeared and changed their phone numbers so she couldn't get hold of them. In the end, under the terms of the livery contract, Cam sent Libby to the sales to try to recoup the money.

"That was only one horse."

"Oh come on, Declan, you must have noticed things have got a bit quiet around here."

"I like them quiet." I look around the barn. Flight's stable – empty. Only three ponies in for the ten o'clock ride. And there's been no new pupils for ages.

Cam shakes her head. "*You* say that because you're an antisocial bastard," she said. "You're not trying to make a living out of it. But look – Flight's gone; Hilary and Jennifer have both moved their horses somewhere cheaper. Lara keeps threatening to go somewhere more *competitive*." She imitates Lara's whiny voice perfectly. Neither of us mentions Nigel and Lorna, bible-bashing bigots who took their three horses away when Pippa moved in and they caught on to what they called Cam's *lifestyle*.

"Let her," I say. "Good riddance."

"Yes, but it'd be good riddance to her money too. Oh, it's fine," she says, as I frown, "I'm not destitute yet. I can sell Spirit if I have to."

Tell her! Tell her you're not going anywhere.

But I can't. The pregnancy's stalking me everywhere – waking and sleeping. There has to be one place where it can't find me. So all I say is, "Well, what do you want me to do for the horses we still have?"

"You can catch Joy up from the bottom field."

I groan. The bottom field's miles away. But it's only a pretend groan and Cam grins. "Might as well get my money's worth out of you while I can. She can stand in for a bit; she's far too fat. Then you can ride her around the farm trail later."

"Why can't Fiona ride her own horse?"

"She's pregnant again."

So it can stalk me here after all.

I sling Joy's purple headcollar over my shoulder and head down the steep lane between the paddocks. The bottom field's for the horses that don't get used much – the three wee Welsh ponies, who are due to be broken in the spring; Sally's Nudge, who's retired because she's lame; tiny freckly Sweep, Cam's first pony; and Joy.

Joy's not keen on being caught and leaving her nice warm sunny spot where she's swishing her tail and munching clover. The other horses follow us and crowd around the gate, noseying and barging, not wanting to let Joy go. I have to fire a few clods of dried-up mud at their arses to get rid of them.

Joy glumps along beside me, putting her ears back at Spirit on the way past the paddock he shares with Willow. Her belly swings as she walks into her cool stable beside the empty one that used to be Flight's. "Lazy mare," I say, scratching her neck. "You've got it too easy." She goggles over the partition at the empty box and neighs. I pat her and leave her.

For a Sunday morning it is pretty quiet and I realize Cam's right. Because I don't have to bother much with the pupils – Cam told me years ago I was great with horses and crap with people – I've never really noticed it. I get caught up on the stuff that didn't get done yesterday. Sitting on the wall in the sun, half-hearing Cam's firm, encouraging voice from the sandschool ("Relax … let the jump come to you … lean forward … forward … good! Give her a pat.") I rub saddle soap into Spirit's bridle and lean back in the sun. This isn't bad, I tell myself. It's a job. There's plenty of people hanging around the streets at home with nothing to do, and no money either.

You have to tell Cam you're staying in case she does get somebody else in.

When I tack Joy up later she glares at me in disgust. She's so fat I have to heave on the girth strap. But when I kick her across the yard to the farm trail she suddenly pricks her freckly grey ears and steps out briskly. She's not fit enough to do more than walk, but it's a gorgeous evening, cooler now, and the flies have gone away. I'm not in a rush home to Mum's questions and predictions and Seaneen's list of names and the email to Hans-Peter Hilgenberg that I've composed in my head but not sent yet. Might go to the library and do it tomorrow on my way home.

Or not.

After the ride I lean on the gate of the bottom field and watch Joy trot down the hill to meet her mates. She snatches at some grass then lets herself fall with a grunt and rolls, kicking up her legs. She clambers up, shakes, then gets down to serious grazing. Sweep wanders up to her with a low nicker and starts biting at her shoulder. They stand nose to tail, grooming each other, Sweep having to stretch his neck up to reach Joy. The Welshies have one of their mad five-minute racing sessions around the field, manes and tails flying, before settling down to graze again.

I wonder if they're happiest of all like this, just mooching about doing their horsey thing, biting at each other's itches, dozing with their lower lips drooping. Left to themselves would they give a damn about jumping and racing and being the best, or is that just us? Even though I keep trying not to, I relive that moment at Balmoral, galloping out of the ring, unable to believe we'd won. I wanted to believe that Flight understood, that he knew he was the best, but when we got back to the truck, all he wanted was his hay net. Probably even Hans-Peter Hilgenberg's beautiful German showjumpers just want to graze and scratch their arses in the field.

For the first time I have to put on the lights on my bike before I leave the yard. I'm way later than usual. Cam's been in the house for ages, lights on from behind the closed curtains.

I whizz down the hill and skirt around the city. The roads are quiet; my legs ache from the effort of getting Joy's lazy arse around the farm trail. I see a long winter ahead, and hope that Cam will be so busy she lets me ride Spirit. Maybe Cam could have an accident – not a bad one like Vicky's; she could just be a little bit hurt. Well enough to do her chores in the yard but not well enough to jump Spirit at shows. But she said she might have to sell Spirit. There's no way I'm going to let myself like him and then have to watch him being led up the ramp of a stranger's truck.

Grounded

Under me, my bike shudders and pulls to the side. I jump off and stand in the verge looking at it, the deflated front tire like a used condom. I unhook the pump and give it a few blasts but it's no use. As fast as I pump the air in, it leaves through the puncture. I resist the urge to kick the bike. Better start pushing. It's about two miles home from here.

When old Dermie gave me this bike he said, always take your puncture kit with you, but I've never bothered. Always been lucky until now.

It's a pain to push, and having to walk slowly makes it too easy to think. Some bastard in a jeep flies past me and blares the horn. For a split second I think it's Emmet McCann in his da's car – Barry got five years for assault. Fuck this. When will I be able to afford a car? I've got just over two hundred pounds saved, hidden in my bedside cabinet with a blue elastic band around it. That'd buy the kind of car that'd leave me doing exactly what I'm doing now: walking home.

The road feels quiet after the jeep blasts past. Then I hear a strange noise. Neighing. Only not neighing. Too high and thin. I look around. Big haulage yard on the left, field of something yellow on the right. Definitely no animals. A ghost horse then.

It comes again, fainter, hardly a neigh at all. But definitely a horse. A horse in distress. The sort of cry that's given up thinking anybody's going to come. But there's no sign of a horse anywhere. The fields are greying in the dusk. Must be a trick. Soundwaves or something. The horse is probably miles away. If it even is a horse.

Like last week. Because wasn't it just here, taking that phone call from Seaneen, that I thought I heard a horse? And I told myself I was doing too much day-dreaming about German showjumpers.

I glance around, ears straining, just in case. Yes, it was exactly this bit of the road. There's the gateway I stood in, the gate still leaning at a drunken angle, tied up with years' worth of fraying baler twine – orange, blue, beige.

The cry cuts the air again. And this time I know it's not a ghost.

6.

I fling the stupid bike at the gate and fiddle with the tangled mass of baler twine before giving up and clambering over. As I let myself down on the other side I see my feet are about to land in a jumble of hoofprints. So sometime there was a horse here. I thud across the dusty hard ground, dodging an old bed and a pile of bust tractor tires.

Another cry. It's coming from the old yard. The closer I get, the darker and scruffier the yard looks – the rusting, corrugated iron barn leaning over the grey farmhouse; the concrete in between pitted and blackened with ancient cow shit. The gate between the field and the yard is too buggered to climb so I have to yank at more baler twine and then pull it towards me. It sticks with a horrible screech but there's enough space for me to squeeze through.

I'm half-running, but when I draw close to the barn I slow down. If there is a horse in there it's in trouble –

maybe got itself locked in by mistake or something – it won't need me dashing in like an idiot.

Some of the sheets of corrugated iron are peeling off in rusty curls. What'll I do if it's locked? But the door's only closed and tied with a thin length of blue rope. As I grab the handle it judders and shakes and sticks and there's a screaming neigh from inside. Hoarse and high-pitched at the same time. "OK," I say. "OK, I'm coming. Good horse."

As I pull the door open the stench hits me so hard I double over, retching. Piss and shit and something – oh God – far worse. I clamp my hand over my mouth and nose. A black buzz of flies swarms out past me.

Christ. What is this?

Another neigh. Definitely a horse. I can't back out now.

Still covering the bottom half of my face, I drag myself through the door.

At first it's so dark that I think the horse in the corner, standing in front of a pile of wooden pallets, is alone, its whiteness shining in the gloom. It turns and stares at me, its eyes black pits in a skeletal face.

A ghost horse after all.

Then the neigh comes again – high and insistent, nothing ghostly about it – from the other side of the barn and I force myself to turn and look, a sort of calm horror making my eyes tell my brain what they see.

The horse lying down in the filthy straw is dead. It lies on its side, the rigging of its ribs like a wrecked ship. A foal stands over it, shaking on stick-thin legs, its head too big for its skinny neck to hold up. When it sees me it lets out a desperate squeal.

Another swarm of flies rises from the carcase of the mare and circles the foal, fighting over the scabs that pockmark its body.

"Ah, Jesus." I stand uselessly in the doorway. Without my mind formulating a thought my hand grabs for my phone. I hit Cam's number. It rings for ages. *Oh please Cam, you have to answer!* I don't know what to do. Police? Vet?

"Declan?" She sounds surprised.

"Cam, thank God, you have to help. I've found these horses. One's dead. And there's a foal. And I don't know what to do. Can you come *now*?"

Immediately her voice is businesslike. "Where?"

"Where? Oh God. Past the new roundabout. Just across from that big haulage place. I'll open the gate for you. You have to drive through a field. You'll see my bike in the gateway. Only *hurry*."

"Are you safe there?"

"Me? *I'm* OK." I push the barn door closed behind me so the horses can't run away, not that they look like they could run too far. "But should I phone the police or a vet or what?"

"I will. Just don't touch the horses. I'll be there in ten minutes."

Glad of something definite to do that gives me an excuse not to go into the barn for a bit, I go back through the yard and over the field. It takes ages to undo all the string; I wish I had a knife. Last week I leaned over this gate and thought I heard neighing. And ignored it. If I'd investigated then, would that mare have lived?

I don't want to go back into the barn but I force myself, pulling the front of my hoodie up over my mouth and nose. The ghost horse has moved out of its corner but when it sees me it backs up again and strikes out with a front leg. It doesn't look as white now my eyes are more used to the gloom. Its face is rubbed raw and scabby and its ridged backbone sticks up like a cow's. Its whole body is a mess of tufts and tats and sores. It looks at me in horror and lays its ears back flat. It grabs at one of the wooden pallets with its teeth and holds on.

"Whoa, pet, it's OK, nobody's going to hurt you," I say. I don't go any closer. Something butts me in the back and I jump. It's the foal. I turn and look at it, trying not to let my eyes take in the wrecked carcase beside it. "Hello," I say. My voice comes out quite normal even though I'm muffled by my hoodie and trying not to breathe. "What happened you?"

It looks up at me, big eyes staring out of its tiny, rough little foal face on either side of a huge star. It's so caked in shit and bits of wet straw that I can't even guess what colour it is. Its thick coat is filthy and rubbed bare in places. It noses at its mother's body. "Don't," I say and try to pull it away. It wriggles and totters.

Lights sweep the back wall of the barn and the ghost horse gives a squeal and flings itself around.

I edge to the door and open it a crack. "Cam? Be careful."

She stands in the doorway, her hair sticking up in red tufts, and lets out a low *whooo*. "Oh my God," she says. "What on earth's happened here?" She sounds really cross.

"Cam, did you mind me ringing you? Only –"

"Of course I didn't mind. I'm not angry with *you*. But ... how could anybody do this?"

"Have you headcollars in the jeep? We could lead them out."

She shakes her head. "Safer to let them stay here till the police come. They must have been here for weeks. Another few minutes won't make any difference." She coughs. "Sorry – need to get out of here. Declan, don't touch that foal. Seriously, you don't know what you might catch. Come on."

We close the door behind us again and lean over the gate, taking deep breaths.

"I feel awful leaving them there," I say.

"Let the police deal with them. How did you know they were there?"

"I heard them." I tell her about the puncture. "D'you think somebody died or something?" I glance over at the grey ramshackle farmhouse. "Ah Jesus, Cam, d'you think there's a *body* in there?" I have the horrible image of an old farmer dead and rotting in bed or lying somewhere with a broken leg.

We both shudder.

"God knows," Cam says. "The police will search the place."

In a way I hope there is a body. Because then it's just a tragic accident. If not, if somebody put them in there, left them there, deliberately ...

A car passes but doesn't slow. In my pocket my phone beeps a text and I check it just for a distraction. But it's only Mum saying she's away over to Stacey's and she's left my dinner in the oven.

"I've never seen anything that bad," I say. "Have you?"

She shakes her head. "A few knackers at the sales, the sort of thing McCluskey takes for meat, but no, nothing like this."

Something about the word "knackers" scratches at me. "They'll be OK, though? I mean, now they've been found?"

"I don't know, Declan. I wouldn't put money on it. God knows how long they've been in there. They're starving, dehydrated, crawling with lice, probably diseased –"

"But you see those before and after photos in all the ads for animal sanctuaries. *They* get better, and some of them look just as bad as that."

"Maybe," she says. "But they don't show the pictures of the ones that are too far gone to be saved, do they?"

"Oh *Cam*!"

She pats my arm in a very un-Camlike way. "Who knows?" she says. "Anyway, you've done your bit, finding them. Look – here's the police coming through the gate."

A PSNI Land Rover lumbers over the field. They haven't brought anything to take the horses away, I think. They're just going to shoot them and not give them a chance. Then another vehicle trundles through the gate, a wee horse truck with the USPCA logo on it.

The field's suddenly busy with noise and lights and people in uniforms. Cam strides forwards to meet them; I hang back. Stupid of me; it's more than three years since I was in trouble with the police, but …

"OK, so what have we got?" There's a policeman

and policewoman and two USPCA men and a vet who's a girl and looks dead young.

Cam pushes me forwards. "Declan here found them; I'm just the backup."

I swallow. "Three horses," I say. "One's dead."

"We wondered if someone had died – in the house, I mean," Cam says.

The policeman shrugs and says, "Looks as if it's been empty for a long time. But we'll check the place over. You guys go ahead and do what you have to do."

The vet and the older USPCA guy go on into the barn and I hear one of them say, "Bloody hell," before he comes out and there's a lot of head-shaking and I hear the words "humane" and "destroyed".

"No!" I say. I follow them all back into the barn even though I know they don't want me to. "You can't just kill them."

The older guy looks at me as if I'm about twelve. "Sometimes it's the kindest thing," he says in a know-all voice.

"But ..."

"Look, leave it to us," he says. "We're the experts. We see this sort of thing all the time. Unfortunately." His colleague, who's fat and quiet, crosses the barn to the ghost horse who flares its nostrils at him and snorts. But he talks dead patiently and in the end the horse lets him put a headcollar on and stands trembling. "Poor old girl," he says. I hadn't got close enough to see she was a mare.

Know-it-all looks at the vet, who's examining the foal. It just lets her. "Lesley?"

"Touch and go," she says. "I'd say they've been here

weeks. It's amazing they haven't died of thirst."

"There's a puddle in the corner – the roof must be leaking."

"What killed the mare, d'you reckon?"

The vet shakes her head. "Starvation – the foal took all the goodness? Or she might have had an infection. We'll have to arrange incineration."

"But you won't put them down, will you?" I ask.

"We'll see if they respond to treatment," Fatty says. "Been too many of these kinds of cases recently."

Know-it-all takes photos of the barn and the horses, for evidence I suppose, and then they start to lead the horses out. The foal totters along without protesting; the ghost horse pulls back and when Fatty tries to get her to walk on she bites his jacket. "This one's a fighter," he says, rubbing his sleeve.

Good. Fighters survive.

The vet goes on ahead to put down the ramp of the horsebox and I help her. "Don't worry," she says. "They must be tough to have survived this far."

The foal goes on to the box as if it doesn't care much what happens any more. The ghost horse pulls back and rears up but then totters and nearly falls, and after that she just walks on with her head drooping nearly to the ground.

As Fatty puts up the ramp behind them, I turn to Cam in a sudden panic. "We can't just let them go. Where are they taking them?"

"Rosevale," Fatty says. "D'you know it? It's a sanctuary. Old lady runs it on her own. We're having to use it as overspill because we've got too many horses coming in. Ten last week. All as bad as this."

I shake my head. He starts explaining where it is and I hope Cam's listening because my head's not taking anything in since he said *ten last week, all as bad as this.*

"Can I give you my number?" Cam asks. "Obviously we'd like to know what happens to them."

Tell them. I try to psych the thought into her head. *Tell them you can give them a home.*

The police come out of the house. The policewoman rubs her arms even though it's a warm evening, but she's smiling.

"Nothing there," she says.

"Looks like it hasn't been lived in for years," the policeman says. "Kids been drinking there, using it as a toilet, but nothing else."

"So where've the horses come from?" I ask.

"Abandoned? Or lost and wandered in and couldn't get out again? Who found them – you?"

I nod.

"Was the door closed properly? Can you remember?"

"Yes. And tied with rope."

"Look, we need to get these horses away," Know-it-all says.

The police Land Rover's blocking the horsebox so the woman goes to move it and the man turns to me. "Well done, son," he says. "We'll have to get a proper statement in the morning. We'll be in touch."

He takes down Cam's address and number and then mine, and I see him trying not think that our addresses don't exactly go together – hers in the posh rolling farmland around Drumbo and mine in a skanky estate in West Belfast, but he's probably been on some course on not being judgemental so he only says, "And you two are …?"

"He works for me," Cam says. "If you come to my yard, you'll find us both."

Yeah, and I bet he'd rather go there than come to my house.

"I'll take you home," Cam says. We get into the jeep and she drives it across the rutted field. We stop at the gate and I grab my bike and throw it in the back. I suppose somebody will be back for the mare's body. "Will you for God's sake get back in?" Cam calls out, but I stand for a second listening, as if I'm expecting to hear the ghost horse's neigh.

7.

I click my seatbelt. I can't stop shivering so Cam turns the heating up.

"Stupid," I say. "It's not even cold."

"Shock,' Cam says.

"And horror."

"God, yes. You read about these things, but ..." She shakes her head. "I wouldn't like to be cleaning out that barn."

We don't say anything for a bit. Cam changes gear for the hill that's always such a slog when I'm cycling up it.

"Will they let us – me – go and see them?" I ask.

"Declan, they probably won't make it," Cam says. "You've done your bit, finding them. It's maybe best to put them out of your mind."

"But ..." I can't believe Cam. She *loves* horses. Her whole life is horses. How can she just say forget about them? Does she not feel the same as me, that we're kind of responsible for them now? "But Cam, that wee foal.

It was so pathetic. Do you not wish you could take them home and look after them?"

"You can't rescue every neglected horse, Declan! Let the USPCA do their job."

"They put them down after a week!"

"I think that's dogs."

"But you heard that fat guy – he says they're running out of room. You have empty stables!" The image of that scabby, ribby foal walking into one of Cam's big stables, all fluffy clean deep shavings banked around the walls, and bulging nets of sweet haylage, is so delicious. If it was my yard, I'd do it.

"I run a livery yard and give lessons," Cam says. "I can just about afford to feed the horses I have."

"You could put them in the bottom field. They'd love it. Oh, *Cam*." I can't understand why it's not obvious to her.

Cam sighs. "It's a lovely idea. But you have to be practical. Those horses are traumatized. They need intensive care. Specialist care. Not to speak of what they could be carrying. Anyway, you're going away."

For a moment I don't know what she's on about. I haven't thought about Germany all evening. Or about Seaneen being pregnant.

"I'll stay! I'll stay and look after them."

"Declan. Don't be daft."

And maybe because I don't want her to know how daft I've already been I miss another chance to tell her that I am staying anyway.

Cam's phone beeps. "That'll be Pippa. She'll be worried. She wanted to come but I knew she'd be too upset.

I'll call her when I drop you off."

When Cam drops me at the end of Tirconnell Parade, I see her lift her phone to her ear and her face breaks into a tired smile when she starts talking to Pippa. It makes me want Seaneen.

I'll go home and text her. I need a bath. Can't get the stench of filth and death out of my nostrils. I'm glad Mum's out; I don't want to talk about the barn. If Seaneen comes around we can actually get a bit of privacy for once. And even if she wants to talk about the baby, it'll be better than thinking about those horses. Are they at that Rosevale place now? Maybe they died on the way. Where did they come from? Would the USPCA give them to me? I could get around Cam. I could work for their keep; she wouldn't need to pay me as well.

Yeah. With a pregnant girlfriend? I can see myself telling the Brogans that I can't provide for their grandchild because I have two half-dead horses to care for.

I push my key into the lock, hoping there'll be hot water. In the hall I pull my boots off. I realize, too late, that they're stinking from all the crap I walked on in the barn – no wonder I could still smell it. Then, with one boot half-off, I freeze.

The house isn't empty.

There's no TV or anything, just a feeling.

Don't tell me Mum's started sitting in the dark again? Not that as well as everything. Is it because of the baby? But no, sure she's happy as Larry about the baby now. And she's at Stacey's. I'm imagining things.

I switch on the living room light and, just in case,

shout out, "Hello? Mum?"

A rustle from the kitchen. Then a crash. What the …? One time Mum left the window open and next door's cat came in and wrecked the place.

I dash to the door and yank it open. It's not a cat. It's a dirty little urban fox on the rob.

Cian tries to make a run for it out the back door, two packets of cigarettes falling out of his hands, but I'm faster. I throw myself at the door in front of him.

"What the hell are you doing in here?" I push him against the door and hold him by one shoulder. I'm not that tall but I'm far stronger than him.

"I'm not … I wasn't … I was only … Your mum–"

For a second I think, *oh God, I've made a mistake.* Mum's over at his house; maybe she asked him to come and get her cigarettes for her.

But his face is pure guilt. And the pockets of his hoodie are bulging.

"What've you got in there?"

"Nothing." His hands cross over his front but I grab them and force them away. He reeks of alcohol. A bottle of pills rattles on the floor. Mum's anti-depressants.

"What else have you stolen?"

"I don't have to tell you!" His eyes flash with sudden spirit. "Lay off!"

I delve into his pocket and pull out a box of strong codeine painkillers that have been hanging around the house ever since I came off Flight last year and wrecked my back. Then a wad of notes. Wrapped in a blue elastic band.

I throw Cian back against the door as hard as I can,

ramming my knee into his groin. He starts whimpering. "You wee bastard, you've been in my room." I shake him hard. I haven't been this close to a fight since I broke Emmet McCann's nose at school.

Cian jukes away and scrabbles at the door, but I lock it and put the key in my back pocket. I shove him down onto a chair at the table. I set the pills and the money down in front of him. "Right, what else?"

"Nothing." Then he says, "Well ..." and pulls out a bent packet of Silk Cut from an inside pocket. He sits there, head down, snivelling.

I stand against the door into the living room and take out my phone. "Right, I'm phoning the police."

He looks at me with narrow eyes. "Wise up. You know you won't." But his voice has gone high-pitched the way mine used to when I was scared and trying to hide it.

"Why wouldn't I? Didn't I catch you red-handed?"

"Aye, and they'll believe *you*?"

"Why not?"

He gives a sneer. "Your ma's told mine all about you. You were put away when you were younger than me. So don't think you can go all holy Joe with me. It was only a few stupid cigarettes."

"And the rest." I ignore what he says about me.

"You guys don't even have any liquor."

He sounds so disgusted, like we should have provided better stuff for him to steal, that I nearly laugh, but the sight of the wad of tenners on the table stops me.

"You break in here –"

"I never! The door was open." His hand creeps towards the pills. I remember the way he downed the beers the other night. "Your ma's around at our house. I heard her saying she forgot to lock the back door. I just" – he shrugs – "thought I'd chance it. Don't tell me *you* never."

"State of you – scrounging drink off me the other night, stealing off me and my mum now. There's people around here could get you sorted out for that – know what I mean? I'd only have to say the word."

This is crap – I don't have those kinds of contacts. Emmet McCann and his mates are meant to have bashed some wee hoodlum's head in with a baseball bat for robbing houses at the other end of the estate, but I stay clear of all that. But Cian doesn't know that.

"You fucking wouldn't." But his face is tight with fear, the freckles standing out, his eyes as huge and black and terrified as the ghost horse's. Only that's crap – it's only 'cause the horses are filling my head.

"Is that why you had to get out of whatever hole you've come from?"

He flinches. "Fuck off. You know nothing about me."

"And you know nothing about me. So don't you dare sit there in my house and tell me you've only done what I've done. 'Cause that's crap. You're just a thieving wee hoodlum."

He tries to make another run for it but I pull out a chair and sit opposite him, blocking him. Under the alcohol his sweat reeks. His hand still fidgets along the table. He's like Mum when she used to be going mad for a drink.

"Look," I say. "You're right in a way. When I was your age I was a wee shit. And I ended up getting locked up in Bankside."

He looks up. "What was it like?"

"You'll be finding out soon enough if you keep on like this." I never think about Bankside now. "Horrible. Like school only you can't get away. And full of bastards. And I mean *bastards*. So maybe you'd be right at home."

He twists his mouth.

I take the money from the table and shake it at him. "See this? D'you know how long it took me to earn this? And save it?"

He gawks at me like I'm speaking a foreign language. "So?"

"So …" I can't be bothered talking to him any more. He hasn't a clue and he never will. "Get your arse out of this house and if you take anything belonging to me or my family ever again, I swear you'll regret it."

"Are you going to tell my ma?" His eyes are wide and dark.

"Why? Afraid of her, are you?"

"No!"

I jab my finger at him. "You get in my way one more time and I'll tell everybody. Starting with your ma. OK?"

"OK."

"Right, get out." I take my time unlocking the back door. He scuttles away into the night.

8.

I lean back against the humped-up pillows and Seaneen wriggles herself up the bed so she can lean on my shoulder. I stroke her hair.

"I hate the thought that he was in here, poking through my stuff," I say, for about the tenth time. I look around at the posters of horses on the wall, the few rosettes, the piled-up magazines, my certificate from college, Flight's name plate. I can't bear to think of that thieving wee dirtbag in here, laughing at all this. Then again, he probably just went straight for where he knew he'd have a good chance of finding money. Probably didn't even notice anything else. At least he didn't wreck the place.

"I know," Seaneen says. She squeezes my hand.

It's after eleven and neither Seaneen nor I want to move. I'm so tired I could fall asleep right now, just snuggled up like this. As soon as Seaneen got here she knew something bad had happened. She cried when I told her about the foal and the dead mare. She said

Cam should take them, I should take them, she would help me pay for their keep. She said when the foal grew up it would probably end up winning the Grand National and they'd make a film about it because of its terrible start in life. "That wee foal," she kept saying, and her tears wet my neck.

"Do you not feel sorry for him?" she asks now.

"The foal?"

"Cian."

"*No*. Don't tell me you do."

"Just … his ma doesn't seem to know what to do with him. She has those two wee girls done up like princesses, but she treats him like some kind of wild animal."

"Well, he shouldn't act like one." But *wild animal* makes me think of the ghost horse.

"When you came out of Bankside," she says, tracing her finger down the front of my T-shirt, "you were like that."

"Don't be stupid."

"You were, Declan. Not wild but … aloof. That's what made me want you. The challenge." She gives one of her sudden grins just before things get too heavy and nuzzles into me and says, "Can I stay over?"

"What'll your mum say?"

"Well …" She turns over and lies on her back, nearly breaking my arm. "Sorry, love. What can she say? Sure I'm pregnant now anyway."

"We've never slept together. I mean – actually *slept*."

"I know. Do you want to?" She sounds shy.

"I don't want you to go," I say. I'm scared that when I close my eyes the ghost horse is going to be waiting.

"Will Theresa mind?" she asks.

"Nah, sure she loves you. She said …" But I don't want to tell her that Mum said she could move in here, because even though just at this minute when it's all cozy and nice I think there'd be worse things in the world than living with Seaneen, living with Seaneen *and* my mum *and* a baby would be pretty crap.

"What?"

"Oh, you know – you're a nice wee girl. All that."

She giggles. "I bet she wasn't calling me a nice wee girl when you told her I was pregnant."

"Um … well, I think she blamed me more."

"She won't look in on you when she gets back, will she?"

"Wise up."

"Well, then, I will stay." She reaches for her phone which she's left on the bedside cabinet and texts her mum. Then switches off the phone so Mairéad can't ring her back.

We lie for a bit and then I think, well, we can't go to sleep in our clothes, so I start taking mine off and she does too, and then I find I'm not as tired as I thought I was.

"Is this OK?" I ask before it gets too late for us to change our minds. "It won't hurt you or the … the baby?"

Seaneen laughs and kisses me. She seems so much happier than in the park yesterday. "You won't hurt me or it. You can't even make me pregnant."

"Better make the most of it then."

★ ★ ★

94

I'm trapped in the barn. The space gets smaller and the air gets thinner and every time I try to move I'm stumbling over bits of dead horse.

I wake up choking, burning, and squashed against the wall. Seaneen's still asleep, turned away from me, her curls half-covering her face and her cheek resting on her elbow. I half sit up but she doesn't stir even when I accidentally catch a bit of her hair. Looking down at her asleep I feel this weird mix of stuff.

I love her.

I resent her.

And I'm scared of what's inside her.

She looks cute and sort of young, her cheeks pink with sleep. I reach down and touch her face lightly. She wrinkles her nose, opens her eyes and looks amazed to see me for a moment before realizing where she is.

"Declan," she murmurs. She rubs her face on the pillow, eyes screwed shut again. Then she moans, launches herself off the bed and stumbles out of the room towards the bathroom. Two seconds later I hear her throwing up. I don't know what to do. I try not to listen. There's silence for a bit and I think, oh God, what's happened to her, and I don't know if I should go in the bathroom, which I don't really want to, or just leave her to it. Then the toilet flushes, there's the whoosh of water into the sink and next minute she comes back into the room looking like shit.

"Are you OK?" I ask. Stupid question.

She sits on the bed and hugs herself. I'm scared she might do it again but I make myself sit beside her and put my arm around her. She takes my hand and hides her face in my neck. Her hand is freezing. I rub her back with my free hand and suddenly remember the first morning we met Cian.

"I'm OK," she says. "I got up too quick. Don't worry, it's normally just once. I'll be OK in a minute."

"Can I get you anything?"

"Mum gives me ginger. And a couple of cream crackers."

"I don't think we have those. There might be some custard creams."

She suppresses a retch and shakes her hand at me. "Uggh." She takes a deep breath. "OK. I'm fine. I have to go home and get ready for work anyway."

"You can't go to work."

"'Course I can. I'll be fine." She pulls away and starts putting on her clothes slowly. Her tits are bursting out of her pink bra but her jeans don't look any tighter than usual. "Declan," she says, like I'm an idiot, "stop looking at me like I'm going to die."

"You should go back to bed."

"I can't spend the next seven months in bed. Anyway, this is only meant to last another few weeks."

I shudder, remembering the way I felt on Saturday morning. Imagine feeling like that every single day for *weeks*. "I'm glad men don't get pregnant," I say.

"Yeah, just as well. Declan, you're sitting on my sock."

When she's gone, I go and get washed. There's no smell in the bathroom; she's opened the window. I wouldn't have thought of that.

9.

From: declankelly1994@sunshinesky.co.uk
To: Anneliesemuller@hphilgenberg.com
Subject: job

Dear Anneliese
I am sorry but I won't be able to come and work
for Mr. Hilgenberg. My circumstances have changed.
I am sorry for any inconvenience.
Declan Kelly

IV. HIDING

Grounded

1.

If I'm going to stop going back to that barn every time I fall asleep I need to see the foal again.

I force the bike up the last punishing stretch of hill before Rosevale. I can see the sign at the end of the drive – Rosevale Horse Sanctuary. I got their number and address from the phone book. The woman on the phone said she didn't normally let members of the public in, but since I had found the horses she would make an exception. She sounded a right bossy cow, with one of those foghorn Englishy voices, but I want to see the foal again, so I wrote down her directions and here I am.

It's an old higgledy piggledy place, not derelict like the death barn, but not smart and painted like Cam's. A jumble of stables and sheds huddle at one end; scruffy, saggy-fenced paddocks and pens tucked into every space. As I wheel my bike up the drive, a donkey with the longest ears I've ever seen looks up from pulling at a hay net tied to a fence and lifts up its head in a loud *Eey-aw-aw-aw!* Its neck is covered in scars.

"Hello?" I call. I lean my bike against a low stone wall. Heads look out of stable doors. I don't see the foal or the ghost horse.

An old woman with a tired face comes out of the nearest stable, carrying a bucket. She empties its contents – water streaked with blood – down a drain before turning to me and growling, "Who let you in?" I recognize the voice from the phone.

"Um – the gate was open. I phoned. Yesterday? About the foal and the ... the grey mare? From the barn?"

I wish I'd asked Cam to come for moral support. She's just as posh as this old biddy and always looks like a proper horsey person in her brown leather boots and nice puffy bodywarmer. I've come straight from work in track bottoms and a sweaty T-shirt. Mind you this old bag's in ancient trousers with a busted zipper and a washed-out sweatshirt that says "Riding for the Disabled 1982".

"Oh, yes," she says. "USPCA brought them in, few days ago?"

"Yeah."

"Terrible." She shakes her head. Grey hair sticks out around it like the petals of a daisy. "They can't cope. None of us can. Seven last month. Tethered. Beside the highway. Doris Rose." It takes me a moment to catch on that she's telling me her name.

I shake my head. I don't think I'm expected to say anything. She rinses out the bucket and refills it with clean water. Then she squirts some antiseptic in from a bottle sitting on top of the wall.

"Come on," she says and I follow her back into the stable she just came out of. It's small and low, must have been designed for sheep or pigs, and standing at the back of it, its head drooping over a thick bed of straw, is the foal. It's light chestnut, far lighter than I imagined it being. I recognize its star, and the big soft brown eyes that have been haunting me ever since Sunday night, eclipsing the black angry pits of the ghost horse's eyes.

"Hello, baby," I whisper, stretching my hand out for it to sniff, but it doesn't move.

"Know anything about horses?" the old bag demands, pulling bits of cotton wool out of her pocket.

"I just got my national diploma in horse care and management."

"Huh." She hands me the bucket. "You can hold it," she says like she's giving me some big treat.

She bends over the foal and starts cleaning a wound on its back. I hadn't noticed properly in the barn, but now that it's more or less clean you can see there's more swellings and sores and raw patches than there is normal skin and hair.

"Infected," she says. Her voice is gruff but her hands on the foal are gentle and quick. It totters and runs backwards at the sting of the water, but she keeps her hand on its chest and talks to it and soon she has all its wounds bathed.

"Will he – she? – be OK?"

"Colt." She shakes her head. "Don't like the infection. Injected him. Who knows? Right, next."

I think the next one must be the ghost horse but when I follow her next door I'm kind of relieved to see an old donkey lying on the straw. It starts up in alarm when it sees us but then relaxes, lipping at the edge of the bucket hopefully with its tiny soft mouth.

I think it's wearing a headcollar until I realize that the bands criss-crossing its grey head are the deep cuts and sores from a headcollar left on so long the hair must have grown around it. Mum's finger swelled up once, when she was drinking, and she had to get her engagement ring cut off. The donkey's head looks just like that.

"God, that's nasty," I say, as she cleans around it. The donkey stands and lets her, sniffing at me. I have Polo mints in my pocket. "Is he allowed one?"

"Oh yes. Why not?"

But the donkey doesn't seem to know what to do with the Polo. It holds it inside its lips and then lets it drop on to the straw.

"How many do you have?" I ask.

She stops and puts her head on one side, counting up on her fingers. "Seventeen here. Four on loan."

"So you do rehome them then?"

"Some. Not all suitable."

I hear the words coming out before I know they're going to. "I would take the wee foal."

She doesn't say, "Oh, that's wonderful, how kind of you; that's just what I was hoping for." Instead she raises her thin grey brows as if to say she's never heard anything so stupid. "What would you want with a foal, boy like you?" She shakes her head as if taking in my shabby track bottoms and earring and my Belfast accent, and adding them up to something she doesn't like much.

"I just … because I found him." I don't tell her I imagine the foal growing up to be a brilliant showjumper, overcoming his bad start in life, taking on

the best in the world. He'd be mine in a way no other
horse ever would because I'd rescued him, taken him
from the body of his dead mother.

None of this is stuff I can say out loud to this tired-
looking old woman with her bucketful of bloody water.

"Takes a long time for a foal to grow," she barks.
"No use to you for four years. Ever raised a foal? Let
alone an orphaned runt like that?"

I bite my lip. "Do the police or the USPCA know
where they came from?" I ask to change the subject.

She takes a fresh piece of cotton wool and wipes a
pussy scab off the donkey's cheek. "Abandoned. The vet
scanned the mare for a microchip in case she was stolen
but there was nothing. But like I say, horses are being
abandoned all the time. I keep saying I can't take any
more in but what can you do? You find a corner somewhere."

I don't know why I'm sort of scared or reluctant or
something to see the ghost horse, but old ma Rose –
Doris – strides ahead of me to a stable in the far corner,
looking over her shoulder to be sure I'm following.

And when I look over the half-door – we don't go in
– it's not a monster or an alien or a wild thing. Just a
skinny white-grey horse with a dark grey mane and tail.
She stands in the far corner from the door, knee deep in
straw more or less the way I've imagined, pulling at a
hay net with absolute concentration. Her face is rubbed
raw and because she's so pale the scabs on her body
stand out even redder and angrier than the foal's, but
she looks as happy and involved in her dinner as any
normal horse.

"She'd be happier outside, but the flies would torture her. Lovely sort," Doris says in a low voice different from her usual bark. The mare's ears flicker and she goggles at us in suspicion but then goes back to her hay.

"Will you be able to get her a new home?"

Doris purses her lips. "Nothing wrong with her that a bit of TLC won't cure."

Just then she sneezes, and the mare squeals and dashes around the stable with her back humped and her eyes rolling. It's the whites of her eyes that make me shiver: the layers of terror and trauma and hatred.

"Bit sensitive," Doris says, wiping her nose with an old-fashioned man's hanky. "All right, old lady, easy now."

But even when the ghost horse starts eating again her ears twitch constantly and she snatches only a strand at a time in between staring at us in horror.

"If they could only talk," Doris says, moving away and starting, in a pretty obvious way, to walk me down the drive, "they could tell us a tale. Old Ned – the donkey – he's well over thirty. Found in a back yard in Lurgan, tied to a fence. Lived on crusts."

I shiver at the idea of the tale the ghost horse, the foal, and the dead mare could tell. I don't know if I'd want to hear it.

* * *

"Declan! Your hat!" Spirit skitters away from Cam's pounding feet on the gravel drive.

"What? Oh!" I reach down and take my riding hat from her. "Sorry." I put it on, and Spirit takes advantage of me only having one hand free to snatch at the reins.

"You would be if he dumped you on the road and you landed on your head." Cam shakes her head, kind of teasing, kind of not. "You gave Willow Sweep's feed yesterday. With his medicine in it."

"I said I was sorry." I play with Spirit's grey mane, the same colour as the ghost horse's.

"It's just not like you. You won't last five minutes at Hilgenberg's if you don't get your head sorted out." She reaches over and untwists Spirit's throat lash.

"Look – about that."

"You're not having second thoughts?"

"I … maybe."

"Gosh." Cam's the only person I know who says gosh. "Well, let me know in plenty of time if I *don't* need to advertise for a new groom." She seems to be working hard at keeping her voice neutral. She gives Spirit's dappled neck a pat. "OK, have a good ride. And keep him *working* – no lolloping about." She goes to walk back up to the yard.

"Cam?"

"What?"

"Job adverts sometimes say 'own horse welcome'."

"So?"

"So *if* I ever got one – *if* I stayed, I mean – could I keep it here?"

Cam wrinkles her forehead like she can't keep up with me. "Of course," she says. "I'd have to take something for its keep from your wages, though. I can't afford to keep a horse for nothing. Anyway, we'll talk about it if you find something. Spirit might be for sale at the end of the season."

"I think he's out of my price range. By about ten thousand pounds."

"He won't be if you don't get his arse out around those roads. Go on – there's seven saddles to clean when you get back."

"Can't wait." I squeeze my legs against Spirit's sides and, glad to get going at last, he steps out down the drive with his long purposeful stride.

★ ★ ★

I tell Seaneen first. Her face lights up and she hugs me. We're in my bedroom. "Och, Declan! That's so cute. We can have a foal *and* a baby. They can grow up together. Can the baby ride the foal?"

"Of course not; don't be stupid."

"Well, how would I know?" But she doesn't sulk or anything. "What about the horse? Are you taking it too?"

"No," I say quickly. "The foal'll be easier to rehabilitate."

"Not as traumatized?" Seaneen says wisely. "It's the same with kids. The younger they are, the better chance they have of recovering from bad stuff. We learned all about that in my course."

"Plus I can't afford to keep two. 'Specially with the baby." It's the first time I've mentioned the baby to her. I don't tell her my wages will be cut to pay for the foal's keep. Maybe we could rent a wee house with a field near the yard. I conveniently ignore the fact that Cam lives in one of the poshest bits of Northern Ireland. Houses around there are sold, not rented, and never for less than a quarter of a million. Let alone the fact that I can't imagine Seaneen living in the country. We still haven't talked about what's going to happen when the baby's born. She still looks slim and normal, apart from her tits getting bigger, which I have to say isn't a problem.

"What'll you call him?"

"Dunno." I say it like it doesn't matter, but I know he has to have a special name.

"What colour is he?"

"Chestnut. With a star."

"Chestnut. Like Flight?" She grins the way she always does when she gets a horsey thing right.

"Not as bright. But they change colour. He could end up grey or anything."

"Aww, I can't wait to see him. I'll buy him some apples. He'll get spoiled rotten."

I imagine him grazing in the bottom field, up to his hocks in clover. Joy will mother him and Sweep won't let him get cheeky and coltish, keep him in his place.

"Call him Flame," Seaneen says. She hasn't even seen him but Flame is a brilliant name – full of life and heat and colour.

I give her a quick kiss. "That's perfect," I say. "Flame."

For the first time getting the foal feels like something exciting instead of scary.

★ ★ ★

On Friday I look into Flight's old stable. It'll take about eight bales of shavings to put down a good bed. At seven quid a bale. Maybe Flame wouldn't need a stable. He could go straight out into the bottom field. But the flies are bad – they'd make a meal out of his cuts and scabs. Maybe his wounds have healed now, though. It's a week since I saw him, a few days since I've been hugging the secret of bringing him home. Only Seaneen knows so far but my next step is to tell Cam. No – my next step is to phone Doris and persuade her to let me take him. But if she's as desperate for space as she says, she won't say no, especially when I tell her I work for Camilla Brooke and he'd be going to her yard.

I put off phoning her till after tea. I got home early for once and Mum was all pleased with herself because she'd made a shepherd's pie. There's no signal in my bedroom and I'm not going to let Mum hear the conversation so I go out into the back yard and walk down to the end of the garden. I'm so nervous I hit the wrong name and end up having this confused conversation with a girl called Roisín I met in Wicklow. But eventually I get through. It rings for ages and then the posh voice barks out, "Rosevale Stables, Doris Rose speaking."

"Mrs. Rose? It's Declan Kelly."

"Who?"

"The one who found Fl – …the orphaned foal? And the grey mare? In the barn?" I push at a dandelion with my trainer.

"Oh yes. And what can I do for you?"

I swallow my excitement. "It's just – I'd really like to rehome the foal."

There's a pause and I think for a moment I've lost the signal but when I take the phone away from my ear and check it, there's five bars.

Grounded

"Hello?"

"I'm sorry," Doris says. "The foal is dead."

2.

I didn't cry when Flight went. I didn't cry when Seaneen got pregnant. So I don't know why I'm sitting on the back step pushing my fingers into the corners of my eyes and trying to swallow the welling ache in my throat. I've only seen the foal twice. I should be relieved, really, because it was a crazy idea. Like Doris said, what did a boy like me want with an orphaned foal?

"Declan?" Mum nearly falls over me on her way to the bin with a bagful of peelings and leftovers.

I glance to the side and dash my hands across my eyes and sniff up some snot. "Hiya, Mum."

But she's not fooled. "Och son, what's wrong?" She sits down beside me, the rubbish bag between her knees. It leaks gravy. I angle my leg away from it.

"Nothing, I'm fine."

"Is it the baby?"

Not *that* baby, I think, but I haven't told her much about Flame and there's no point now so I just say, "No, it's nothing. Mum, that bag's disgusting."

She gets up and puts it in the bin. Flies buzz out when she opens it. I bat one away. I hope Mum'll go back in now but she sits back down beside me. "I know it's not what you'd planned," she says. "But sure you've got a job and a home. Many's a one hasn't."

"Yeah."

"And Seaneen's a great wee girl."

"I *know*."

"And she'll be a lovely wee mother."

I grit my teeth. "For Christ's sake, Mum."

"Sure I wasn't much older when I had you."

Is this meant to reassure me? "I know."

"And you turned out OK. In the end."

"Thanks."

She looks worried so I say, "It's not the baby. It's just – well, that wee foal died."

"What foal?"

I pull at a hangnail with my tooth. "The one I found. I just wish – if I'd found it sooner it might have made it."

She looks dead relieved. "Och, well, if *that's* all."

"That's all."

★ ★ ★

Seaneen cries too. Bursts into tears walking down the main road from the Spar. She fancied a popsicle and I fancied getting out of the house. "Must be my hormones," she says, but I know she'd have cried even if she wasn't pregnant.

"I should have known I was never going to get my own horse," I say.

Seaneen hands me her Polly Pineapple popsicle so

she can wipe her eyes. "'Course you will. Anyway, there's loads of horses at Cam's you can ride, aren't there?"

"It's not even that. I couldn't have ridden Flame for years anyway. I just wanted to give him a nice life."

She takes back her popsicle and licks away the drips that have formed. "So?" she says. "Take the other one."

My stomach tightens at the thought of the ghost horse. "The mare?"

"Why not?"

I shake my head. "She's not really ... she wouldn't be" – I remember the word Doris used – "suitable."

"Not suitable for what? Having a nice life?"

"Seaneen, no offence but you don't know anything about horses. She's a psycho."

Seaneen shrugs. "OK." She licks off the last sliver of yellow popsicle and tosses the stick into a bin. She takes my hand. Hers is sticky. We draw level with the park. "Want to go in?"

"Not really."

"You're jiggling my hand."

"Sorry."

"D'you want to get the bus up to Colin Glen and go for a walk in the forest park?" Seaneen hates the forest park, which is always full of midges and things that make her sneeze, so she's only saying this to please me because she can feel my restlessness.

"Nah, it'll be dark before we get there."

Seaneen sighs. I bet she's thinking she hopes the baby isn't a miserable ass like its dad.

"Look," Seaneen says. "There's wee Cian."

"*Wee* Cian?"

"You know what I mean."

He's sitting on a swing, a can in his hand, looking at the ground.

"Hiya!" Seaneen calls over.

I jerk hard on her hand. "Don't talk to him! He robbed us."

But she calls over again. "Hey, Cian!"

He looks up this time.

"Tell your mum I tried those ginger biscuits and it helped. Well, a wee bit."

"Wha'?" His eyes are unfocused. Around his mouth is red and scabby. The can in his hand is lighter fuel.

Seaneen turns to me. "He's sniffing something!"

"So? Nothing to do with us. Come on." But Seaneen ploughs on over to him. It's just like that first morning. I stand back in the line of scrubby trees. I kick a bottle. I try not to look at them but there's something about the way Seaneen's standing, arms folded under her tits, feet planted squarely, that reminds me of the way she used to be, back in school, when she fancied me and was always trying to get me to cheer up and talk and everything. At least she can't *like* Cian.

I hear the rise and fall of her voice, but nothing from him, and she soon gives up. She comes back to me, arms still folded, shaking her head.

"Can't get any sense out of him. God love him."

"God *love* him?"

"He's been at that old lighter fuel. I thought *nine-year-olds* sniffed that."

"Right enough. I should have let him have that two hundred quid, shouldn't I? So he could have got himself a better fix. Champagne maybe? Or he might rather

113

have had a nice line of coke?"

"Declan."

"Well, he's a wee bastard."

"I hope he gets home OK. Stacey'll kick his arse if he gets in in that state."

"I hope she kicks it hard."

"Declan, you're all heart."

"It's not you he robbed."

"*Tried* to."

"Same thing."

We walk on a bit. When we get to the estate Seaneen asks if I want to go to her house but I say no. I kiss her goodbye at the corner of Tirconnell Parade. I try to make the kiss say *sorry for being a grumpy shit* but I don't think I manage it.

That bloody Stacey is at our house again. As soon as I push the front door open her nasal whine hits me. I hesitate outside the living-room door.

"That you, love?" Mum calls out.

Who else would it be? "Yeah. Just going up to my room."

"OK." She doesn't even try to get me to come in the way she normally does. They must be in the middle of a juicy gossip. I clomp upstairs, then tiptoe back down and sit on the bottom step. Haven't done this since I was a kid and Gran had her friends in, but all they ever talked about were women's insides and what the priest had said.

"Och, there's no way you'll look like a granny." Stacey says.

Oh God. I nearly go back upstairs. Only I'm still

too restless. I need distraction. Maybe I should go out and walk around a bit, tire myself out.

"I hope that's not the next thing with our Cian."

"Och, no, Stacey. Not at his age."

"I'd be the last to know."

If Mum says again that Seaneen was the making of me I'll have to go in there and shut them up.

"Sure Declan tells me nothing."

Well, that's true.

"Give me girls any time. Maybe the baby'll be a girl. Wouldn't that be lovely?"

"Aye, I'd have her spoiled rotten."

"You can get gorgeous wee things. My Courtney and Madison's room's like a fairy castle."

"At least you've no bother with them. And you keep them lovely."

I don't know why I'm listening to this crap. I think I'm just enjoying the fact that she's in here saying what a good mother she is when her wee lad's out sniffing lighter fuel.

"But I worry all the time. Social services poking around. It's only 'cause of him. He's the only one's ever been any bother. Staying out all night, getting in trouble, not going to school. From the day and hour that child was born –"

"And when did they take him away?"

"Three."

But even Cian can't have been running away and skipping school and getting into trouble when he was *three*.

"He was away five years – I don't know how many

foster homes – and when he came back he was like a stranger. 'Course I'd sorted myself out by then. New man and all. Courtney's dad. I *wanted* him back – I fought for him all those years. I thought we could be a family. But I sometimes wish …"

Mum makes a sympathetic noise.

"When Courtney was born he never gave her a minute's peace. Trying to lift her out of her crib. He dropped her once, banged her on the head, and you should have seen them social workers poking around again with their reports and their files. *Just checking the baby was in a safe environment.* The baby was OK – it was him; he was like an alien."

"God love you, Stacey. Sure Declan was the same when he came out of Bankside. It was like having a stranger in the house."

Because Gran had died.

Because *you* suddenly had to put up with a fourteen-year-old son for the first time.

Because you were too drunk to hack it.

Because you blamed me for Barry leaving.

I bite the inside of my cheek.

"Aye, well, that'll be the next thing for him. He'll not make it to sixteen without getting into serious trouble."

"He must have your head turned."

"And now I've met Darren, and he's lovely, Theresa – I think he's the one, you know, but Cian's always spoiling for a fight, hardly even speaks to him. I sometimes wish he'd do something bad enough so they *would* take him away. Is that terrible?" She goes on without waiting for an answer. "I think he's always blamed me because I've never known who his dad was. I was only a kid, Theresa. I'd been in and out of foster homes all my life; I just wanted some affection."

"God love you. I was with Declan's dad from before I can remember. He wasn't the steadiest, like, but sure neither was I ..."

And off she rambles boringly into the past and I realize my legs have cramped from sitting. I go to my room and lie for ages looking at the streetlight flickering through the curtains and trying to ignore the hum of voices from underneath me.

When I finally sleep I dream about a barn full of dead horses. Flies bigger than bats buzz around my head and when I try to call for help the buttons on my phone keep shifting out of place and have no numbers on them. And in the corner of the barn, instead of the ghost horse, there's Cian playing with the dead foal.

3.

For two weeks I obsess about the grey mare, sometimes as a psycho ghost horse that won't stop haunting me; sometimes as a potential showjumper who's just had a bit of a rough start.

Two weeks of trying to improve Joy who can't see any reason why she should change the laid-back ways of a lifetime. Two weeks of ignoring Lara's comments about how it's lovely to see me having a bit of fun on Joy but of course there's nothing like your own horse and what a pity I won't be able to go to the big show at Cavan but there wouldn't be room in the truck.

"Not that there'd be any point going with nothing to ride," she says, leaning on the gate of the school, having a good look at Joy refusing for the third time to lead off on the right leg. "You should use your stick," she says. I know where I'd like to put my stick. I *can* do it, I want to say. I won at Balmoral. But that feels like another life now.

"Cam needs me to look after this place when she's away," I mutter. Which isn't even true – Jim could cope if he had to.

"Willow's stable walls need painting," she says. "You'd have to dig out all the bedding first but it would give you something to do."

I give Joy a sharper kick than I mean to, just to get away from Lara, and she's so taken aback that she actually strikes off on the right leg and I keep her cantering around the school until I see Lara's skinny arse heading back up to the yard.

"Why are you taking *her*?" I complain to Cam when we're putting the tack away one evening. "Let them make their own way."

"They'll pay half the diesel," Cam says. "It's no joke taking a truck this size any distance, with fuel the price it is."

"But listening to that for three days!"

"Are you jealous?" She fixes me with one of her hard green stares.

"Wise up."

But when Cam and Lara drive off in the truck I feel more left behind and out of it than ever.

It's also two weeks of my mum nagging me about the baby and making *decisions*.

"I told you a million times, I'm not going anywhere, so what is there to decide?" I tell her the day Cam goes off to Cavan. I had to stay at the yard until eight to get everything done and then cycle home, and the only thing I want to do is eat the fries I bought at Fat Frankie's, lie in the bath and go to bed.

She hovers over the sofa, frowning because my socks have left a few bits of grass on the carpet. Sometimes I wish she'd never sobered up. "Where are you going to live, for a start?" She picks up the grass.

I sigh. "Mum, it's not due for ages. Will you stop going on about it?"

"It's not *that* long. Isn't she ten weeks gone now?"

Gone. That's a horrible expression. "Something like that."

"You need to show more interest." She pounces on an invisible speck of mud on the carpet and tuts.

"For Christ's sake, Mum, I'm only in, I'm exhausted, I'm starving, would you leave me alone? There's nothing to be *interested* in yet."

"That's your *child*."

It's not a child. It's just a bundle of cells that aren't showing yet on the outside, that are making Seaneen pale and sick and weepy sometimes, but otherwise she's the same, just Seaneen. We're getting on fine – it's just that when I'm with her it's impossible to forget about the baby. Which is probably why I still haven't told anybody at the yard, so sometimes when I'm there I can forget about it for hours at a time. It's only when I'm doing something mindless, like digging out Willow's bed so I can paint the walls of the stable, which is what's got me so sweaty and dirty today, that I start thinking about it, and then I can distract myself by imagining the grey mare jumping in Dublin. I spear a fat fry.

"Declan." Mum's voice is like a phone that won't stop ringing. "You can't just do your usual trick."

"What *trick*? I haven't got a trick." I wrap the fries up again.

"Refusing to talk about things. Pretending they're not happening." Mum thinks everybody should be *talking* about everything all the time, just 'cause of all that counselling she's had.

"There's nothing to *say*."

"There'll be something to say when it's born, Declan."

I screw up the wrapper. "I'm going out," I say. Fuck the bath, fuck the early night. Not killing my mum is suddenly a priority.

I go out the back, dump the fries in the bin and think about getting on my bike and spinning off for miles. But it'll be dark soon, there's nowhere to go and I really am too exhausted so in the end I walk around to the corner store and buy a can of Coke – I haven't had a proper drink since Seaneen told me she was pregnant. There's a queue and only Cathal Gurney's on the till, so he's not getting through it too quickly. It's not a real job – he's on some kind of scheme for thick people – so I don't know why he's been left on his own.

"Hey, state of you, horse boy."

I glance around and see Cian in the queue behind me.

"You stink," he goes on, wrinkling his nose. His eyes look darker than usual, the pupils huge.

"Watch him," I say to Cathal in a loud voice. The wee old lady in front of me turns and looks me up and down like I just escaped from the mental hospital. She clutches her bag tighter. "Search him on the way out; he's probably stolen something."

I set my Coke down on the counter and walk out. It's either that or thump the wee bastard.

★ ★ ★

Seaneen gets up and closes her bedroom door more

firmly on the theme tune of *EastEnders* from downstairs. "Just phone Doris. At least go up and see the horse."

"But am I mad?"

"Probably." She comes back over to the bed, leans forward and kisses the end of my nose, then pulls away. "God, Cian was right even if he was off his head; you are a bit whiffy."

"You always say sweat's sexy."

She sniffs and looks thoughtful. "This is more like … horse wee."

"But am I? Mad?"

"You were going to take the foal. What's the difference?" To her a horse is just a horse. A head, four legs. Something she'll visit and feed apples to as long as it doesn't move too quickly or fart or snort or kick out.

"I told you. She's more complicated."

Seaneen shrugs. "Everything's complicated."

"No – I mean … I don't know. I want her, but I don't want her. I'm – there's something about her that scares me," I admit for the first time.

Seaneen's hand lies for a moment across her belly even though there's nothing to see yet. Her nails are bitten. "Declan, I'm scared of *this*, you know. I mean – I *want* it. I wouldn't wish it away now, but I'm terrified. Will it hurt? Will there be something wrong with it? What if I can't be a good mum? All that."

"And I'm going on about a horse. I know it seems –"

"*No.*" She gives me a quick hug. "I don't mean that. I mean, just because it's scary doesn't mean it's not the right thing to do. You found her. You should keep her. And when you go and see her I'm coming with you."

★ ★ ★

Doris falls in love with Seaneen at first sight and takes her to see all kinds of pathetic creatures that she never showed me. I trail behind them for a bit then go down to the paddock where the grey mare is turned out and watch her for a bit. Even in two weeks she's like a different horse. Still skinny and tatty in places, but the scabs have faded and dropped off, and she grazes watchfully but intently under a huge old tree at the far end. It's a cool, breezy evening and when the leaves rustle too loudly she shivers. I don't go into the field; I just watch her being a horse for a bit.

I find Seaneen in one of the stables with a miniature Shetland foal on her knee. It's about the size of a cat or a lamb. She kneels in the straw and holds it and it lips at her hair.

"It must think it's hay," I say, leaning over the half-door.

"Thanks."

"I thought you were scared of horses."

"Big monsters like that Flight. Sure you couldn't be scared of a wee baby like this." She runs her hand over its fluffy neck.

"They grow up."

Seaneen looks over at the foal's mother, which is about the size of a Labrador, her brown eyes peeping from under a bushy spring of black mane. "Doris says she was found in a garden shed. Somebody got her for their daughter's birthday. Hadn't a clue how to look after her, just got her off a man in the pub. Didn't even know she was having a foal."

Doris stops outside the door. "Come and see the mare," she says. "I've got some apples for her. You might as well get to know her."

We wander back to the paddock, with Doris demonstrating to Seaneen the right way to hold a treat with her hand out flat. We all lean over the fence while Doris shows the grey mare the apples and waits for her to approach. She'll never come, I think, but slowly, a step at a time, checking all around her, the mare walks towards us. Her ears are on the flick all the time and she keeps one eye fixed on us, but she keeps coming.

"You see, she's much happier out of doors now the scabs are healing." Doris opens the gate and waves me and Seaneen through, then follows us. The mare stops when she sees so many people coming into her space. She puts her ears back, but the smell of the apples seems to be enough to overcome some of her natural fear and when Seaneen reaches out a hand with an apple slice on it, the mare stretches out her neck, makes a quick grab for it and stands back, eating it. Seaneen stays totally still, hardly breathing, her face breaking into a wide grin. "Och, God love her," she whispers.

I take a slice too and reach out my hand, and the mare looks at me with those sunken black eyes. I get the feeling she'd rather have Seaneen. *Come on*, I will her; *come to me. Please trust me.*

She stops a couple of feet from me. I can't stretch out my hand any further. She makes her neck like a giraffe's and snatches the apple so fast I hardly register that she's got it. I want to reach my hand out and touch her shoulder but I know she won't let me go that far. Up close you can still see her ribs clearly but her backbone no longer sticks up like a cow's. "Good girl," I whisper. Her ears twitch and she backs off a few paces.

Behind me I can hear Doris saying quietly to Seaneen, "She doesn't trust people. She's had no reason to."

There's no apple left now, and the mare decides she's had enough of human company and trots away down the field. She carries her tail high when she trots and looks almost pretty.

We all lean over the gate again. Doris seems more relaxed today, maybe because it's evening, or more likely because people always relax and want to chat with Seaneen.

"So, Doris, don't you think Declan could give the horse a good home?" Seaneen asks, pulling at a bit of hair that's got tangled in the wind.

"I'd be keeping her with Camilla Brooke," I say quickly. "I work for her." I've come in jodhpurs and boots today just to let her see I'm not a hoodlum but a serious horsey person.

Doris's face lights up. "Little Camilla. I used to hunt with Henry and Harriet – her parents."

Seaneen's eyes widen at the mention of hunting but she doesn't say anything.

"Well, you'd certainly be all right with Camilla behind you. Taught her in the Pony Club. What was her pony called? Flea-bitten grey, nice little chap?"

She's not asking like she expects me to answer, just trying to remember for herself, but she looks delighted when I say, "Sweep. She still has him."

"Jolly good."

"So it'd be a good home," I go on.

"Long as you're patient. She needs a lot of time. Come and spend time here with her. Get to know her. There's no rush to take her away, is there? Though I admit I'd be glad of the space. Need to get the Shetland mare and foal out to grass soon."

"And I'll come too," Seaneen says. "Cuddle that foal before it gets too big to fit on my knee."

"More than welcome." Doris straightens up her back, putting a hand to it and wincing. "Well, must get on. Horses won't feed themselves."

And she limps off on her endless rounds. I wonder if she ever has any help.

On the bus back to Belfast Seaneen snuggles into me. She smells of straw and horses under her normal perfume. Maybe she'll suddenly get horsey and want to move out to the country. I point out all the nice things to her – the views, any cottages that she'd think were cute and anything resembling a baby animal, and she smiles at it all, but I know she sees the country as somewhere to visit on a nice day. She's all bizz about the grey mare.

"When she took the apple from my hand I nearly cried," she says.

"I know." I take her hand. "I do want her. I just didn't imagine it happening like this."

"Sure anybody can just go and *buy* a horse," Seaneen says scornfully. "Like that cow Lara. That's easy. You'd give this horse a brilliant home."

I fast forward months – a year – into the future and see myself flying around a course of big jumps, clearing every one perfectly, and all the people hanging around the outside of the ring muttering, "He rescued that mare, you know. Brought her on from nothing. They're going to go right to the top."

Never mind the Laras of this world, using Daddy's money to buy something they can just sit on and point at the jumps. The ghost horse and I will take them on and beat them.

4.

It would be OK if it was just me and Seaneen. I even offer to pay for a taxi to the hospital – I wouldn't expect her to go on the bus, especially as she's still feeling sick on and off – but Mairéad says she's never heard anything so ridiculous and she'll drive us. Only she doesn't just mean drive us, she means come in with us, see the scan and all.

"You won't want me if your mum's there," I said when Seaneen phoned the night before to tell me to be ready to be picked up at ten o'clock.

"You mean you don't want to come?" She sounded grumpy, which isn't like Seaneen. Maybe she was nervous as well. "It's your baby too."

"It's not your mum's baby."

Silence.

"Seaneen?"

"Look, it's not much to ask, is it?"

It's terrible at the hospital. Everybody treats Seaneen as if she's about twelve. Not that they aren't nice to her, but they act like she's mental or something. And I'm invisible which suits me. Probably because her ma's hanging around, asking all the questions, acting like she's best friends with the nurse, holding Seaneen's hand, even, when they put this cold stuff on her tummy. It's too weird, seeing Seaneen with her top rolled up, her skin pale and freckly, the wee mole beside her belly button, with her ma standing there. There's a tiny bump now – not a bump, really; just a bit of a bulge.

"There's twins in the family," Mairéad says to the nurse and I nearly choke.

Seaneen twists her head and gives me a nervous grin.

The nurse moves the scanner thing over Seaneen's tummy and we all stare at the screen. I know it's meant to be all special and magical, and maybe it is if you're thirty or something and you *want* a baby.

The nurse smiles and says, "Oh look, there we go!" even though I'm not going anywhere, thanks to this baby. "Only one," she says. "Time enough for twins when you're older!" She laughs as if she's said something dead clever.

There's a shape. An alien bumbling around, all blurry but definitely there.

"Oh my God." Seaneen's eyes go all bright the way they were when she was cuddling the foal. She reaches for my hand as well as her mum's. "Can you believe it? Can you, Declan?"

I don't know how to answer so I don't say anything.

This is what's stopping me going away and having the life I want to have.

Mairéad squints at the picture. "Too early to say what it is, of course," she says, like she's some big expert.

"But we seem to have the recipe for girls in my family."

"It's the father that determines the gender," says the nurse, and Mairéad gives me this dirty look, like I'd better get it right.

The nurse chats to Seaneen about vitamins and morning sickness and the next scan, with Mairéad interrupting every two seconds, and it's all so *female* I could scream. Maybe if I'd felt something when I saw the thing move on the screen … but I didn't. They give Seaneen a couple of pictures of the scan and she looks at them all the way back to the car park.

Mairéad nearly shits herself turning out of the hospital car park. She hesitates and dithers and misses all these chances while the driver behind hoots and bangs on his dashboard and then, just when it's *not* safe, she rams her foot down and jumps out into the honking traffic. We'll do well to get home alive, never mind live long enough for Seaneen to actually have the baby.

There's construction and a funeral. We inch up the Falls Road in second gear, juddering so much that Seaneen says she's going to be sick and has to sit with the window down. I'm in the back and the thick city air – petrol and fries and dust – oozes past her and up my nose. I pull my sweaty T-shirt away from my body to try and cool down.

"You shouldn't be looking at that picture while the car's moving; that'd make anybody sick," Mairéad says.

The lights ahead turn red and Mairéad jams on the handbrake before the car's properly stopped. "So, Declan," she says, in a now-I've-got-you way. "I suppose you'll be thinking about a new job." She smirks at me in the rear-view mirror. For a few seconds I think she must know I'd been hoping to go away before all this, but in the next breath she says, "They're looking for somebody to do shifts at the Spar."

"I have a job."

Mairéad puts the car into first gear and lurches forward. "I know you have your wee job with the horses. But Seaneen says you only get the minimum wage."

"Mum, I never!" Seaneen turns around to me. "I only said, you'd think after doing your two years in college you'd get paid more." She turns quickly around again and I can tell from the way she leans back against the seatbelt that she really does feel sick.

Familiar panicky rage huffs down my nostrils with the recycled city air. I nip one arm hard to distract me from wanting to hit Seaneen's ma and throw myself out of this barely-moving car into the traffic. Watch the red pinch of skin turn slowly white and go back into shape.

"I didn't go to college for two years to work in a frigging shop," I say. Mairéad works in Tesco's.

"Could you not get a better-paid job with horses?"

"If I went away." The words hang in the car.

"Mum, you need to stop, I swear. Please." She doesn't mean, as I think at first, you need to stop hassling my boyfriend who hasn't done anything wrong; she means, you need to stop the car before I throw up in it.

It's the third of July. This is the week I was meant to start at Hans-Peter Hilgenberg's.

★ ★ ★

Doris is surprised to see me. She's struggling with the gate of the paddock beside the drive, which is hanging on one hinge. "I had a day off," I explain, "so I just came out." Even though it's the truth my voice sounds tight and unnatural to me.

"Jolly good,' she says. "Blasted donkey," she goes on. "Burst through the gate at feeding time. Been here six months and still can't get used to the fact that he doesn't have to fight for his grub."

"Maybe I could fix it for you?"

"Oh." She looks at me in surprise, her eyes narrowing into slits in her wrinkly face. "Any good with gates?"

"I can try."

Turns out I'm not that brilliant with gates but I'm a lot stronger than Doris and, using mostly brute force, manage to cobble together a way of getting the gate to work. By the time it's done and I head down to see the grey mare, the icy bad temper that followed me the whole ten miles here on the bike is melting.

The mare, grazing near the tree again, looks whiter and smoother than last time. Quieter too, says Doris, who's come down with me. Doris rattles the gate and the mare's long ears flicker but she doesn't shy or run away.

"Spend some time with her," Doris says, pulling at the baler twine which ties up the gate. "Don't be in a hurry. Just *be*." She sounds like an old hippy sometimes, for somebody who used to go "hunting with Henry and Harriet".

I sit under the tree and don't try to get the mare to come to me. I set out some apple slices nearby. The mare ignores me. I flick one in her direction and she goggles in alarm but then catches on to what it is and slowly, step by step, approaches it. She stretches out her neck, wrinkles her nose and sucks it up. Then she stands and, after a moment or two, goes back to grazing. I lean back against the rough, cool bark and watch the mare. She grazes with more intensity than any horse I've ever seen, as if the grass might suddenly disappear. In the distance I hear all the sounds of Rosevale. Some of them are the sounds you get in any yard, but there's no ringing of iron-shod hooves, no clatter of jump poles or kids boasting about their ponies. There's the chink of buckets. Neighs and ee-aws. Sheep maaahing in the next-door field, a whole conversation of it. The clattering whoosh of a hose being pulled out. I only realize I've had a headache when I start to feel it lift. I close my eyes and breathe in the smells of grass and air.

I wake to the warm huff of breath on my shoulder, and a snort. Cold wet horsey spit sprays my neck.

I turn my head and there she is. Shining white, her dark mane parted down the length of her thin neck. She looks as if she can't believe how close she's come to me, all of her own accord. She stretches her neck out for the last piece of apple, which is right beside my left foot. I don't move. Or breathe. Her eye stays on me. It's purplish dark and soft, wary but not a black pit of hatred and fear any more.

"Hey,' I whisper in the quietest voice I've ever used. "Little ghost horse."

I raise myself onto my knees and very, very slowly stand up. She starts away but only for a few steps before she stops and looks at me with interest. Maybe it's just that she smells the apple juice from my pockets. But whatever the reason, she stays and lets me touch her. I rub my hand down her shoulder. She shivers and then relaxes. Bits of her skin are still bare and pinkish with corrugated scabs. Her eyes run constantly because she's sensitive to the light after being in the dark for so long. She flits her head away when I try to touch it, but she lets me stroke her neck and shoulders. I murmur nonsense to her the whole time. "Folly? Do you want to be my horse?" I whisper. I don't know why I've started calling her Folly; it just suits her.

Folly's ears flicker.

★ ★ ★

Cam and I sit in her kitchen. I don't think she's changed anything since her parents died, because it's kind of old-fashioned. It's tidier since Pippa came on the scene, but you're still as likely to find a bridle and a few tubes of wormer on the table as a place mat or a salt shaker. Span jumps on my knee and starts nosing at a bit of dirt stuck to my sweatshirt.

"You're sure about this?" Cam hands me a cup of milky coffee and sits down opposite me. "You won't get itchy feet in the middle of the winter? Because if I'm going to have to replace you I'd rather do it now. I don't want you leaving me in the lurch in January when the pipes are frozen and the yard's a sheet of ice and I've twelve horses going mad in the stables."

"I promise I won't do that." The baby will be born in January. "Cam? There's something else. I've kind of got a horse. Well, I *have* got a horse."

"Good God." She cups her hands around her own coffee and shoos Spick down onto the ground from where he growls jealously at Span. "How have you managed that?"

Without me, I think she means. I never imagined

getting a horse without Cam's help.

"It's the grey mare." I concentrate on stroking Span's ear so she can't see my face. "From the barn."

Cam's quiet for a moment, as if she has to struggle to remember. We never mentioned the death barn after the first few days. I wonder if she's forgotten or if, like me, she can't stand thinking about it. "Gosh. Are you sure? That's a lot to take on. You'd be better with —"

"I know. But listen. She's nowhere near as nervous as she was then. I mean, you saw her at her worst. I've been going up to see her most days after work. She lets me groom her and all."

"But … going up *where*? And why didn't you tell me all this?"

"She's at Rosevale. Doris Rose's sanctuary?" Cam should *know* all this – the police, or maybe the USPCA, told us the night we found the horses that they were going to Rosevale.

"Doris is still alive? She used to be a dragon at Pony Club."

For a second I see Cam, all red plaits and Pony Club tie, on a younger, livelier Sweep, and Doris telling her off for not having her stirrups shining.

"She seems to run the place all on her own. I try to help a bit when I'm there but mostly I just work with the mare."

"Well, well. You're a dark horse, Declan – no pun intended."

"But do you mind? I mean, I know she's rough, but she's improved. She doesn't look like a toast rack any more. You could hide her somewhere if you don't want the customers to see her. I know she won't be a good advert for the yard."

"That doesn't matter," Cam says. "Anybody can see we're not in the habit of starving our horses here. As long as she hasn't got anything."

"Well, she's been at Rosevale for a month now. She's been wormed, deloused, de-everythinged."

"What age?"

"Six or seven."

"Broken?"

"Doris thinks so." I don't tell Cam that the clues Doris has spotted have all been pretty negative – sore areas on her back that may be the result of a badly fitting saddle, scars on her girth, roughness at the bars of her mouth. "So that's good, isn't it? I won't have to start right at the beginning." I'm trying to make Folly sound as good as possible.

Cam hesitates and lifts up my empty mug. "Sometimes that's easier. You don't know what bad experiences she might have had. You'll probably have a lot to *un*do."

I haven't really let myself think about this. But I have ridden some difficult horses over the last few years, and some young, green ones. I'm a good rider and I'm brave. And the difference is, she'll be *mine*.

"But you'll help me, won't you, Cam?"

"Of course I will. Only, well … don't expect too much. She's had a bad start."

There's no arguing with this. Whatever chain of events led to Folly being locked up starving in a barn, it can't be a happy story. Cam's only saying the things I told myself for weeks when Folly was still the ghost horse, haunting my nightmares and freaking me out.

But it's different now.

Cam changes tack. "I'm sorry, Declan; I'm not being negative. I think it's wonderful. Your first horse." She stands up and Span jumps down from my knee and wags her tail. "OK, better go and do some work. Don't look so worried. You're taking a chance, that's all. It's no more than I did, two years ago."

"With what?" I can't remember Cam buying a horse two years ago. Unless she means the Welshies, bought cheap as shy yearlings.

She laughs. "Not a horse! On *you*. People told me not to expect too much. But you turned out OK." She grins like she's remembering me when I knew nothing. When I joyrode Flight and nearly wrecked him. "More than OK."

"Oh." I don't know whether to be flattered or insulted. A bit of both, I think.

5.

Folly clatters off the ramp, losing her footing and panicking, and jumps and trembles at the end of her lead rope. It burns across the palm of my hand. I jerk on it but she only wheels around and goggles in alarm at this strange new place.

"Easy, baby," I beg her. She lifts her head, ears quivering, and squeals.

"We'll turn her out straight away," Cam says. "She'll settle when she sees the other horses. And the grass." She doesn't sound that convinced. Old Jim purses his lips and keeps his distance.

It takes both me and Cam to lead a jumpy Folly down the lane to the fields. We're putting her in the small paddock we use for convalescent horses or newcomers, where they can see the other horses but have their own space.

We manage to get her through the gate and she pauses just inside the field, head up, eyes huge and black. Here at Cam's yard, which isn't full of rescue cases, she looks very, very skinny and rough. She's the ghost horse again, terrified and outraged.

"She'll graze in a minute," Cam says. "Stop looking so worried."

We lean over the gate, like we've done so many times, watching so many horses. But nothing was like watching this horse fling herself up and down the fence in panic. Because this animal with the angry eyes, the red pits of nostrils and the heaving, sweating flanks, is mine. My responsibility.

I twist a blade of grass around my finger and will her to stop, to put her head down and graze and be content.

Folly dashes up and down, wearing a path in the grass already, shuddering to a halt so close to the fence that each time you think, this time she won't be able to stop.

I don't know how Cam can stand beside me so calmly, sucking a Polo mint. "I wonder how she's bred," she says. "Looks more or less thoroughbred to me — those legs and that chest. Though the colour's unusual…. She could have been bred to race. A lot of horses who end up on the scrap heap are racehorses who haven't made the grade. Who knows."

This isn't what I want to hear. A horse bred to race, trained to race, can be difficult to retrain.

But right now all I want is for Folly to stop pacing and throwing herself about and settle down. She ignores the lovely rich grass. Stops every few strides to neigh at Spirit and Willow who are grooming each other in the next field, ignoring her. From the bottom field, friendly Nudge lifts up her head and nickers back, throaty and curious.

"She's going to break the fence," I say. "Look, next time, she's not going to turn, she's not going to stop."

"She won't break the fence. And if she does she can't go anywhere except into Spirit and Willow. And she'll get a nasty shock from the electric fence."

"But she's not ready for a nasty shock! Oh Cam, she's going to hurt herself. Look, I should go in and get her." I reach for the gate.

"Declan." Cam puts a hand on my shoulder. "You could get hurt. She'll calm down. She's just nervous. Everything's strange to her. Go and take Joy around the farm trail. I don't want to see you back here for an hour."

"I can't – what if something happens?"

"I've run this yard for eight years. I'll manage. I have Lara for a lesson; I can keep an eye on Folly from the school. Go. It's an order."

I go.

Joy's fit enough now that the hills of the farm trail don't make her sweat and huff, and when I put her at a couple of logs she pops over them happily. Two years ago this would have been enough for me – to take a horse, any horse, around the farm trail, going where I want, being in charge. But today all I can think of is Folly. I know she'll break out. Easy for Cam to say she can keep an eye from the school – it's five minutes away. When things go wrong with horses they tend to go wrong in a split second.

By the time I get back to the yard I know Folly has burst through the fence, maybe scared herself so much she's had a heart attack. Or she's tried to jump the gate and broken her leg. It's almost a shock not to see the vet's car in the yard.

I can't hear anything weird. Just Cam's voice in the school: "You need to pick up the left lead immediately. Now. Good."

I throw myself off Joy and drag her behind me to her stable to untack her. "Come on, you lazy brute!" Joy likes to rub her face on you when you get off, and she's offended to be lugged around like this. I yank her tack off, getting her reins all tangled the way I did when I started riding and everything was a mystery to me. I dump her expensive tack outside her stable, ram the bolt home in the door and dash down to the field.

The fence is in one piece. Folly is in one piece. *Oh thank you God; I will never ask for anything again.* She's grazing; not with the single-minded intensity she did the last couple of weeks at Rosevale – her ears flicker and she looks up every few seconds – but she's grazing. She's rolled in the muddy patch beside the gate and looks like a skewbald, big splashes of brown spattered over the white. I let out a long slow breath.

"OK?" Cam calls from the school.

"Yeah." I bend over and get my breath back properly.

Lara canters Willow around in circles. She's looking in the direction of the field. I wonder what she thinks of Folly. I lean on the gate again and survey my horse. I try to imagine I don't know where she came from. I try to pretend she's not my horse. What does she look like?

Dirty. Sweaty, her coat roughened with dried-up patches. Skinny, ribs still showing clearly. She looks like what she is: a knacker.

But out of my memory comes Seaneen's voice:

"Anybody can go out and buy a horse with their daddy's money."

I'd love to go and get Folly and groom her and make her all clean and shining. But that's not fair. Showing her off doesn't matter. Letting her settle does. So I open the gate very quietly and walk up to her.

"Folly," I say, very low. She doesn't know her name but I like to think she knows my voice. She looks up, goggles at me, then settles back to grazing. I'm happy to be ignored. "Good girl," I say. "Clever Folly." I get closer and she lets me stroke her neck. The sweat has dried into wavy curls. "Poor old girl," I whisper. "It's OK. This is your new home. You're never going anywhere bad again, I promise."

But I don't think she believes me.

6.

"Declan." Cam appears beside me at the gate of Folly's paddock, holding Joy's headcollar rope. She's just been to turn her out in the bottom field. "For God's sake, go *home*. Has your bike even got lights?"

"It has *a* light."

"Folly's fine. And I'm here. I can check on her from the landing window."

"D'you not think she's a bit less settled than she was?"

"She was interested in Joy going past, that's all." Folly lifts up her head and gives a high-pitched neigh. "She's a bit anxious, maybe, but you standing around here looking at her every two seconds isn't going to change that."

"She drank loads. What if she gets colic?"

"Declan." Cam puts both hands on my shoulders and pretends to drag me away from the fence. "If you get mowed down by a truck because you're cycling home in the dark you needn't think I am going to look after that horse for you." She smiles. "So *go*."

"I'll be here extra early in the morning," I promise, walking beside her back up to the yard where my bike is in its usual place against the wall. I won't sleep, worrying about Folly. Mum's out tonight with Colette; Colette's taking her for dinner for her birthday. This will be the first time they've met since the night I landed, drunk, at Colette's house. I want to time my arrival back home so that I don't have to see her.

At the end of Cam's road I nearly turn back for a last check, but a Land Rover beeps at me and I remember what Cam said about getting mowed down in the dark so I force myself to turn left and freewheel down the hill. I count everything to distract me – fields with horses in them, road signs, houses for sale … It only half works. After five minutes the rain starts – a drizzle at first, then proper cold rain that makes my hoodie heavy and freezes my hands on the handlebars. And gives me something new to worry about – Folly getting chilled from sweating up then getting rained on.

I hate cycling past the barn. But the other road home is three miles longer and far hillier. I still don't like looking over the overgrown messy hedge and seeing the roof of the barn in at the far end of the field, but every time, I can't stop myself from standing up on my pedals and checking it out. Tonight somebody's dumped an old car seat, a portable barbecue and two TVs on top of the usual litter of beer cans in the gateway. If I hadn't stopped that night, Folly would be lying in there dead now. I put my head down and cycle past.

I change gears as the hills get steeper. The bike tires whizz through puddles. I give myself a good talking to.

Grounded

It'll be OK. She'll settle down and bond with me and I'll make her a champion.

In my mind I'm jumping Folly around the same course I did at Balmoral on Flight, only she's even better, faster, surer. And *mine*. I turn into Tirconnell Parade. It's properly dark now. There's no light in any of the windows of our house so Mum mustn't be back yet. With any luck, if I go straight to bed, I won't have to talk to her or Colette.

That Cian's sitting on the wall outside our house, tracing wet shapes on the ground with the side of his trainer. I stop the bike and stand straddling it. "Get off and sit on your own wall."

"I'm only sitting here. You don't own the wall."

I remember shouting over the same thing to old Mrs. Mulholland, Seaneen's granny, when me and Emmet McCann – before we were enemies – and a whole load of people used to sit on her wall. She'd come barging out, arms crossed under her big mono-boob, and shout, "Will you get off my wall; you have your own frigging walls."

Like anybody ever wanted to sit on their own wall.

She stopped when we got big enough to scare her, and then we got even bigger and stopped getting our kicks from sitting on walls sharing a bottle of Strongbow.

And now the old bag's dead and this wee rat lives in her house and sits on people's walls. But there's something about the way he's sitting, with the rain misting his hair in droplets, as if he hasn't so much chosen to be here as found himself here.

"Why are you sitting out here in the rain?"

He shrugs and keeps moving his foot. I glance over

145

at his house and see an unfamiliar Honda Civic parked outside. And remember something else. That I didn't only sit around on people's walls to annoy them and I didn't always do it with my mates. Sometimes it was raining like now and I was on my own and it was boring and cold but it was better than going home. To Barry or Mike or Colin or the one before Colin with the motorbike, who was nice at first and then not, whose name I can't remember.

And Stacey said she had a new man.

"Your ma throw you out?" I ask.

Cian shrugs again. There's something different about him tonight but I can't work out what.

"I hear she has a fella."

He screws up his mouth.

I'm about to go on past with a dirty look to show him I'm above worrying about whose wall he's sitting on, when my phone buzzes in my pocket and I grab for it so fast I nearly let the bike fall. When I see it's a text from Cam I'm nearly scared to read it. *Folly settled. Grazing. So go to sleep and stop worrying!!*

I must let my breath out really loudly because the nosy wee bastard goes, "What is it?"

"None of your business," I snap. Then find myself saying, "It's my horse." I get a rush of pride at the words.

Too late I remember the way Cian got on in the Spar, calling me horse boy, saying I smelled, but instead of making fun he says, "Your own horse? No way."

"I just got her." The temptation to talk about Folly is stronger than the dislike I have for this kid.

"Got a photo?"

After a small hesitation I show him my phone – just show it, don't let him take it in his thieving mitts.

"It's awful skinny," he says.

I snatch the phone away. "That's because she was rescued. You should have seen her a few weeks ago."

When I look at his snipey wee face it's full of something I've never seen in it before: interest. So instead of telling him where to go I say I found her starving in a barn.

"So is it like finders keepers?"

"No. I had to fill in forms and all. It's all official."

My hands are cold and wet on the handlebars. I don't need to be standing here with this loser. I could be in a nice warm house – a nice warm *empty* house for once – maybe having a lovely long hot bath without Mum yelling through the door about the hot water.

I don't know why I'm not.

Just because this kid reminds me of me, not wanting to go home and deal with some new man. Or not allowed to. I remember Stacey saying she just wanted him out of the way when – what was his name? – Darren was around.

Just because he's shown a bit of interest in Folly. I don't even *want* him to be interested in Folly. I remember when I first saw Flight, it was like having a crush, but Vicky was always there, whispering "mine".

But I also think about Seaneen: Seaneen wouldn't be going in to a hot bath and leaving him sitting out in the rain, keeping watch until it was safe to go home.

For God's sake! This kid walked into our house and helped himself to whatever he wanted! I don't owe him a thing.

Still I find myself saying, "If you want to come in for

a cup of tea, you can. Get dry."

Cian looks startled for a moment, then shrugs, says, "Might as well," and heaves himself off the wall like he's doing me a favour. So I regret asking him before I even put the key in the door. What if he goes up to the loo? He knows where my £200 is now – I put it back in the same place. Will I have to search him when he comes downstairs? This is a stupid idea.

I leave the door into the kitchen open while I make the tea and stick four rounds of bread into the toaster. Cian sits on the sofa, arms folded like he's worked out I'm keeping tabs on him.

"How do you like your tea?" I shout in.

"*Tea*? Have you no proper drink?"

"No." I bring the tea in – he's got it milk, no sugar and if he doesn't like it he can go back out and sit on the wall and I hope his ma keeps on having sex or whatever she's doing for another few hours. And I hope it keeps raining. When he takes the tea and reaches out for a slice of toast I see his eyes clocking the packet of cigarettes on the arm of the sofa and I realize what's different about him tonight. It's the first time I've ever seen him when he hasn't been on something, or at least looked as if he was.

He munches through most of the toast and drinks the tea happily enough. He keeps looking around the room. Casing it probably.

"Is that you on that big red horse?" he asks, jerking his head at the framed photo Vicky gave me for my eighteenth. It wasn't long after she'd bust her leg and I'd started competing on Flight. It's one of those professional pictures that photographers take at shows and it's a really good one. I hate Mum having school photos of me and all but I've never minded this being on display. At least it proves it was all *real*.

"Yeah."

"My ma said you were a jockey."

I can't help a grin at that. Jockey sounds better than shit shoveller. "No. Showjumping."

"So it's not a race?"

"No. But sometimes it's against the clock."

"But that's not the horse on your phone?"

"No. That's Flight. He was sold." I chew on a bit of toast.

"So you have a different one?" He sets his mug down on the arm of the sofa.

"Yeah."

"And does it jump like that?"

"Not yet. I have to train her."

"I used to have a dog," he says. "One time."

I can't imagine Stacey with a dog, unless maybe one of those ratty things that live in handbags.

"A Labrador. Gypsy."

"I wouldn't have thought your mum would go for big dogs."

"Not *her*," he says like I'm stupid. "Somebody else."

I'm about to say, "Oh yeah, I heard you got fostered," but I stop myself because I remember how annoying it is to have strangers knowing stuff about you. When I got out of Bankside, loads of teachers, ones that didn't even teach me, ones that had damn-all to do with me, would give me sideways looks in the corridor like they'd had a *meeting* about me or something. So instead I just put on this innocent, sort of interested face, and Cian pauses then says, like he's telling me something important, "Helen and Sam."

I hand him the last slice of toast. "How come?"

"Foster care," he says. I wait for him to say more, but he doesn't. He just looks at me with those weird fox's eyes narrowed. I know he's waiting for me to ask him something.

"So why was that?"

He shakes his head, then shrugs. "I don't know. Don't remember. Mum says I was too much for her."

"Do you remember being taken away?"

"Nah." He wipes toast crumbs from his mouth and says, "Have you really not got a proper drink?"

"We don't keep it in the house."

"Is your mum an alcoholic?"

I consider this. She hasn't had a drink for over two years. But she says it's always there, in the back of her head. Sometimes she goes to her AA meetings a lot and I know she's finding it harder. "Yeah,' I say. "A recovering one. So next time you come here robbing, you know that's one thing you won't find."

He looks down and bites his lip and I feel guilty. A tiny bit.

"I was out of my mind," Cian says. "I'm always doing stupid stuff."

"So why do it?"

He shrugs. "Nothing else to do."

I haven't sat through years of Mr. Pastoral Care Dermott for nothing. "That's bullshit."

"Yeah? So what did you do when you were my age?"

"Well – hung out. You know. With my mates."

"Drinking?"

I shrug. "Suppose."

"Smoking? Sitting on walls annoying people? Nicking cars? Drugs?"

I sigh. There's no point lying. "Yes to most of those. Only not drugs. And it was *a* car. Once."

"See?"

"But there's other stuff you could do. Go to the youth club. Boxing?" Some of the ones I was at school with are well into their boxing. Go all over the place with it. "Football?"

"Nah. I just like having a laugh."

I feel like I should say something to him. Something – I don't know – wise or helpful or something, the kind of thing Seaneen would think of, but all I can come up with is, "Well, I didn't see you laughing too hard tonight."

7.

"Good girl." I set Folly's hoof down on the floor of her stable – Flight's old stable – and straighten up. It's taken ten minutes to pick out three hooves, and the sweat's running down inside my T-shirt. Thank God horses only have four legs. It's taken us weeks to get to this stage. Weeks of gut-twisting worry, praying that she'll let me touch her without flinching and shifting to the back of the stable, and then occasional breakthroughs like her letting me lift a back hoof for the first time. I've hardly been home except to sleep. Seaneen complains that she never sees me. That there's another woman in my life now. It started as a joke but lately she's been sounding pissed off.

"C'mon. Last one." I run my hand down her back leg. "Up." She lifts the hoof but then strikes out with it so I have to yank my hand away before it gets kicked. "No." I keep my voice firm and low. The ring of hooves outside makes Folly start and prick her ears. A shadow falls across the stable door and Lara looks in. She's on

Willow. She looks smugly relaxed, feet out of her stirrups, reins loose. Willow pins his ears back at Folly and
Lara kicks him and hauls on the reins so he backs up a
couple of steps but she doesn't get out of my way.

"I can't believe you're *still* picking out her feet."

I ignore her and pull again at the tiny frill of white
hair at the back of Folly's leg. "Up, girl."

This time the hoof remains firmly on the ground.

"You should hit her. You're too soft. It's just badness."

Without looking up I say, "It's not badness. She's
scared. If she gives me her hoof she can't run away."

Lara gives me a "Duh!" look. "She's in a *stable*. She
can't *go* anywhere anyway."

"Exactly. That's why she feels more vulnerable.
Especially because she was locked up."

Lara sniffs. "You spoil her. She doesn't look scared to
me. See the whites of her eye? That's a sign of a mean
horse."

"The only mean horse around here is yours," I say.
"Who kicked the farrier? Who chased Spirit away from
the drinker in the field?"

"It's just pathetic to see you wasting so much time
and money on something that's never going to amount
to anything."

"She'll amount to more than that bad-tempered
brute."

Lara laughs. "You won't be saying that when you're
on the phone begging McCluskey to take her to the cat-
food factory." She hauls Willow around and trots off to
the school.

I run my hand over Folly's thin white shoulder,

scratching at the last dregs of an old scab. She wouldn't have let me do that a few days ago. "You're never going to McCluskey," I whisper. "I promise." As soon as Lara's gone Folly lets me lift her hoof and pick out the dirt, but just as she puts it down there's more hoofbeats outside. I sigh. At Rosevale there was never anybody about but Doris and she was always too busy to get in your way. Sometimes I worry that Cam's is going to be too noisy for Folly, even though Cam complains that things are dead this summer. And Folly looks much worse here, where everything else is fat and shining.

But when I see it's only Sally, leading Nudge, her brown cob, I relax, and even Folly doesn't look as outraged as she normally does when someone walks past.

Nudge stops when Sally does and nuzzles into her shoulder. She's the nosiest horse in the world and now she sticks her head over the half-door. "Be nice," Sally warns. But Folly touches noses with her and they sniff a bit without any squealing or trouble, before Folly loses interest and goes back to her hay net. I worry about overfeeding her, but she's so much condition to put on and she gets stressed standing in her stable.

Sally looks in and smiles her slow quiet smile. "How are you getting on?" she asks.

I run the softest body brush over Folly's white shoulder. "I just wish she wasn't so nervous. Sometimes I think she hates people."

"Well, she'd have good reason to. Poor baby," she says directly to Folly who's now so intent on her hay net that she ignores us, even though I'm grooming her, which normally makes her twitchy. "Lucky, though, being found by you. Quite a story, isn't it?"

"Depends if she turns out OK." I can't tell even Sally the ridiculous over-the-top dreams I have for Folly. I know it's not fair, putting so much on a horse. But what else is left?

"Ah, she will." Sally speaks like there's no doubt. "She just needs time."

"That's what Doris says. And Cam. Lara says she's vicious and will end up on McCluskey's truck. *After* I've wasted a fortune on her."

"Her!" Sally rolls her eyes. "She told me I should get Nudge put down and get myself something useful."

"Bitch." We both look at Nudge who's still standing perfectly at ease beside Sally, resting a leg. She nudges Sally in the side and we both laugh.

"Have you decided about putting her in foal?" I ask.

"Not going to. I love the idea of it, but I have to think, could I manage another horse, have I time for a foal, and what's going to happen to it in the long run? I know I'm not up to training a young horse properly. And there's so many unwanted horses now." She nods at Folly who's relaxed into an acceptance of being groomed, as long as she can keep eating at the same time. "Did you hear about those wee ponies down in Dublin? They were sold for a Euro, fifty cents even. Ending up being beaten around housing estates and living in backyards."

I imagine Folly in our garden, blinking under the streetlights, eating leftover chips from Fat Frankie's. Kids like Cian asking me for rides on her. Or just taking her. I shiver. "You should have seen the wee foal that was in with her," I tell Sally. Even now, with Folly standing beside me, warm and alive, I don't like thinking about Flame.

"Well, this one's a survivor. Wait till the end of the summer. A few weeks of grass. You won't recognize her."

Sally always cheers me up. If I could tell anyone at the yard about the baby, it would be her. But I couldn't tell her before Cam.

* * *

Even though Mairéad and Gary are out I can never relax in Seaneen's living room. The twins are asleep upstairs but the carpet and sofa are littered with the pink plastic junk that seems to breed around them. I flick through a hundred channels of crap.

"Ah, isn't this great?" Seaneen puts down her pregnancy magazine – how can there be a whole magazine about something so boring? – leans back against the sofa cushions and reaches for my hand. "Declan?"

"Yeah. Sorry. Just tired."

"I'm not surprised. You're at that yard all hours. Why are you always so late?"

"Told you. I have to look after Folly. It takes time." And staying late with Folly gives me a great excuse not to spend too much time at home, where Seaneen wants to talk about names and Mum's taken up knitting.

"But I haven't seen you all week, and all you want to do is yawn and watch TV."

"You were the one had to stay in and babysit."

Oh God. Is this going to be me and Seaneen in ten years, sitting in a Belfast housing project with our brats asleep upstairs – one of them nearly ten? And where'll Folly be then? She'll be about sixteen – just past her prime as a showjumper. Maybe she'll have a foal. I'd put her to a really good stallion. *Her* foal won't end up abandoned in a barn.

"Declan?" Seaneen jiggles my arm and I drop the remote.

"Sorry. Look, you should come and see Folly. You were the one encouraged me to get her."

She sighs. "I thought she'd just go in a *field*. I didn't think you'd spend all your time with her."

Seaneen's not sick these days and she doesn't look as pasty. Her hair's bouncy again and even curlier. But she's starting to *look* pregnant, with this growing bulge that I try not to look at. I like it when she wears baggy T-shirts but the magazine she's just put down has a picture of some pregnant singer letting it all hang out with a big sticky-out belly button that's the grossest thing I ever saw. If Seaneen starts going for that look I'll be mortified.

"I told them at work," she says.

"Told them what?"

She sighs. "About the *baby*. I want to keep working as long as I can. Because I haven't been there long enough to get maternity leave."

I try to sound intelligent. "So what does that mean?"

"I'll have to resign." She shrugs and then lays her arm across her belly. "I would've anyway. I'm not leaving our baby in a nursery when it's no age, not like some of them."

I hate it when she talks about the baby like it's a real thing. If I've ever thought about it I suppose I assumed she'd take it to work with her; maybe they'd let her dump it there for free or at least cheap, like me having Folly at the yard.

"I'll go back part-time when he or she's older. The

twins'll be at school and Mum says she'll mind the child." Seaneen never says *it*.

"So – you'll still be living *here?*"

Seaneen picks up a purple feathery dressing-up shoe and strokes it. "I don't know, Dec. Will I?" Her eyes look big.

"How should I –"

"It's your baby too."

"I never said it wasn't. Look, I haven't gone any-where. I'm *not* going anywhere. I never for one second said I wasn't going to stay with you."

"You never *said* it."

"I never thought it; whatever. Same thing."

"It's not the same thing." She moves to the other end of the sofa, and flicks over to some medical drama on Sky. I could get up and go home, but I don't. Only I don't move any closer to her, either.

★ ★ ★

Seaneen looks around the yard, nose twitching. She's got this thing about smells now. "Where is everyone?"

"Cam's gone to a big show on the north coast. She's brought some of the liveries. It's Jim's day off." I don't tell her I picked this day on purpose so we wouldn't meet anybody.

We stroll down through the paddocks. It's August and there's a breath of autumn that makes me zip my hoodie. Cam put Folly in the field beside the school last week, with the Welshies for company, and after the usual squealing and hoof stamping and dashing around the field with their tails up, they settled down OK.

Seaneen leans on the gate and squints into the field. The wind catches her curls and blows them around her face. She spits hair out of her mouth. "I can't see her," she complains. "She must've escaped."

"Don't be daft. There she is, under the tree. Folly!" I raise my voice, crossing my fingers that she'll respond. Sometimes she does; sometimes she doesn't. She lifts her head, ears pricked. She looks around and takes ages making up her mind. Then she trots up to the gate, long grey mane flying in the breeze, hooves skimming the ground, a world away from the ghost horse who cowered in the barn.

Seaneen turns to me. "No way is that her! Where's her scabs?"

"Healed up." I can't prevent a huge grin as I take Seaneen's hand. "*Now* you see why I've been so busy?" Actually, Folly looking so good has got more to do with her stuffing her face with Cam's good grass than with the hours I've spent with her in the stable. But Seaneen won't know that.

"Come on." I undo the gate. "Come in and see her properly."

But Seaneen hangs back. Her cheeks are pink in the wind.

"You came into the field at Doris's. She's a million times quieter now."

Seaneen flips her hand at the three Welsh ponies, who are way down at the bottom of the field and have no notion of moving.

"*They* won't come near you. They're happy, eating."

"It's just" – she places her arm protectively across

her stomach – "with the baby …"

"I don't know anybody who's ever been kicked in the stomach by a horse. But if you don't want to …"

Seaneen hesitates. "I'll talk to her over the fence,' she says.

But Folly's given up on us. She sees we haven't got anything for her and trots back to her tree.

We go for the bus. It feels like a stupid waste of an afternoon. All the way home, Seaneen says, "You know, I can't see what takes up the time. If she's just eating grass in the field all day …"

"I'm training her," I explain. "Getting her ready to ride. That's the whole point."

"Oh," Seaneen says. "So that'll take up even more time?"

It's the first time I've looked at Seaneen and seen Mairéad. And I have a horrible feeling it won't be the last.

8.

My heart slumps at the sight of Mairéad coming down the aisle of the liquor store towards me.

She looks at the can in my hand. One can of Harp. One wee can to quench the dust and sand that have scratched at my throat the whole way home.

"Drinking on your own?" she says like she's just caught me with a litre of Buckfast in an alleyway. She nods in a knowing way. She looks me up and down and her nose twitches. I know I'm sweaty, and sand from the school clings to the mud on my boots. It's the smell of hard work. Isn't that the kind of thing girls' mums are meant to love?

I look at the three-bottles-of-wine-for-a-tenner in her own basket. "Mairéad – did you want something?"

She hoicks her basket up her arm. "I don't want us to fall out, Declan. You're the father of my grandchild." God, I wish she wouldn't put it like that.

"But?" I prompt her.

"Me and Gary have been talking. You need to start sorting things out."

"What sort of things?"

"Somewhere to live?"

A fat man pushes past us on his way to the whiskey.

I don't keep my voice down. "Why? Are you throwing Seaneen out?"

A red flush creeps up Mairéad's neck. "Don't be stupid. I just meant – I thought you were sticking by her. Because she's got rights, you know."

"I *am* sticking by her." I am fed up having this conversation.

"Well, you're not very involved."

"I came to the scan!"

"That was one hour! Where are you all day long? Where have you been the night? Our Seaneen's waiting on you."

"Mairéad, I have a job."

"Seven days a week? Night, noon, and morning?"

"I have to look after Folly."

"Folly!" She snorts.

I turn away and walk to the checkout but Granzilla catches me up. "Don't think you can just walk away from that child."

I don't know if *that child* means Seaneen or the baby. All I know is when I get out of the liquor store and start wheeling my bike home, which is ridiculous when you're trying to drink a can of beer at the same time, her heels tap along beside me. "I mean it, Declan. Our Seaneen lets you get away with murder, but I won't. And Gary won't."

I wonder if Seaneen *would* let me get away with murder – with murdering her ma. The wine bottles clink in her carrier bag.

Mairéad changes to a creamy kind of voice. "Och, Declan, you've never had a father, have you? So you don't know what you missed out on. But I'm not having that child growing up like that." She changes her carrier bag to the other hand. "She's eighteen weeks now. You can't keep letting on it's not happening." She heads off down her own street, her arse wiggling exactly the same way Seaneen's does, only hers is wider. She half-turns to call back at me, "You have to start being *adult* about it," so she doesn't see some kid in a hoodie dash past, head down, shoving her into the road and nearly making her drop her bag. I grin, until I realize the kid's heading straight for me and if I don't grab him he's going to mow me down. He hurtles into me but I block him. The kid keels over and nearly falls, his breath huffing in slobbery wheezes.

"Steady on." I grab him by the wrists to hold him up. It's Cian. His face under his hood is white, his eyes wild. For a second he blinks at me without recognition. Down the street a car revs.

"What's up with you?" I ask.

I look down at his wrists, caught in my hands. His sleeves have ridden up, exposing deep red scratches on his arms. He pulls away and hugs himself. He shakes his head. "Nothing," he mutters.

"Is somebody after you? Where are you going?"

"Nowhere."

A Honda Civic roars past us, and Cian flinches like

it's going to mow him down. His breath is ragged and shaky.

"That your ma's fella?"

"Ex," he says. "He just dumped her."

I remember Stacey's whiny voice, "If he wrecks this for me …" I look at Cian's arms and he pulls his sleeves down quickly. "Did he give you those marks?"

Cian shakes his head. "Think I'd let that bastard near me?" He's all swagger again but the effect's spoiled by the snot and tears. And actually the marks don't look like something a man would make, more like he's been fighting with his wee sisters. If only Seaneen was here. She'd know what to say. She's the one always going around feeling sorry for him.

But even I can't leave him here, crying in the street.

Cian sniffs and rubs his hand across his eyes. "Is your ma out?" he asks and I suppose he's remembering the time I made him the toast.

"No." And if Stacey's had a row with her fella I'd give her five minutes to land around at our house, whining, probably with the two brats in tow. Cian doesn't have to tell me he doesn't want to go home. And I know how he feels. Which is probably why I say, "D'you want to come for a walk?"

"A *walk*?" Even covered in tears and snot, he manages to pour a bucketload of scorn over the word. "You gay or something?"

"Suit yourself; I don't need company."

"Nah, might as well."

So we walk out of the estate and up the main road away from town. I chain my bike to a lamp post and hope it'll still be there when I get back. After two minutes Cian's puffing. "Where are we going?" he pants. "Can we get a few cans?"

"Maybe," I say. "There's a wee shop further up."

He struggles to keep up but he doesn't turn back. "Where are we going?" he whines again. "Sure there's nothing up here."

"This is the way I go to work every day," I tell him, "on my bike."

"Bloody hell. Rather you than me." He stops and bends over, resting his hands on his knees. "You must be fit."

"You don't have to come. I'm only walking because …"

"Why?"

"Well … d'you never need to just walk? Just get away from people?" After all, he was running fast enough when I met him.

"Nah," he says. Then he goes on, surprising me, "I don't walk. I hide."

"Hide?"

"Yeah. When people piss me off. Around our old way I'd loads of places nobody knew about. This empty house. It was boarded up but I found a way in. Had an air mattress in there and everything."

"And you think *I'm* weird?"

He's keeping up easier now, even though we're still going uphill. He natters on about the old house and hiding stuff in it for a favour for somebody in return for free drugs. He's boasting – I don't believe him, but I'm only half listening.

"So where do you hide around our way?"

His eyes darken and his face closes down. "Think I'd tell *you*?"

It's getting dark, but restlessness fizzes through me. I could walk for miles. I stop at the wee shop and buy us each a can of Coke and I think Cian will get fed up and go home then, but he tags on.

"Have you no mates?" I ask him.

"Have *you* no mates?" he flashes straight back at me. Not around here, I think, not any more. And I wonder why that didn't bother me so much before.

I pull the tab on my can and take a swig.

"Do you know Emmet McCann?" he asks suddenly.

"I … yeah. I wouldn't get mixed up with him if I were you."

"I can look after myself."

"Well, Emmet McCann's not the type to take you for a walk and buy you a Coke. So watch yourself."

The edges of the city are bleeding into rough fields. I hadn't realized we'd come so far until I see the parked hulks of the trucks at the haulage yard. I don't want to go around the next corner. Not in the dark. My feet judder to a halt as if they get the message before my brain, and Cian nearly bangs into me.

"Let's head back," I say.

"Aww. I want to go and check those trucks out," he says, like a toddler.

"Wise up. It's alarmed. And there's an Alsatian."

"How d'you know?"

I sigh. This kid has the memory of a goldfish. Must be all that stuff he sniffs and smokes and drinks.

"Told you. I cycle past here every day. And just up there – past that yard – that's where I found Folly. See that shape – sort of rounded? That's the roof of the barn. The house is behind it." I shiver and Cian notices.

"What?"

"Just … creepy. The thought of that horse dying in there. We even thought there was a dead body in the house. A *person*." His eyes widen, loving that. "Only there wasn't."

"So is it haunted?"

"Could be. Come on. It's dark anyway. I have to get up tomorrow even if you don't."

"I soon will. School." He twists his face. "St. Ignatius's. That where you went?"

"Yeah. It's full of fascists. Mr. Dermott's nice. But you only get him if you're in the thick class."

"I will be."

There's nothing much to say to that. For a while we walk down the hill. Cian stops every so often and looks back at the death barn. I don't look back. He takes out a packet of cigarettes and offers it to me. "Want one?"

I shake my head. "I haven't smoked since I was your age."

"Granda."

The way back seems far shorter. As we turn off the main road into the estate Cian's steps slow to a drag. I remember all the times I didn't want to go home when I was his age. All the fellas I didn't want to go home to. And how it was worse, sometimes, after they'd pissed off leaving Mum crying and blaming me.

"Cian," I say at the top of our street. I don't know if he's checked to see if the Honda Civic's parked outside his house, but I have and it isn't. "You should tell somebody."

"What?"

"If anybody's hurting you." I can't help looking at his

arms. He shrugs them back inside his sleeves. "Your mum?"

He shakes his head.

"If that Darren –"

His voice suddenly goes hard. "I told you, *no*. Wise up." He swaggers across the street. He doesn't thank me for the Coke or the walk. I don't thank him for the company. I suppose for about a minute I hope he's OK and that his mum doesn't take it out on him, but no more than that.

When I sneak in as quietly as I can through the back door, I hear the rise and fall of voices from the living room and my chest tightens in case it's Mairéad, but then I recognize Stacey's whinge, and catch the words, *wee bastard ... spoils everything ... Darren ... best I ever had ... should have known ...*

I sneak up to bed. Sometime in the early hours I hear shouting in the street but I bury my head under the pillow. It's ages before I sleep, though. I can't help replaying that conversation about running and hiding in my head. And Mairéad: *You can't keep letting on it's not happening.*

V. LOSING

I.

"There!" Without asking, Seaneen takes my hand and places it on her belly. The one part of her I haven't touched for weeks. The one part of her I've tried not even to *look* at, though it's getting harder and harder to miss. "Ouch," I say. "That's my sore hand."

Seaneen gives me a funny look. "You're always bruised these days. Look at your arm! Is that Folly?"

I shrug. "Hit it on the gate," I lie, but Seaneen's not stupid. Yesterday when I tried to lunge Folly she swung her arse around and kicked me. I thought my arm was broken but when the numbness wore off it was just bruised.

"Declan, that horse is going to kill you."

"Don't be daft."

"Can you not just leave her in the field, eating the grass? Why do you have to train her?"

"It's not just training. It's … I have to get her to

trust me."

Seaneen starts to say something but seems to change her mind. Instead she picks up my other hand and puts it on her bump. Something jabs me. I yank my hand away. "Jesus."

"You're not meant to say *Jesus.*" For a moment I think she's telling me off about cursing in front of our unborn baby, but then she gives a wee smile as if to tell me she's not serious – only it's an *uncertain* smile and I'm not used to Seaneen being uncertain. I think she's hurt that I pulled my hand away so quick.

"Sorry. Don't want to hurt you – it."

Seaneen stops smiling. "Feeling your baby kick,' she says sulkily. "You're meant to be overwhelmed with emotion."

"I am." That's the truth anyway. Only I don't think it's the right emotion.

We're in my house, sprawled on the sofa. We have it all to ourselves because Mum's over at Stacey's. Darren seems to have taken off right enough, and Mum keeps telling me Stacey has "self-esteem issues" and she's just glad to "be there for her" and other expressions that would make you puke.

"And you're coming to the scan next week?"

"I said I would. Tuesday." I've already told Cam I had to take my mum to an appointment. She said she'd see to Folly for me. Next Tuesday will be the end of August. The summer will be over and I still haven't ridden Folly.

Seaneen gives a wriggle. "This is the one where they can tell you the sex."

I sit up. "No!" The word flies out of my mouth before I've even thought it.

Seaneen looks disappointed. "Ah, d'you want it to be a surprise? That's dead sweet. Only I want to know. Bronagh says she wouldn't want to know either. But I think she's just saying that because I do. And she's *so* jealous. She wants one. She says she doesn't but I know better." She says it like a baby's a tattoo or something. "Some people think it's bad luck to know. Do you?"

I shake my head. What worse luck can there be than the baby existing in the first place? "It's not that, I just … I dunno, Seaneen." I scratch the slow-healing rope burn on my hand.

"Would you rather keep it as a surprise?"

I don't want to know what sex it is because it's just going to make it more *real*. I know it's real *now*. I'm not in denial about it. It's not just cells and stuff making Seaneen sick any more; it's a *being*, there inside her, pushing its tiny feet against the drum of her belly, making her look pregnant and weird. But knowing it's a boy or a girl, that'll just do my head in. It won't be *it* any more. She'll start going on about names. Mum'll stop knitting yellow and white and start on to pink. Or blue.

"Do you care what it is?"

I shake my head.

"Neither do I. Long as it's OK. Does anything run in your family? The twins have eczema but I never had anything like that."

I shake my head. "Dunno. Don't think so." Alcoholism, but I don't say that.

"I hope it doesn't have curly hair like me. I hope it has lovely dark eyes like you. Declan?"

"What?"

"Do you not worry about it being OK? I mean, turning out OK? Like you keep saying about Folly?"

"Um, yeah, 'course." I try to sound interested.

"I wouldn't want it to be like half the wee hoodlums around here. I think a girl would be easier. What do you think?"

I don't know what I think. But I stay. And I listen. Well, half-listen.

★ ★ ★

I set my coffee cup down on Cam's kitchen table. "No, 'course you should go," I say. "I can come in and see to everything here."

"But it's Tuesday – your mum's appointment?"

"My mum's …? Oh. It doesn't matter. She won't mind." I stare at the leaflet again. "It looks brilliant. I wish …" Next year, I tell myself, next year Folly and I will go to a Marsha Graham masterclass.

"I just forgot the vet was coming. I could put him off but I need to get those passports sent off for the Welshies and they all need their tetanus boosters. It's a nuisance that Jim's away."

"No, it's fine. Mum'll understand. I suppose Lara's going too?" I keep my voice neutral. I hate the idea of Lara getting the benefit of Marsha Graham's teaching, but at least she won't be at the yard annoying me. With the place quiet I might even get the chance to make some proper progress with Folly instead of mucking about, which is all I seem to have been doing. Or making excuses not to work her so people

SHEENA WILKINSON

can't see how bad she is.

"Look," Cam says, putting the leaflet on top of a pile of show schedules, *Farm Week*s and feed receipts, "if you really can come in, you can get George to do Folly's markings as well. You need to get her passport sorted out."

Another expense. "I can't aff –"

"I'll pay. Call it a thank you for messing you about. But are you *sure* your mum will be all right without you?"

"Totally positive." I cross my fingers.

* * *

Cycling into the estate I still haven't made up my mind how to get out of the scan. Pretend to be sick? But what if Seaneen sees me cycling to work? Pretend there's some sort of big crisis at the yard?

No. I can't keep hiding stuff. I'll tell her the truth. Be *adult* about it. I go straight around to hers, without changing out of my horsey stuff, just to get it over with.

Seaneen's green eyes darken and narrow. "OK," she says. We're in her hall. The TV blares from the living room. Granzilla's making fries in the kitchen. I can hear and smell them but I have a feeling I'm not going to be invited to stay.

"OK," Seaneen says again. "Let me get this right. You won't come to the scan –"

"Can't. I *can't* come –"

"Because the vet is coming to do some routine thing? Fill in some *forms*? Something he could do any time?"

Oh God, so much for telling the truth.

"It's not that simple. George is … you have to book

him weeks in advance – he's the best … And the Welsh ponies need their tetanus injections."

"The *scan* was booked weeks in advance. And why does it have to be you?"

"Cam's at a showjumping thing. Jim's away. There's nobody else. I'll make it up to you, Seaneen. And sure your mum'll go, won't she? She's better at all that kind of …"

She turns and walks off down the hall. I don't know if I'm meant to follow her or what. It'd be easier just to leave. Just at the bottom of the stairs she stops and flings over her shoulder, "You coming?"

I don't think I have any choice. It reminds me too much of the night she told me she was pregnant. In her bedroom I try again. "Seaneen, I'm sorry, but you know I'm no good at that kind of thing – hospitals and that. I felt stupid last time. It's not … not really me."

She gives a bark of laughter. "Oh, sorry! Not really you. You think this is really *me*? You think I *want* to be fat and tired and ugly and have to give birth?"

"No, 'course not. I know it's harder on you." Too late I realize I should have said she wasn't ugly.

She grabs my arms and makes me look at her. "Declan, if I'd known how immature you were going to be about this baby, I'd have –"

"What?" The pain of her fingers digging into my bruises makes me say what I've never said. "Had an abortion? Pity you hadn't."

She pulls away from me and her hand goes to its usual protective position across her bump. "How can you even say that? Kill our baby?" She squeezes her eyes shut for a moment as if it hurts her even to say the words. She gives me a cold hard look. "I mean I'd have … I'd have finished with you. And never let on it was yours."

"I wish you had." Oh God, where did this all come from? These words must have been very near the surface to jump out like this.

"You see? You don't want it!"

"Of course I don't bloody want it!" I shout. "But it's not a matter of *wanting,* is it? It exists. We have to get on with it."

"No, *I* have to get on with it. You can fuck off if you want to." Her green eyes shine with tears. "I'm the one that has to go through with it. And I'm the one who'll be left with it when you leave."

"I haven't bloody left, though, have I?" I rub my hands over my face as if I can push away the red mist that's making me want to tell her how much I nearly did. How much I still wish I could. How what's keeping me here has more to with a frightened, frightening horse than with whatever's inside Seaneen's belly. "Look, Seaneen, it's *one scan* I can't come to. That's all."

"It's not all. Mum and Dad are right. You're pretending this baby isn't happening."

"That's bullshit, Seaneen."

"It's not!" The tears are running down her cheeks now and she doesn't try to rub them away. "You won't talk about what we're going to do, where we're going to live, *anything.*" She bends over her folded arms like she's in pain. "I hope this poor baby doesn't turn out like you, you selfish bastard."

I yank her arms away and make her look at me. "Don't you dare say I'm selfish. You have no idea what I gave up for you and this baby." I don't care if Granzilla can hear. I don't care if Gary comes up the stairs and beats the shit out of me. I hope he does.

"Oh yeah? What?" She hugs herself. "What have *you* ever given up for anybody?"

"I was meant to go to Germany!" I spit it out. "I had this job lined up. A brilliant one. I should be there now, only I didn't go because of you and the fucking baby. So don't tell me I'm selfish."

Her eyes widen. I watch her face taking this in, working out what it means, and then I turn and bash out of the room and out of the house with her screeching after me, "So fuck off to Germany then and don't come back!"

2.

It's only six a.m. and not even properly light but I can't stay in bed any longer with Seaneen's words bashing around my brain. I'm at work so early that the curtains are still pulled across Cam's bedroom window. I stuff my jacket and phone – which I haven't switched on since last night – in a corner of the tack room and grab some headcollars. By the time Cam comes out, I have everything in that needs to be in – the Welshies for their passports, Spirit and Willow. I don't like helping Lara but Cam's pointed out to me more than once that it's my job to work with *all* the horses: I don't get to pick and choose. Just like everything else in my life.

I bring Folly in last, and she noses at my hand for a treat. Her teeth pull the skin on my wrist and I smack her nose. She flinches away and I feel guilty. If I hadn't started giving her treats she wouldn't have gone looking for them, but I had to, because she's getting harder to catch.

She sulks in her stable but cheers up when I throw an armful of haylage over the door.

"Gosh, Declan, you've everything done? What time were you here at?" Cam asks.

"Uh – sevenish, I suppose."

"You're a star," she says with a yawn. She goes to fetch a grooming kit and looks in over Folly's half-door on the way past. Folly lunges at her, ears back, teeth bared.

"Sorry," I say. "She hardly ever does that now."

"She's not as settled as she was, is she?" Cam says. "Maybe she's in season or something." I pretend not to hear, and follow Cam into Spirit's stable. I make a start on grooming his silvery mane.

"Declan!" Cam says. "That's a dandy brush. Do you want to break all the hairs?"

"Sorry." I exchange the harsh dandy brush for a soft body brush.

"Don't mix anything up when George comes." Cam gives me a funny look like she doesn't really trust me on my own.

"'Course I won't."

"And can you poo-pick the bottom field?"

I groan. "Yes."

Poo-picking's the last thing I want to do today. I don't mind the work so much, but it's so mindless it leaves you far too much time to think. What I want today is something physical and difficult, something that will use up all my energy and all my thoughts.

George's big Range Rover swings into the yard about lunchtime. Cam and I have filled in the passport forms in advance with the names and details. All I have to do is bring the ponies out one by one and hold them while George checks out all their markings and fills them in on a chart. They're all perfectly mannered and patient, even when George sticks needles into their necks to microchip them, standing in the hot yard like textbook ponies, bright eyes peeking from under their bushy forelocks.

"Very civil for youngsters," George says.

"They've had plenty of handling."

"Makes all the difference,'" he says, scrawling his signature across the bottom of the form. "A good grounding. Now – that it?"

"One more if you've time. My own mare." I still get a thrill out of saying this.

George looks at his watch.

"Won't take long." I pull open the bolt on Folly's door and the thrill of saying *my own mare* dims a bit. Unlike the Welsh ponies, she's been pacing up and down ever since she finished her haylage. Teeth marks on the top of her door show that she's been biting it again. A light film of sweat darkens her neck and behind her front legs. She blinks in the sunlight, then rolls her eyes at George, and pulls back in alarm when he lifts up her forelock to see if there's a whorl under it.

"So," he says. "Easy, girl, stop that. Where did you get this?"

"Long story," I say. "She had a bad start."

George looks at the form, where I've already filled in her name and age and breeding – unknown. "Six? Riding?"

"Um, I haven't tried yet."

"Folly?" he asks. "Let's hope she doesn't live up to her name, eh?" He grins.

I don't smile back.

"Right, just the chip now. Sure she hasn't already been done?"

I nod. "She was abandoned. The police vet checked – just in case she was stolen."

"Well, I'll scan her again just to be sure." He runs the wee machine up her neck.

Panic pushes at my chest. Just say the police vet missed something? Just say she is stolen and I have to give her back? She's caused me more worry than anything in my life ever but I can't lose her now.

"No," he says. "Nothing," and sticks the needle in. Folly starts when she feels it and a bubble of blood beads on her neck, startling against the white. "Ah, it won't kill her." George dabs it away with a sterile wipe, leaving a pinkish smear. "Right." He straightens up. "Ten to two. Time I was away."

Ten to two. Seaneen's scan's in ten minutes. I don't let that thought develop.

You should be glad. You wanted out, didn't you? Deep down?

I don't know.

Fuck off to Germany then.

When George is gone I let the Welshies out – Mary, Mungo, and Midge are their names but we always just call them the Welshies; I suppose that'll change when we start working with them properly. They go for a scamper around their paddock, manes and tails flying, pretty heads tossing. They're like cartoon ponies. I lean on the gate for a while. I should go and put Folly out now, and then get down to some poo-picking in the bottom field.

But the restlessness hasn't gone.

Folly neighs from the yard. Various horses lift up their heads and answer. I should put her out. I should poo-pick. When I get back to her stable she bangs a hoof against the door. I hang over the door and talk to her, but she doesn't want me; she wants her freedom. She's paddled all the bedding into a mulch of shit and wet shavings. "Ah, horse, you're restless too, aren't you?" I say. Her ears swivel at my voice.

She's probably just bored. She doesn't *get* all that mucking about in the school with lunge reins and stuff. Going around in circles.

That's what *I've* been doing: going around in circles. And now Seaneen's cut the rope.

So why don't I feel happy?

I imagine me and Folly cantering up the long springy ride at the edge of the farm trail. I can almost feel her under me, part of me, obedient to the smallest shift of weight or adjustment of rein, like Flight used to be.

I go into the tack room. Joy's tack should fit. Fiona doesn't need to know.

When Folly sees the saddle over my arm she puts her ears back but then comes forward and stretches her head down for a sniff. I suppose she smells Joy, whose white hairs speckle the blue numnah. I tie Folly up outside the stable. She's still sweating but it's a hot day, more like June than nearly September. "Half an hour," I promise her. "Not even. Fifteen minutes. Just show me you can do it. Just a wee walk around the school. Just let me prove you can do it and then you can go and scratch your arse in the field for the rest of the day.

"Please," I whisper in her ear. "Just be good. Just be a normal horse."

Grounded

I'm all thumbs, like I never put on a bridle before. When Folly feels the cold metal of the bit against her teeth, she clamps them shut and steps back to evade me, treading on my foot. "Ow!" I push her off. I rub the bit on my jeans so it's not as cold. Maybe I should dip it in treacle? There's some in the feed room. Really, just to let her mouth it would be enough for now. We can do more tomorrow.

No. It has to be *now*. I slide my fingers in at the sides of her mouth and next minute it opens and the bit slips in. I have the bridle up over her ears and buckled before she realizes what's going on. She stands mouthing the bit. She looks suspicious but not traumatized. The soft black leather makes her face even whiter and finer. It's the kind of bridle I'll never be able to afford.

Now the saddle. I let her sniff it again then place it very gently at the bottom of her neck. She trembles but that's all. I slide it down as smoothly as I can until it's sitting properly. It's not a brilliant fit – she's narrower than Joy – but I'm only going to walk for fifteen minutes; what harm can it do?

I do up the girth loosely. And then she's ready. She looks gorgeous. She looks like a normal horse. She looks like I could get on her and jump around a course of show jumps.

I ram my hat on and lead Folly out into the quiet sunny yard, making sure she doesn't catch her stirrups in the barn doorframe and spook herself.

The sun strokes my shoulderblades under my T-shirt. I don't let myself think about Mairéad and Seaneen driving home from the hospital up the hot fumy Falls Road. Knowing if the baby's a boy or girl. I don't let myself

183

think that I shouldn't be doing this. That I'm mad to try an untested horse without somebody here to give me a leg up, to hold the other stirrup while I get on, to lead her around a bit at first to make sure she's going OK. I know all that. But I want to do it my way. On my own.

I'm about to ride my horse – my own horse – for the first time in my life.

And maybe I want to do something dangerous.

I lead her over to the mounting block and she doesn't react. I pull down on the stirrup nearest me, to let her feel the weight. She flicks her ears and shifts her feet but she doesn't freak. I daren't pull the girth too tight, but it'll be OK, we're only going to walk.

My chest pounds. *Wise up,* I tell myself. *This is not a big deal. You've built it up too much. It's a horse. You've ridden dozens.*

I decide to mount as quickly as I can. If there's going to be trouble I'll deal with it better from the saddle than halfway on.

"Good girl." I gather the reins and spring up. A moment, and then … I lower myself as softly as I can into the saddle. Her ears fly back and her back humps for a second like she's going to buck, but I expected this and my legs are ready to push her on. "Go on." I squeeze her with my lower legs. Keep her moving; don't let her think about it too much.

She walks crabbily, not the easy swing of a happy, trained horse, but I keep my contact light and concentrate on being as relaxed as possible. Inside I'm fizzing but I try not to let Folly pick up on that. "Good girl," I say nearly every step. I'm just going to walk around the school a few times. I won't push it.

At the corner Folly stops. Looks around as if she just noticed where she was. She lifts up her head and lets out a shrill, panicky neigh. From their field the ponies answer. "Come on." I touch her sides with my heels. She runs backwards and stops, shaking her head. I apply more pressure. "Come on, never mind them. You'll be back out with them in ten minutes if you're good." I risk a tiny kick. She's not scared; she's just being grumpy.

She hurtles backwards into the fence. Wood cracks. And she's off.

Head between her legs, back end in the air, body twisting, total rodeo. Instinct makes me try to sit deep, get her head up and get back in control but I haven't a chance.

I hang on for maybe five seconds, then I'm flung through the air and down, Folly looming above me, huge and mad. I'm tangled up in her legs, my foot caught in the stirrup, her hooves flashing above me, and all I can think is, it's OK, she's not shod, and I throw my hands over my face and then my foot's free, Folly's galloping away and my head whams against the fence so hard that everything spins.

I pull myself up straight away. Test my limbs. I'm not hurt. Where's Folly? The sun's in my eyes and I can't see her and for a terrible moment I think she's jumped the gate, but no, there she is, in the far corner, trembling so hard I can see her sides shake from here, dark grey with sweat. Her saddle – Joy's saddle – is twisted around to the side, and her reins are broken.

"Shit," I say. "Shit, shit, shit."

I stand up properly, my head swimming, and walk over to her. She eyes me with horror and when I get within grabbing distance she swings her arse around and kicks out at me before trotting away, the saddle slipping more with every stride.

"Folly, I'm sorry. Come on." I stretch out my hand to her. She skites away. "I won't ride you again," I promise. "Not for a long time." The memory of that crashing fear, being out of control on a terrified, crazy animal, makes me shudder. I've been on a bucking horse before but nothing like that.

But she doesn't understand. And she doesn't trust me. Why should she?

She starts cantering, stirrups banging her sides, making her freak even more. Below in the paddocks the ponies pick up on the panic and start to gallop up the field.

All I need now is for Cam and Lara to land back in the yard and see the mess I've made.

Food. She'll come for food.

I leave the school and go into the lovely cold dark of the barn. Folly's headcollar rope hangs from the ring where I tied her, mocking my stupid hopes.

I get a scoop of mix out of the feed barrel and head back to the school. The heat's intense after the cool of the barn, and I have to squint to see properly. Folly's in the corner now, back to me. Diarrhea trickles down her back legs. The middle rail of the fence is in two jagged halves meeting at an angle. Don't know if it was Folly's back end or my head did that. My head feels huge and heavy. I take my hat off which helps a bit. Folly grabs the top rail in her teeth, the way she did with the wooden pallets in the death barn.

I rattle the bucket and when she hears it she turns

and comes over, kind of half sideways, like she doesn't really want to, but the pull of food is too strong. Like a druggie who'll do anything for a fix. She thrusts her head into the bucket and then it's no problem to take her reins, undo the girth and get the saddle off, and then take her back to the stable. The reins aren't broken, just unbuckled, but I hardly dare look at Fiona's saddle.

I should wash her down, she's so sweaty, but I have to sort out the school and the saddle before anybody comes, so I just give her a quick rub down with a wet brush as best I can. I check her all over and she's not hurt as far as I can see, but she twists and fidgets away from me, and when I lead her through the paddock gate she hardly waits for me to undo her headcollar before she's off galloping down to the ponies, swinging around so fast I have to dodge her flying hooves again. I lean over the gate for a few seconds, but she doesn't look back, just grazes in the far corner with one ear flicked towards the yard, ready for a quick flight if I dare to come near her again. It's like the ghost horse is saying, *I'm still here. Under the healed-up scabs and the new flesh, there's still something scary.*

And as I head back to face the broken fence posts and Fiona's scraped saddle, I know they're not the only things I've wrecked.

3.

I sit on an upturned bucket in the cool of the barn, Fiona's saddle upside-down on my lap. I've rubbed the saddle soap in and rubbed it off about three times. I've tried oil and something called leather balsam I nicked out of Lara's tack box, but now the saddle just feels sticky and you can still see the deep scrape down the seat, like a scar. You always will.

I shoo the yard cat away from sniffing around the saddle soap and straighten up, noticing that the hot ache in my head is building up to a nagging throb. I set the saddle over my arm and take it to its rack in the tack room where it sits, clean and damaged and accusing. My phone's lying in a corner of the tack room. No idea what it's doing there. I put it in my pocket.

At least Fiona doesn't come up much these days. Maybe she'll think somebody scraped against it by accident in the tack room.

You could just tell *her, Declan,* a voice a bit like Colette's or Cam's goes, inside my head. *You know, apologize, confess, be* adult *about it.*

Shut up, I order it, and head out to see what I can do about the school fence rail. The sun still beats down, turning the concrete of the yard a dazzling pale grey and making my eyeballs cringe. A wee breeze lifts and scuts dust and clumps of horse hair around. Nothing else moves. I don't normally like the yard like this, with all the horses out, no curious, friendly faces looking over half-doors; no sounds of munching or sudden nickers of recognition; no ring of hooves on the yard, but today I'm glad there's nobody to witness me, not even a horse. Especially not a horse.

Witness. It's not like I committed a crime. I only rode my own horse, or tried to.

But the pounding inside my head and the memory of Folly's desperate, broncoing fear keep telling me something else.

OK, fence rail.

At first I think the rail's magically fixed itself because I can't see anything, but then I realize I'm looking in the wrong corner of the school. The rail's wrecked OK, its splintered edges jabbing forwards into the school. It looks awful, and it's dangerous, and I don't think I can fix it. But I can't just leave it. Wishing my head would stop throbbing, I go to find a hammer or something, or another bit of wood. Cam has a load of tools in a box in the corner of the barn, though Jim usually does the maintenance.

I hesitate in the doorway of the barn. What did I come in for? My tack cleaning stuff's sitting out in the middle of the floor, Lara's leather balsam lying on its side, seeping into the concrete floor. I bend down and grab it but the bottle's empty. Stupid cat must have knocked it over. Easiest thing to do is just chuck the bottle in the bin and never let on. Lara can buy more.

But what did I come in here *for*? I start to tidy up the tack cleaning stuff but when I bend down my head goes really weird, pain pulsing at my skull. I close my eyes against it. Jesus, what is this? I'm feel like I'm about to puke. I breathe in slowly. No, I'm not, not if I keep still. But the ground tilts under my feet. Don't look down. Never mind the tack cleaning stuff for now. I sit back down on the upturned bucket and hold my head. Why do I feel like this? Maybe it's a migraine, only I don't get migraines. But if I sit here for a bit in the dark it might go away.

Where is everybody though? The place is dead; it'd be a perfect opportunity to ride Folly, prove she's as good as anybody's horse. I don't want to let some stupid headache stop me doing that. I concentrate on keeping still. It might be just the sun. In a minute I'll go and get her headcollar and fetch her up from the field. She has to come in anyway because the vet's coming. And the ponies. Better get the ponies in too.

It's cold now in the barn, my arms goosebumpy, my insides shivering. But if I stay like this, eyes closed, it'll be OK.

* * *

"Declan?

"Hello?

"Where are you?"

I'm about to call out, "In here!" when Cam's face appears around the door of the barn. She's got her show clothes on – white breeches and good shirt.

"I've been calling you for ages," she says. "Can you give me a hand getting the ramp down?"

"What ramp?"

"Duh – the truck?"

"Truck?"

"Gosh, Declan, are you going to sit there and repeat everything I say? Come on, I need you to give me a hand. Bloody Lara went straight home in the car with her mum, lazy cow. You can sort out Willow."

"Have you been somewhere with Willow?"

"Declan?" She comes closer. She's frowning. "What's up with you? You sound really strange. Have you been *drinking*?"

I'm at *work*; how would I have been drinking? Cam's acting really weird. "I'm fine." I pull myself to my feet. My head spins. I follow Cam out into the yard, but when my eyes hit the glare outside I have to shut them fast, and then open them just a slit, enough to see my way to the truck, but everything's blurry.

"Where are you going?" I ask Cam, reaching for the clip that holds the ramp up, but my hand keeps missing it and banging against the wood. "What horses are you taking?"

"Declan?" Cam reaches up and puts her hand on my arm, stopping me. "What have you done?"

"I haven't done anything." I've no idea what she's on about. "You said to get the ramp down. Are we going to a show?"

"Oh, for Christ's sake, what's *wrong* with you?" She stands back and scans my face. A horse stamps and neighs from *inside* the truck. So why is she asking me to put the ramp down?

"Look – you're ready to go," I point out. "Is it a show? Am I coming?"

Cam takes a deep breath and leads me away from the truck. I'm so surprised I let her. She sits me down on the wall and says in a trying-to-be-calm voice, "Listen. Concentrate. You're not making much sense. Have you had a fall? Have you hit your head? I hope you have because it's either that or you're losing it."

"I think I already lost it." I look down at the whirling ground and the pain crashes at my skull and I have to hold my head still because it's going to fall off. Then Cam's moving horses around, fast, and won't let me help. And then we're going somewhere only she's forgotten the horses; it's just me and her in the Land Rover.

"You forgot the horses," I keep saying.

"Shh." She takes her hand from the steering wheel and puts it on my knee. "You're concussed, I think. We're going to the hospital. Oh God, maybe I should have waited for an ambulance. You're not going to pass out, are you? Did you fall? Did one of the ponies kick you in the head? The horses are all in their fields OK; I checked."

"I don't know!" I mutter. It hurts to talk out loud. "My head's sore. I don't remember. You forgot the horses. What show are we going to?"

"Oh God." Cam puts her foot down and the fields and hedges rush past in such a sickening blur that I have to close my eyes tight or I'll puke all over Cam's Land Rover.

"Declan, what day is it? Do you remember the vet

coming?"

Her voice stabs at me through the sick waves of pain, but I daren't open my mouth to speak and I don't know any of the answers anyway.

★ ★ ★

Hospital. Been here before, I think, when I got on the wrong side of Emmet McCann's da. Or maybe that was a different one. I remember waiting for hours. I don't think they make us wait long this time, but I'm not holding on to things very well; it's like being drunk only it hurts more.

I lie on a narrow bed thing in a cubicle with green spotty curtains. Even when I close my eyes the green spots stay.

The doctor looks about my age but she can't be. She's very cute, with glossy black hair in a plait. She shines something in my eyes that makes me want to sneeze.

"Can you tell me what today's date is, Declan?" she asks.

Haven't a clue, but then I'd normally have to think about that one.

"OK, your birthday?"

That's easy, 15 December. I think. Near Christmas, anyway.

"Hmm." She stops shining the light in my eye. "And you don't remember what happened?"

Cam breaks in. "Like I told the nurse – I came back to the yard and found him like this. Disoriented."

"I don't even remember being at work today. I thought I was going mad."

"No madder than the rest of us," the doctor says.

"That's debatable," Cam says.

"No, it's very common with a head injury to lose your memory of the events leading up to it," the doctor goes. "It's nothing to worry about."

"But …" How can it be nothing to worry about, forgetting a whole day? Ending up in this state with no idea how it happened? When Cam says, "The most likely thing is he's fallen off a horse," I get a tingle, like being on the edge of waking up, but then it's gone again.

"We'll do a CT scan, just to make sure, see if your brain's swelling," the doctor says. "We've no way of knowing if you lost consciousness, so we'll have to err on the safe side. Have you vomited?"

"No. I don't think so."

"We'll send you down for the scan as soon as possible," the doctor says. "In the meantime, just rest." Like I'm going to jump up and start dancing.

"I'll call your mum," Cam says after the doctor bustles out.

"Don't – she'll worry."

"Declan, she's your mum; she's *supposed* to worry."

"But …" It's too complicated to tell her that I try not to let Mum worry in case it sends her back on the drink. Seaneen would understand. I wish Seaneen was here.

Seaneen – something about Seaneen. Oh God, we had a row. *Fuck off to Germany then*. When was that?

A nurse comes in just as Cam's taking her phone out of her pocket. "You can't use that in here," he says.

"Sorry – I'll go outside. Actually, Declan, give me your phone; you'll have the right numbers."

"Don't phone Mum. Please. I'll be home in a few hours and she can see I'm fine. If you say *hospital* she'll panic. You don't know her."

"Declan, apart from anything else, I need to get back to the yard," Cam says. "I don't know what happened. I need to check the horses are OK. I had a quick look around before we left and everything looked fine – but *something* happened to you and that means something may have happened to one of my horses too."

One of my horses. Again that tingle.

She holds out her hand for my phone. I can't win. She goes out. I keep my eyes shut. I feel her come back I don't know how much later, but it's easier not to talk. Then I hear a voice and it isn't Cam's or the doctor's.

"Hey Dec," Seaneen says.

My eyes snap open in time to see Cam's mouth open in shock as she looks at Seaneen's belly and then at me.

"Seaneen," she says. She can't keep her eyes off the bump. "Right," she says. "Well, now Seaneen's here I should get back to my horses."

"Cam –"

"What?"

I swallow. "Can you keep an eye on Folly for me?"

"Folly!" Seaneen cuts in. "Psycho, more like. I knew she'd end up killing you."

"I'm not dead."

Cam stares at me. "Folly?" She narrows her eyes. "You haven't been trying to *ride* her, have you?"

That tingle again. Red in front of my eyes and a sudden wallop of fear. "I – I suppose I must have been."

Cam shakes her head. "God, Declan, I thought you'd learned sense. A yard full of people to help you and you

195

wait until … You know, you asked for this." She suddenly sounds really pissed off. "You're lucky you *weren't* killed." And she parts the curtains and stalks away.

Seaneen looks after her in surprise. "What's up with her? She looked at me like I'd two heads."

"Dunno." I close my eyes again. I thought people were meant to get *sympathy* when they were hurt. When Vicky broke her leg she'd everybody dancing around being lovely to her.

"Look," Seaneen says, and her voice is harder than Seaneen's voice ever is. "I came because Cam couldn't get hold of your mum. She didn't give me much choice. But that doesn't mean … Don't tell me you've forgotten about last night?"

"I know we had a … a fight. I didn't remember if it was today or yesterday." The pain bashes at my skull.

A nurse sweeps in. "They're nearly ready for you," she says. "Somebody will come and wheel you down. You'll have to take your earring out. Any other jewellery?"

I fumble with the stud in my ear and give it to Seaneen to mind for me but she sets it on the bedside table.

The nurse looks at Seaneen and smiles at her belly. "Congratulations," she says. "When are you due?"

Seaneen places her hand over her bump. "January," she says in a much nicer voice than she's been using with me.

"Everything going OK?"

"Yeah. Had a scan today. You could see …"

I close my eyes again. Women can go on like this for hours.

"Declan," Seaneen says. The nurse has gone. "Look.

My dad's waiting for me in the car park. I only came because Cam said somebody had to. And I" – she nibbles her fingernail the way she does when she's upset – "was worried about you. Even though –"

"What?" It's hot in here but the air around my face goes suddenly cold.

Her voice hardens again. "You haven't even *asked* about the baby. You knew I was having the scan today. Or had you forgotten that too?" Her voice is suddenly hopeful.

"I hadn't forgotten. I just – I have other things on my mind here." Maybe this comes out wrong. But I have just had a bang on the head.

"Exactly." She wrinkles her mouth as if she's trying not to cry – but she can't be; Seaneen hardly ever cries. Only she cried last night. I remember that. "Declan, I saw the baby today. On the scan. And it was" – she shakes her head like she can't find important enough words – "amazing. You could see … this perfect wee person. But *you* should have been there."

If I'd gone to the scan with her I wouldn't be lying here waiting for a bloody brain scan with my head about to explode. "I'll make it up to you."

"No, I don't want you to." She takes a deep breath. Her chest rises and falls. "You were going to leave, so … I don't want you around any more."

Fuck off to Germany. But she didn't *mean* that.

"Seaneen, I'm sorry about the scan, but –"

"No, *listen*." Her eyes fill with tears. "This is hard enough for me. When I saw the baby on the scan I knew … that's a *person*, Declan. A *child*. And he deserves better than a dad who doesn't want him. No, shut up, you *don't*. You never have. And I'm not going to spend the next year or two years, or however long it takes, waiting for you to admit that and clear off. Because you *will*, Declan; you know you will. And I don't want to have to tell that child that his daddy's gone. I'd rather do it on my own from the start."

"So you're dumping me?"

"I have to. And don't pretend you're not glad."

And she stumbles out through the green spotty curtains.

4.

I get the scan. It's a bit scary but it doesn't hurt. The machine whirs and buzzes in a cold room, and then I have to wait for ages.

Mum arrives in a panic; she was in town with Stacey and forgot her phone and she'll never forgive herself and she always knew those old horses would kill me in the end. Finally the doctor comes back with the results. There's nothing much wrong. A simple concussion. I have to go home and rest. She gives Mum a list of things to watch out for and a prescription for painkillers. I hope they're strong. I hope they knock me out for days.

And through the pain and the worry about Folly, Seaneen's cold, clear voice, again and again. *Don't pretend you're not glad.*

When the doctor says rest at home for at least a week, I go, yeah, yeah, of course, planning to make my escape back to work as soon as I can. Lying around the house – no way. I haven't been home during the day for years and I don't intend to start now.

Only I reckon without three things.

One is the headache. The pills take the edge off it, but even so I sweat out hours lying still in bed, knowing that if I move too fast, even just sit up, the sickening swoops of pain are waiting for me. I flick through old horsey magazines, but every few pages an article about reschooling a nervous horse or a photo of a grey horse makes me lay the magazine down.

The second thing that stops me escaping is Mum. She's turned into bloody Florence Nightingale. She never leaves me alone with her wee cups of tea or food that I can't eat. She never stops asking, "Do you want anything? Can you see all right? Will I bring in the TV from my room? Are you hungry?" And when I say no, I'm fine, she doesn't get the hint; she hovers, all hopeful, like she's begging me to give her the chance to look after me. Finding things to tell me. She tells me Vicky's home from wherever, devastated because she didn't get her grades for Cambridge. She tells me Stacey found a stash of pills in Cian's room and he hit her when she told him she'd flushed them down the loo.

She doesn't mention Seaneen and neither do I.

I tell her I want to be left alone and she goes downstairs all droopy.

I hear the hoover and the TV, the sounds of Mum's days. She's busier than she used to be. She does a lot of housework and her friends call in; their voices drift up the stairs. She never used to have friends, only boyfriends.

And the third thing that stops me escaping, even when the headache dulls down to a bearable ache and the room stops its drunken spinning, is me. Because the thought of going out in the street, up to the yard, into town, anywhere, is just too much. I'm grounded, rooted to my room, stuck here. Sometimes I think I'll never move again.

On the third day, or the fourth, or maybe the seventh, I don't know, I'm lying in bed when the doorbell rings. It bores into my head like a drill. Mum's out but I'm not moving. It's probably Stacey or the window cleaner or something. But it drills on and on and the only way to make it stop is to get out of bed and deal with it. I drag myself up, hating the whiff of a body that hasn't had a shower for days, and pull on some track bottoms. "I'm coming, for Christ's sake!" I yell down the stairs. The stairs rear up at me, even though I'm going down them. I have to grab the banister rail, like Gran when she was old, like Mum when she was drunk. The bell rings on.

Maybe it's Seaneen.

As I grab the front door handle I realize it's probably Mairéad and Gary. They've lain in wait for Mum to go out and now they're going to pounce. But *she* dumped *me*, I get ready to tell them, pulling the door open.

It's Cian. Bloody Cian.

"What the —"

"Let me in, *please*." He's nearly crying.

"Should you not be at school?" I've kind of lost track but I don't think it's the weekend.

"Look, please, let me in — I'm in trouble."

"Why am I not surprised?"

"No — *real* trouble. Please." His face is white, the spots around his mouth standing out like a rash.

I don't want him coming in. Then again I don't want
to keep standing on the doorstep half-dressed either, so
I stand aside and he pushes in past me.

"Right, what is it?" I ask, sitting down on the sofa
arm.

"I owe somebody money. Emmet McCann."

"Drugs?"

"He let me have some – I'd no money and he said I
could take them and pay him later. I thought he was
dead on. He's been letting me get stuff for weeks. Only
now he wants the money and I can't pay him back."

"Are you stupid or something? That's the oldest trick
in the book. McCann won't let you away with that."
Well, I suppose Cian knows that or he wouldn't be snivelling to me about it. "Anyway, what's it to do with
me?"

Cian looks at the carpet. "You've got money. I saw
it that time …"

"*Saw* it? You mean tried to rob it?"

"Declan, I'm desperate." He glances around as if
Emmet McCann's hiding behind the sofa. "He's going
to get me, I know he is."

"You should have thought of that."

"But I *needed* the stuff!" he cries. "Declan – please.
I'll pay you back, I promise! There's nobody else I can
ask. Please!" He's shaking. If I'm the closest thing he
has to someone who can help him, that's pretty
pathetic.

"No," I say. I don't even have to think about it.
"There's no way I'd give anybody one penny for Emmet
McCann, let alone – how much is it?"

"Two hundred. Just a loan."

"I haven't even *got* the money any more," I lie. "It's all gone on Folly."

"But …" He starts to blub and wail. "He'll kill me, Declan, I swear."

"I can't help that."

"But what am I going to do?"

"It's not my problem." I can see the kid's terrified. But maybe it'll make him wise up. "Look, you'll have to go."

He rubs his hand over his face. "But there's nobody else."

"Sorry." I walk out to the hall and open the front door. I watch him shuffle down the street, not towards his own house. My hand twitches. I could have given him *something*. Not two hundred, but something to get McCann off his back. I nearly call him back and give him forty quid or something.

But I don't.

The living room is clean and tidy, but the sour smell of Mum's smoke makes me push open the window and stand there for a bit, breathing the air from the street. Standing makes my head swim so I flump onto the sofa. Something stabs my thigh. I pull out Mum's latest knitting effort. It's pale blue and fluffy, on its way to being a jumper. I stroke it. How can just winding wool around some needles and jiggling and clicking them about turn a ball of wool into something you could actually wear? You don't need to do this any more, Mum, I think, and wonder what she'll say when I tell her Seaneen dumped me. I shove the knitting out of my way and pick up the remote control from the coffee table but there's nothing on that anybody with two brain cells would watch. I don't feel like trying the horsey channel.

I look at the tiny half-jumper and then wrap it around the needles so it doesn't look so … human. Seaneen dumped *me*. I never ran out on her. She wants to do it on her own. That's fair enough. Plenty of girls around here doing exactly the same thing. And Seaneen's got loads of support with Granzilla and her dad and those bratty twins. They'll love having a baby in the house. They won't need me. What do I know about babies? And I'll send her money. It's not like I don't have any sense of responsibility.

Responsibility. Folly. I sigh. I should phone Cam. But my phone's up in my room, I don't feel like braving the stairs again so soon. Except I know Cam's number by heart, and the house phone's sitting right beside me on the coffee table on top of a pile of Mum's TV magazines.

"How's Folly?" I ask as soon as she answers.

"Fine." Her voice is brisk.

"I'll be back as soon as I can." I'm not even sure how long I've been off for.

"We're managing."

"Cam, are you annoyed with me?"

She doesn't say anything and I wonder if she's hung up.

"Cam? Did I – have I done something?" I'm still haunted by that lost day. I know I must have ridden Folly, or tried to, and been thrown off, but I don't remember. When I try there's just a fog and a creeping fear that spreads over my mind like a bloodstain. But has Cam found evidence of something else? Something even stupider? Did I – oh God, did I *hurt* Folly and Cam won't tell me?

"Cam? Are you keeping something from me? 'Cause I'd rather know."

There's a funny noise, halfway between a snort and a laugh. "*Me*? Keep something from *you*? Are you shitting me, Declan?"

Cam doesn't say things like *shitting me* unless she's seriously annoyed.

"What … what do you mean?"

"Eh – the baby? When were you going to tell me?"

"Oh! Is that all?" Relief that it's not Folly floods me.

"*All*? Declan, you let me believe you stayed because of *me* – well, the yard. The job. I was feeling *guilty* because it wasn't enough for you. Looking for ways to make it more worth your while. And all the time …"

"But I …" And then I grind to a jagged halt. Because it'd be a lie to say I stayed because of Folly. In the first place it *was* the baby. I don't know why she sounds so angry, though. Not just angry – hurt. "Look, does it matter *why* I stayed? I stayed. And now there's Folly and –"

"I thought something as big as that, you'd tell me."

"But it's got nothing to do with the yard."

Again that faint snorty laugh. "It's got everything to do with the yard when your mind's not on the job." But I know she means more than that. She thinks I should have confided in her. Because Cam's been more than my employer. She gave me my first chance. The most important break I ever had. And she thought I stayed because I appreciated that. When all along …

"I'm sorry." As usual, my crapness with words stops me saying what I really mean. That I wanted there to be somewhere where I could hide from the baby. And the longer I left it the harder it was to say, *oh by the way …*

"Right. So was there anything else, Declan? Because I have horses to get ready."

I swallow. "Cam? You do – you do *want* me back, don't you?"

She sighs. "Yes. But I wish I could think that bang on the head had knocked some sense into you."

"And Folly's really OK?"

"She's fine. Look, I have to go."

I curl up on the sofa, ignoring the sweaty smell of myself, and try not to let myself imagine the yard. I close my eyes and think of Folly, her warm smell, her soft white coat. I want to run my hands down her neck, soothe the trembling in her. I want her to be gentle and happy and brave, like other horses. An awful dread creeps through me that that's never going to happen. I should be there with her. I shouldn't be lying around here; there's nothing wrong with me, only a bit of a headache.

"Declan!" Mum drags the Tesco's bags into the living room and plonks them on the ground. "Are you feeling better, love?"

"Yeah, fine."

She stares at me. "Sure? You look a bit … Is it just your concussion or is there something else? Because I'm not stupid, Declan, and I'm your mum."

For years I could have had my leg falling off and Mum would have been too drunk too notice.

"I'm just bored. I might go back to work tomorrow."

"No, you will not. A week, that doctor said. Now, I'll just put these away and then I'll make us a nice wee cup of tea."

I could offer to help put the groceries away to stop

her fussing around me like this, but I might as well make the most of not being expected to do anything.

When Mum comes back with the tea she's not alone. "Look who I found at the back door! Stacey must have heard the kettle boil."

Stacey gives me an uncertain smile. She's changed her hair colour to a kind of red, a bit like Cian's. Could be her natural colour. Getting off the sofa and going upstairs to my nice peaceful bedroom is suddenly a very attractive option, but Mum stops me when she sees me starting to make a move. "Och, love, stay where you are."

"No, I'll leave you to it."

"Don't let me chase you away, Declan. I could do with your advice, anyway," Stacey says, sitting down at the other end of the sofa.

"*My* advice?"

"About my Cian."

I sigh. "I'm not really the best …"

Stacey leans over towards me and I draw away in case she can smell me. I need to go and lie in the bath for hours. Her lipstick's come off on the rim of her cup and when she takes her cigarette out of her mouth it's ringed in red too. "That bloody school," she says. "He's suspended for a day already. First week."

Impressive. "What for?"

"Oh." She waves her cigarette around and I cough. "Telling some teacher to fuck off."

I shrug. "I never liked that school."

Mum rushes in. "Och, Declan, that's not true! Sure you did so well." She turns to Stacey. "He did awful well in the end."

I got five GCSEs: two Bs and three Cs. Not exactly a high achiever. But I know I'm not going to escape from Mum and Stacey, and I suppose talking about Cian's easier than thinking about Folly or Cam or Seaneen.

"Whose tutor group's he in?"

Stacey looks blank. "He doesn't say much. He's in the bottom class. He's not stupid," she adds quickly. "He just doesn't bother."

"Aye, sure that was you, Declan, wasn't it?" Mum says, lighting up.

I cough. "I suppose."

"But what made you *change*? Because if I could get my Cian to –"

"The horses. I needed to get the grades to get to college. And people helped me." I don't look at Mum. The best way she helped me was by going away to dry out and leaving me with Colette. If it hadn't been for that, God knows where I'd be now.

Stacey sighs. "You see, he's got you, Theresa. Cian's only got me." And she looks at Mum like Mum might know how to help her, like Mum's somebody *useful*, like Colette or Cam or somebody.

"See, if he had a hobby, Stacey," Mum says. "Once our Declan got into the horses I never saw him."

"I never see Cian as it is," Stacey says. "But you're right, if he had a hobby ..."

And off they go, same old things they've been saying for weeks. I want to tell her that her kid's in real trouble, that he's seriously out of control, that he needs more than a *hobby*.

Then Stacey's voice goes all soppy and she seems to forget about Cian. "Och, Theresa!" she gushes and picks up the blue knitting. "That's so cute. Blue. Does that mean …?"

"It's a boy," Mum says. "Seaneen had a scan the other day. A wee grandson."

I swallow. A boy. "Mum … about the baby …"

She fixes me with a surprisingly tough look. "Oh, I know," she says. "Seaneen told me the other day; I met her in the street. But I turned around and I said to her, doesn't matter what you and Declan do, that wee boy's still my grandson."

The need to get away is so urgent it's like suddenly needing the toilet.

"OK," I say. "Going to go and have a bath. See you."

But I don't make it as far as the bath. I close my bedroom curtains and lie in the half-dark, listening to the rise and fall of their voices through the floor and wondering why I feel so sad.

5.

Every night I say, I'll go back to work tomorrow. Every morning I wake up late after a crap night – dreaming of babies and Seaneen and Folly all mixed up in one sweaty, choking nightmare – and think it's not worth it, and my headache's still not properly gone, and I'm tired and I don't feel like moving, and anyway my bike's still up there so how would I get there? It's too far to walk, it's an awkward journey by bus and a taxi would cost too much. If Cam really needed me back she'd bring me my bike. If there was anything wrong with Folly she'd have let me know.

Then one afternoon I get a text from Vicky.

When am I gonna meet your new horse? Fiona tells me she's been causing a bit of mayhem! Mind you, haven't we all wanted to bite Lara?

I stare at the screen. What's she on about? *Lara* wouldn't be anywhere near Folly. Then I feel ashamed. How would I know? I haven't been there. Anything could have happened. I haven't much credit but I don't trust this to a text, so I press *call*. "What did you mean about Folly and Lara?" I ask as soon as Vicky answers.

"Thanks very much, Declan, I had a lovely time, thanks for asking."

"Sorry, yeah, good. But what did you mean about Folly?"

She sounds surprised. "Well, just about her attacking Lara. I know I shouldn't laugh but ..."

Oh my God. I knew Cam was keeping something from me. "Vicky – d'you really want to come and see her? Folly, I mean?"

"Yes, of course." I can't tell if she means it or not. But she has a car.

"Can you pick me up now? I'm at home."

She sighs. "I didn't mean *now*, Declan. I meant sometime before I go to Durham."

"Please?" I hate asking her.

"I'm never very sure of how to get to your house."

"Thought you had GPS?"

"I was going to... Oh, OK." She gives in. "I suppose it'd be nice to see Cam."

I wait at the window so when the white Fiat swings around the corner I can make a quick getaway before Mum starts asking Vicky about her holiday and all. They can't stand each other but they always pretend they're mates and it'd make you puke to listen to them. I let myself into the car. Vicky's very brown, showing off her tan in a pink vest top even though it's not summer any more. Vicky's a big girl, taller than me and broad, but I can't help looking at her flat stomach. No bump for Vicky. "OK?" I say and start doing up the seat belt before she has a chance to take the key out of the ignition.

"I heard you got a bang on the head." She does a seven-point turn in an area where there's space to turn a bus. "Did it knock any sense into you?"

"Probably not." I suppose she knows about the baby. Not that it matters now. But she and Colette are weird; they tell each other everything, so I suppose Colette's put her in the picture. She doesn't mention it, though. I ask her about her holiday and she jabbers on about Thailand and beaches and temples all the way out of the estate, but all the time keeping a careful look out for whatever she thinks is going to jump out of the hedge and attack her. Only when West Belfast turns into the arse-end of South Belfast and we start climbing the hilly country roads towards the yard does she relax.

"So what are you planning to do with your horse?" she asks as we pass mares and foals in fields and a herd of miniature Shetlands.

I squash down the memory of how bad things had got with Folly. The need to impress Vicky rushes to the front of my head. "I want to jump her. I hoped she'd be ready for some of the winter leagues, but … Well, maybe not, but next year …" Then I change the subject. "My mum said you're not going to Cambridge?"

"Didn't get the grades."

"But you got all As!"

"Needed A stars."

"That's mad. How can four As not be enough?"

She shrugs. "I'm going to Durham and it's gorgeous, so it's fine."

"So what about you and Rory?"

She shrugs a brown shoulder. "I'll have my car. And

we've survived two years of being in separate countries."

"And I suppose if you split up it'll be easier not living in the same place." Instead of having Seaneen in the next street.

"Thanks Declan, always so positive." Vicky turns into Cam's road.

The yard looks the same as usual, except I notice it needs sweeping. It's Saturday so there's a fair amount of bustle. Jim, walking past with a bale of shavings on his shoulder, grunts at Vicky – he's never liked her – but nods at me and says, "Is that you back, son?"

"Um, yeah, I suppose. Came up to see Folly anyway."

He says something that might be "huh" but might just be a clearing of the throat.

Some of the crap Saturday riders, Casper and Bella and some I don't know, hanging around gossiping after their lesson, flock around Vicky and ask her about her travels. Next minute she gets her iPad out and starts going through a million photos of white beaches and Rory in shorts. I leave them to it and break away. I grab Folly's headcollar from the hook outside my stable door, registering that Willow's stable is empty and the plaque that said Willow has been unscrewed. Has Lara *left*? My heart pounds as I skirt past the school on my way to the fields. What has Folly done?

At first I don't see her in the bottom field, just the Welshies grazing in a clump, and panic surges through me. *She's gone.* Then I see her white tail whisking the air. She's only hidden behind Mungo.

I let myself into the field, my hands suddenly slippery on the gate catch. "Folly!" She lifts her head at the sound of my voice and so do the ponies, but then they all start grazing again. I walk up to the little group, noticing that the field needs poo-picked.

"Wait for me, Declan! Thought you wanted me to see this new horse?"

Vicky strides up, blonde hair bouncing on her shoulders, and Folly darts sideways in alarm just before I can put a hand on her.

"Sorry!" she says. I stifle a sigh of irritation. After all, she did give me a lift here, and it's not her fault Folly's nervous.

"Folly!" I will her to look at me, to nicker a welcome, to walk straight up to me, to show Vicky that she's my horse and that she likes being my horse.

By now Folly's spied the headcollar in my hand and she turns her arse to me with a double-barrelled flick of her heels.

"Friend*ly*." Vicky flinches away.

"Sorry. She's a bit … oversensitive. She doesn't usually do that."

"Apparently she took a lump out of Lara's arm."

"Well, Lara shouldn't have been anywhere near her. She must have done something on her. Lara's never liked her anyway."

"Chill out, Declan! God! I'm only telling you. Folly isn't the only oversensitive one. Lara's got her new horse anyway. It cost seven thousand pounds."

"That's only seven thousand pounds more than my horse."

I inch closer to Folly, rustling in my pocket even though there isn't a treat there. She's not fooled, though, and trots away again, her head in the air. I decide not to catch her after all. I need to get my bike home before dark. I drop the headcollar on the ground and eventually Folly lets me stroke her, though she feels poised for flight at any second, and even the usually puppy-friendly Welshies have picked up on her vibes and are eyeing us with long-lashed suspicion. Vicky keeps her distance, and a cautious eye on Folly's back legs.

"See you, Folly," I say in a casual voice. "Back to normal tomorrow. You can start doing some work again." For a moment there's the tingle of remembering and fear but as always it's gone before I can reach for it.

"Declan, remember when you first got into horses? And I was really jealous, because you seemed to have this bond with Flight?"

"Yeah?"

"Cam said you were good with horses because you didn't have any *expectations* about them. You just saw them as horses. As themselves. Not as showjumpers or whatever."

I shrug. "That's 'cause I didn't know anything back then."

"OK." She frowns, as if making up her mind about something. "But I always remembered that. And – well, maybe you knew more then than you do now."

I throw the headcollar over my shoulder and try to look as if none of this matters a damn to me. "Look," I say, "She's *fine*. It's not like I just went out and bought her for thousands of pounds, you know. Not like Lara with her bloody seven thousand."

Vicky leans across to me and touches my shoulder. "Does that hurt?"

"What?"

"That chip on your shoulder."

"Ha ha."

"Declan?" She keeps her hand on my shoulder and swings me around to look at her. Her blue eyes are quite kind. "It doesn't matter what other people think. If she's the horse for you, that's fine."

"Yeah, I know." I start walking back up the field. "Well, she is."

★ ★ ★

You wouldn't think a few days off could make you so unfit, but my bike feels about a ton heavier as I slog up the hills, and home has never seemed so far from the yard, not even on winter evenings, struggling through slush in the dark. By the time I turn into the estate all I can think about is a hot bath and bed – especially as I've promised to go back to work tomorrow which means getting up early and doing it all again.

A silver jeep sitting sideways across the waste ground outside the Spar, abandoned rather than parked, forces me to swerve, and when I look up there's Seaneen talking to Emmet McCann. I see her in profile. She has to tilt her head to look up at him and the swell of her bump sticks out.

What the hell is Emmet McCann doing near Seaneen? He'd better not be harassing her. She's got a Spar bag in one hand and she looks more pregnant than the last time I saw her. Except that's stupid; it hasn't been long enough. It's just the shock of suddenly seeing her.

Emmet McCann's put on weight too. He's as square

as a fridge and his scalp shows through his shaved hair. His belly, not much smaller than Seaneen's, pushes against his football top and the part of me that isn't busy looking at Seaneen thinks he's even more like his da than ever. Even his voice, loud and annoyed, used to getting its own way, is like Barry's. But neither of their voices has the power to scare me these days. If he's hassling Seaneen he'll have me to worry about. I slow my bike. I'm close enough to hear what they're saying.

"Well, if you do see him, tell him," he finishes. "I mean it."

"Whatever," Seaneen says, and I can imagine the upwards flicker of her eyes even if I can't see it. I'm reassured by the fact that she's not scared of him. Or attracted to him.

McCann gets into the jeep and roars off through the gap, nearly knocking me off my bike. I have to grapple for control of the pedals and wreck my balls on the crossbar.

"Bastard."

Seaneen stands right in front of me. She's wearing a pink jumper I never saw before that skims her hump. Her cheeks are pink as if she's been flustered by talking to McCann.

"All right, Dec?" Her voice is tight.

I jerk my head in the direction of the retreating car. "What did he want?"

"You don't want to know." She sounds tired and fed up and keeps her eyes from making contact with mine. A ringlet falls across her face in the way that always drives her mad. She pushes it away but it springs back. "Wee Cian," she says. "He's after him."

I don't tell her I already know. "Why's Emmet asking *you*?"

"He's just asking random people who live near Cian. He was in the shop asking Cathal Gurney." My hand itches to reach out and push that ringlet out of her eye. "So if you see Cian," she says, "will you warn him? I mean, you of all people …"

"I know." I was never that scared of Emmet McCann. But then he wasn't a drug dealer when I knew him, just a bully. But I was scared of his da all right. I remember that crushing helplessness. Of every street being full of shadows. Of Barry McCann's voice being enough to shrivel me inside. "I will, yeah."

"OK, so … see you."

She walks away. From the back she doesn't look pregnant.

As I'm going to bed I get a text. *It was really hard seeing you. I don't want to keep bumping into you when the baby's born. I hope you do find a job somewhere away from here. You know it's what you want. It's only worth it if you go and follow your dream.*

I know what she means. If Lara had bought Flight and kept him at Cam's it would have killed me a lot more than him going to Wexford. But I don't know how to reply. In the end I don't, and I delete her number from my phone. Even though I know it off by heart.

6.

As soon as I walk into the barn the next morning a new head looks out over Willow's old stable door with a friendly, curious nicker. It's a shiny black with a diamond-shaped star under a silky forelock and huge purplish eyes fringed in long black lashes.

"Hello," I say. I stroke its velvety nose and it nuzzles against my palm, licking it the way Flight used to. "Hey, you're gorgeous, aren't you?" I unbolt the stable door and go in. It's a mare. She steps back politely at my entrance and lips again at my hand, not like she wants to bite, just in the confident expectation that a human visitor means something nice might be going to happen. Her coat shines with health and grooming. She is far, far too good for Lara.

"Ah, you've met our new arrival?"

"Oh, hi Cam." I feel stupidly shy meeting Cam. Last time she saw me I was acting like a nutter. Having the new horse to focus on makes the first few minutes easier, before the busy routine can swallow us up.

"Where'd this come from?"

"Scott's. Lara had her on a week's trial. Passed the vet on Friday. Hasn't put a foot wrong. Jumps every-thing you put her at; forward-going but sensible; a lamb in the stable; nine years old. Done a few Grand Prixs."

"Too good for Lara."

"Now, now. Lara's livery bill pays your wages. Patrick was here with his dad to deliver the horse. He said you should give him a ring if you want a bit of help with Folly."

"So where's the lovely Willow? McCluskey's?" I ask to change the subject. I can joke about this because wherever Willow is, it's not the cat-food factory.

"Scott took him. Some boy up in Derry's trying him out."

"And what's this one called?"

"Aisling's Promise. Promise for short. OK, we can't stand around admiring horses all day long. There's a bit of a backlog. And I've a lesson at ten."

"Have I time to just go and check on Folly before I start?" I'm a bit nervous about mentioning Folly. Cam hasn't said anything about her biting Lara yet, but it can only be a matter of time.

"Of course."

Seeing Promise reminds me that all the horses will be coming in soon. I can't imagine Folly in the stable most of the time, turned out for a few hours during the day, but Cam brings everything in for the winter to let the fields rest. I decide not to think about that yet.

Folly's grazing with the ponies. She looks up when I call her, then trots off in the other direction, snatching tufts of grass as she goes in a way that would be cute if it was someone else's horse.

Stupid to feel so rejected; it's not like I was even planning to catch her. And it's not personal; she just doesn't want anybody to interfere with her nice quiet life of eating and dozing. Who could blame her?

Cam wasn't joking about a backlog. Even though most of the horses are still out, so there's only Promise's bed to do, I don't stop all day. Nobody's poo-picked or cleaned tack in my absence. Every time I finish one boring, menial job, Cam shouts over with another.

"The truck needs to be swept out."

"The school needs to bed poo-picked."

"The yard needs sweeping."

I'd nearly think it was some kind of punishment except I haven't done anything wrong, and all these things do need to get done. But it's hard not to feel resentful, pushing the fourth wheelbarrow of dung up the ramp to the muck heap and watching Cam and Lara return from a hack around the farm trail, the sun glinting off their horses' shining flanks, their easy laughter floating up to me. Under saddle Promise looks magical, moving lightly over the ground, relaxed and easy in her new life.

And for the first time in ages I can't stop the thought: what would I be doing right this minute if I'd gone to Hilgenberg's?

Except I suppose German showjumpers shit too.

I don't get a chance to bring Folly in until evening. It's noticeably darker than it was a week ago at this time. This time it's hard to believe it's not personal. She turns her arse on me the minute she spies the headcollar in my hand and I have to flinch from her flying hooves.

"Come on, girl, stop fooling around." I make my voice gentle. I make my voice stern. Every time I get within grabbing distance she trots off. Eventually I get her, but she snaps her teeth at me every few seconds. Then she lifts up her head and lets out a high-pitched indignant squeal and next minute we're surrounded by the ponies in a flurry of flying manes and tails and little hooves. I have to hold really tight to stop Folly cantering off after them, and she spins around me, the rope burning into my palm. For a second I'm tempted to say, what the hell, and just let her go, and pretend to myself I didn't really want to bring her in, but I can't give in to her.

I can see Jim standing at the top of the lane, having a smoke and watching with interest. By the time I get to him I'm sweating and Folly's fussing and pulling.

"Aye," he says, coughing. "You've your work cut out there."

At the sound of his cough Folly skitters sideways. When I get her to the stable, she flicks back her ears, digs her feet in and won't go forward. Jim comes up and chases her from behind, which forces her in OK, but she stands in the corner, flanks heaving, neck dark with sweat, eyes rolling.

"Could do with a bullet, that thing," Jim says, leaning over the stable door. "Why don't you get yourself something you can have a bit of fun on?"

I ignore him. I ignore the fact that he's worked with horses for over forty years. I ignore the fantasy of starting again with a different horse, a *normal* horse. What would I do with Folly? I'd be like Stacey, having more brats even though she couldn't cope with the one she had. I push past Jim to get Folly a bucket of feed, which she attacks with her usual enthusiasm, but without taking her eyes off me.

"Aye. I'm too old for the likes of that," Jim says with a sideways spit.

"Well, you don't have to go near her," I say, going for my brushes. "Silly girl," I tell her as she stretches out a suspicious nose to sniff the soft body brush. "I'm not going to hurt you." She doesn't look like she believes me. For a while I groom her quietly, and eventually she starts to relax, but tenses again when a shadow falls across the door and I hear Lara's voice.

"Oh, you're back," she says. "Did you hear what your brute did to me?"

I think it's wisest to act innocent.

"No, what?" I straighten up and lean over the door with the brush in my hand. I rub it against the top of the door and dust flies out of it, making Lara cough.

Lara rolls up her sleeve and shows me a blackish bruise just above her elbow. "You're lucky I was wearing my coat or she'd have broken the skin. All I did was go and check on her because Cam was too busy."

I don't know what to say. "You must have scared her."

"Scared her!" Lara makes a noise halfway between a laugh and a snort. "She was always a nutter but now she's actually vicious. Just as well you're back because nobody'll go near her now."

"Well, keep away from her." For a moment I like the idea of a one-man horse. In my mind I smile at Princess Anne while she hands us our Olympic gold medal. Folly bends her head to let Princess Anne put the winner's sash around her neck. "And does one understand that nobody else can do anything with her?" Princess Anne asks.

Then I remember that I can't do much with her myself.

"Look, do you want something?" I ask. "Because I'm busy here and my horse clearly doesn't like you."

Lara stalks off with her nose in the air but a minute later Cam takes her place. "Can you not be so rude to my customers, please?" she says. "I've just had a complaint from Lara."

"She asked for it."

"You should have apologized to her. That was a nasty bite."

"*I* didn't bite her."

"Don't be so childish. Folly's your responsibility."

"Well, you shouldn't have asked Lara to go and check on her. Folly doesn't like Lara. Probably heard all the nasty things she's said about her. 'That horse's only fit for the knackers' and all that crap."

"Declan, you haven't showed up for ten days. I don't think you realize the kind of pressure that put me under."

"It wasn't my fault I had concussion."

Cam gives me one of her very straight looks that makes you feel as if she's peeling off a layer of your skin. "Are you sure about that?"

"I don't remember," I mutter.

"Come with me," she says. I don't know what she wants but you don't argue with Cam when she's in this mood so I trail after her. She leads me to the school. In one corner there's a bit of fence that's obviously just been repaired. "This was broken," she says, and before I can say anything she marches over to the tack room, where she takes down Joy's saddle. A deep gash and some smaller scrapes spoil the shiny black leather. Cam looks at me and raises her eyebrows. "You wouldn't need to be Sherlock Holmes," she says.

"Oh my God." My hand flies up to my mouth. "I must have borrowed it." My voice comes out in a guilty whisper. "I'll pay for it," I say with more confidence.

"With what? Those saddles cost £1,500."

"Why are you being so nasty?" I sound like a sulky kid, but I can't seem to stop myself.

"Why are you being so childish?" she snaps back. "You've got a *horse*, Declan, not a toy! God, out of everybody I know, I never thought I'd have to have this conversation with *you*."

"You never wanted me to get her."

"I was cautious. A horse with that kind of background was always going to need patience and special handling. Maybe more than you're capable of."

"But you said – you said *time*. You said they all settle."

"If you let them." Cam sighs. "And I don't know what you've been doing with her but she's getting worse, not better."

I rub my hand over my face.

"Look, I'm sorry if I sound hard on you. Fences and saddles can be fixed – I don't want *you* getting hurt."

"Is Fiona raging?"

"Fiona lost the baby. Last night. She's in the hospital. So the saddle's not the foremost of her worries."

"Oh." Why can't Seaneen have that and then we can

get back to normal, I think before I can stop myself, and then I think no wonder bad things happen to me when I go around having thoughts like that.

"Anyway, Declan, I want you to promise me you won't try to work Folly unless I'm in the yard."

"Cam, I'm not stupid."

"I wouldn't necessarily agree with that." She indicates the damaged saddle. "Seriously, Declan. That horse is potentially dangerous. Either you promise or … or I won't have her in the yard. I mean it, I can't take the risk." She gives me her most determined look. "I have customers to think about. Some of them are children."

"But nobody needs to go near her but me!" I almost sob it out.

"It's not that simple."

"I'm not some beginner, you know. What did I go to coll –"

"When it comes to a complicated animal like that you are. Look, I have to go, Declan." She sounds fed up with the conversation. "Pippa and I are going to her mum's for dinner. Can I trust you to lock up?"

"Of course you can."

Cam's usually right about horses. But not this time.

Their words chase me home. *I won't have her in the yard … Could do with a bullet, that thing …*

7.

Mum stands in front of the mirror above the fireplace, getting ready to go out. She turns around and smiles at me. "OK, love? First day back go all right? I'm going to the cinema with Margaret. We might go for a coffee after. I'll be back about ten."

She has all these new friends from her support groups. They're not all ex-alcoholics. Margaret is something to do with some women's group.

I flop down on the sofa and grab the remote. My legs twitch with exhaustion. "Is there any dinner?"

"Heat yourself up a pizza," she says.

She rummages in her make-up bag and takes out a big brush. She dabs it over her face. "Oh," she says, as if she's about to tell me something important. "Stacey's got a big night tonight."

"Uh?" I flick through the channels but keep the sound down.

"Aye. Her and Darren's meeting up. He texted her and said he missed her. She went out and got herself a new dress and all. Isn't that good?"

"I dunno. Is he not a bit of a thug?"

"Darren? No! He's a computer programmer."

"I thought Cian …" Then I remember that Cian never said Darren laid a finger on him; it was me who assumed he had.

"Och, Cian." Mum sniffs. "*He* did his best to wreck it as usual. But he's babysitting his wee sisters tonight. Well, he's grounded for getting suspended, so he has to watch them at the same time. I said to Stacey, 'you need to be tougher on him'."

Neither *grounded* nor *babysitting* sound like Cian. Too *normal.* I wonder if his ma knows he's hiding from the local drug dealer. But it's not my business.

"God love her," Mum says. "Sure all she wants is a wee bit of happiness." She blots her lipstick and turns around and smiles at me. "Right, will I do?"

"You on the prowl, Mum?"

"Och, Declan!" She looks quite pleased but then she goes serious. "I don't think I'm ready for a relationship just yet. I still have some self-esteem issues to work through."

I never know what to say when she goes all Californian on me.

"Do you want me to record *Midsomer Murders*?"

"Thanks, love."

When she's gone I mooch into the kitchen and stick a pizza in the oven. The whole time I was off work I never felt like eating, but now, after slaving in the open air all day, I'm starving. I eat at the kitchen table, flicking through the new *Horse and Hound*. There's hardly any jobs. One of them says "own horse welcome" so I read it more carefully. It's in Suffolk. I don't know exactly where that is but it says "miles of coastal hacking" and I imagine me and Folly cantering along a beach under a huge sky. Imagine her stepping smartly off a horse truck in a blue rug, looking around her new yard with bright, confident eyes, happy to accept whatever's in store, knowing from experience it'll be OK. But I realize I've turned her into Promise or Spirit or Flight – a *normal* horse – and catch myself on.

I take the magazine back into the living room and read a feature about some town in Yorkshire with loads of racing yards. Middleham, it's called. I know nothing about racing, though we had a visit to a racing yard at college and some people specialized in racehorse man- agement, but I bet I could just turn up there and go around the yards until somebody took me on. They have loads of staff in racing yards. I'm wiry and light and brave – I could exercise the horses. It'd get me over the winter anyway. I know I promised Cam I'd stay but there'd be nothing she could actually *do* if I just went.

And it's not just selfishness. Seaneen *wants* me to go.

I don't know where Folly fits into this fantasy.

For the first time it occurs to me that horses, like babies, are a lot easier to get than they are to get rid of. Not that I want rid of Folly. I want …

But I don't know what I want.

I must doze off because next minute there's this awful banging at the door and somebody shouting. Not Cian again! But the voice is crying, "Theresa! Theresa!" and it's a girl.

It's Stacey's wee girls. They're both crying their eyes out and shrieking and it takes me a few seconds to see that the wee one's neck above her soaking wet pink vest top is bright red.

"Jesus!" I say. "What's happened you?"

She roars louder than ever and the bigger one says, "Madison pulled the kettle over! We were going to have hot chocolate but it wasn't my fault."

I drag them in although I haven't a clue what to do with them. "Is Theresa not there?" the bigger one says.

"No."

The wee one sits down hard on the bottom stair and starts to whimper, which is less annoying than the shrieking but also a bit scary, like she's really hurt. I know about horse first aid, but nothing about scalds. Horses aren't normally near boiling water. The only person I know who could cope with these kids is Seaneen. But I get the first bit of luck I've had in days when Mum pushes through the open door and says, "Courtney! Madison! What's happened you?"

Courtney dives at her. "Madison's all burnt! But it wasn't my fault."

Mum looks at me and I shrug. "Don't ask me. They just appeared."

"Well, have you phoned an ambulance?"

"It's only a wee burn."

But when Mum gets the smaller kid to show her, it's not just her neck, it's all the way down her chest.

"Declan! For God's sake, phone – OK, not an ambulance, but phone a taxi and say it's urgent. And then phone Stacey." She thrusts her phone at me, and then bends down to Madison. "Come on, darling, you're OK. Theresa'll take you to the hospital and the doctor'll make you better." She drags the kids off into the kitchen, but the door's open wide enough for me to hear them still howling.

I phone the taxi first and then scroll through Mum's contacts for Stacey's number. It goes straight to voice-mail. I leave a message saying what's happened and that Mum's going to take the kid to the hospital, and then open the front door to look out for the taxi. The sooner it comes the sooner I can get rid of these shrieking kids who make me feel so stupid and unsure of what to do.

But when Mum rushes out, carrying Madison, she says to me, "You'd better take Courtney home and look after her in her own house. She'll be happier there. And keep trying Stacey."

"I already left a message. I haven't got her number."

"I'll text you it. Shh, Madison, good brave girl. OK, Courtney, love, you go with Declan."

She gets into the taxi like somebody who knows exactly what she's doing, leaving behind a still-blub-bering Courtney and me. And I haven't a clue.

"Is Madison going to die?" Courtney sobs. "Is my mummy going to be cross with me?"

"I don't know," I say. "I mean – no, of course she's not going to die. The doctors and nurses will make her better. Come on; we'll go back to your house."

She slips her warm, sticky hand into mine, which feels disgusting but it seems mean to shrug it off. "OK," she says.

The door of their house is still wide open from when they came crying out into the street. I've never been in Stacey's house. I suppose I imagined it would be a bit of a dive, like ours during Mum's vodka years. But it's not. It's still got some old-lady wallpaper from when Seaneen's granny lived here, but other than that it's quite clean and modern and pink. Very pink. Fluffy cushions and rugs and the same bits of plastic crap that are in Seaneen's house. Loads of photos of the kids everywhere – mainly the girls. A purple plastic castle takes up half the sofa.

"We were playing princesses," Courtney says. "And Cian said we could have hot chocolate. But then he never came back."

"Where did he go?"

"To the shop. He said we could have hot chocolate and he would get us Flakes to put on top. But he'd have to go out and get them in the shop. Only he never came back. So Madison started crying and I said *I* knew how to make hot chocolate, but then she went and lifted the kettle down herself. I told her she wasn't allowed, only she wouldn't listen. She was trying to h-h-help." And she bursts into fresh blubbery sobs.

"Ah come on, now, sure it'll be OK." I move the purple castle from the sofa, hoping this might encourage her to sit down. "Tell you what – if you stop crying, *I'll* make you hot chocolate. How's that?"

She stares at me from under her long yellowy bangs and sniffs wetly. Her face is all snotty and blotched. I wonder if she's old enough to be told to blow her nose. I definitely can't do it for her. I wish Seaneen was here. This is her kind of thing.

I go into the kitchen. The kettle's still lying on the floor where it must have fallen, in a pool of cooling water. It doesn't look like much to have caused all that damage. I lift it up and check that the element isn't wet, and then blot the floor with kitchen roll.

Courtney stands in the middle of the kitchen and

watches me with her hands on her hips. She's dressed like a baby prostitute in a tight black T-shirt with a glittery pink face printed on it, and pink leggings with laces up the sides.

"Is my mummy going to be cross?" she asks again.

"Maybe with Cian," I say since she obviously isn't going to stop nagging till she gets an answer. I put the kettle on and find the hot chocolate powder sitting out on the table.

Courtney wags her head. "She's always cross with Cian. That's 'cause he's a bad boy. He smokes in his room, only nobody's meant to know, but I do." She snorts up more of the snot. "I'm in P2," she says. "I'm in Mrs. O'Malley's class. What P are you in?"

"I'm not in P-anything. I'm grown up."

"Madison's not in P-anything yet. She goes to nursery school. Cian goes to the big school but he got s'pended. I'll be six in three more weeks. I'm getting a Baby Annabel."

"Are you?" I spoon the hot chocolate into a Barbie mug and then fetch a Hello Kitty mug for myself. I haven't had hot chocolate for years. I glance at my watch. I've only been here for ten minutes. Why are small kids so boring? How can Seaneen spend all day looking after them?

"Can I have toast and Nutella?" Courtney asks while I pour the hot water into the cups.

"If it keeps you quiet."

She looks at me with her head tilted, as if she's trying to work out if this is a joke. "Are you babysitting me?" she asks.

"I suppose. Look, if you sit down carefully at the

table with that and don't spill, I'll make you some toast and Nutella." I sound like Seaneen. Maybe if I pretend to *be* Seaneen I'll be able to manage. Only where the hell is Stacey?

"OK." She sits up at the table and slurps her hot chocolate. I make the toast and soon she adds streaks of Nutella to the smeared snot and tears on her face. "You'll need to wash your face before you go to bed," I say, still being Seaneen, as I slide Courtney's toast crusts off the plate into the bin.

She folds her arms. "I'm not going to bed," she says firmly. She gets down from the table and springs into the living room. "Not till my mummy comes home."

"If you go to bed and go to sleep your mummy'll be home when you wake up."

"But I'm *allowed* to stay up." She flashes a gaped chocolatey grin at me. "Look what I can do." She checks that I'm looking then bounces up and down on the sofa, her stringy blonde hair bouncing in wisps on her narrow shoulders. God, this is going to go on for hours. I can't *make* her go to bed. At least she isn't crying any more. I phone Mum's mobile but it goes straight to voicemail which I suppose means she's in the hospital and can't use it.

At last Courtney flops down on the sofa.

"Why don't you watch some TV?" I suggest.

"Yeah!" She grabs the remote and flicks through the channels faster than I've ever seen. I think she'll go for a cartoon or something but her face lights up when she hits on some American X-Factorish thing. She knows all the judges, though I've never heard of them, and she sings along with half the songs, standing on the sofa, looking around to see if I'm admiring her and shaking her skinny little six-year-old body in time to the music. It's repulsive. I feel like a pervert just for being in the same room.

Mum rings in the middle of this and says they've taken Madison in to get her burns assessed and dressed. "They're quite worried about the deep one on her chest," she says. "But I can't get hold of Stacey. She never goes anywhere without her phone, so I can't understand it."

"The reunion must be going well," I say in a low voice, with an eye on Courtney, who's too busy dancing and singing to listen.

Mum sighs. "Everything OK there?"

"Yeah. I've given her her supper and all."

"Good for you. God love her. It wasn't her fault."

"Ah, she's cheered up, she's grand."

By midnight, Courtney is conked out on the sofa, her yellow hair strung over her face, legs sprawled. I don't want to touch her but she looks too exposed like that so I put the pink fleece from the back of the sofa over her.

I fight to keep awake with TV and coffee. I look at the photos of the kids on the white unit and big ones on the walls. There's loads of baby pictures of the girls, always in pink, but the only ones of Cian are when he's older. I wonder where he is, and if Emmet McCann's caught up with him yet. I don't want Emmet to *hurt* Cian. But maybe he needs a bit of a scare if he's ever going to wise up.

The front door bangs. Stacey bursts in, her face blurred like Mum's used to be when she had just been with a man she really liked. But when she sees me all her features snap suddenly into place. She throws her huge purple and silver handbag onto the armchair.

"What the … Where's Madison? What are you doing here?"

I tell her as quickly as I can. "We've been trying to phone you all night."

"My phone's disappeared. Haven't seen it since this morning." She runs her hands through her hair, which I notice for the first time is all done in loose curls. "And where the hell's our Cian?" Her eyes are huge with fear and make-up.

"I don't know."

"He was grounded!" Her voice is about one second away from bursting into tears. "The wee bastard wasn't allowed over the door. See when I get hold of him …"

"Look, I'll ring you a taxi," I say, taking out my phone. "And then – is there somebody who can come and stay with Courtney? Only I have to get up for work in the morning, and …"

She turns on me as if I've suggested leaving Courtney up at the traffic lights.

"No, there bloody isn't. You stay here," she orders like I'm one of her kids. "Oh God! This'll have social services sniffing around again. You can bet. That wee bastard. I wish I'd never had him." She speaks as if I'm not here.

Courtney stirs and mutters something, then rolls over and buries her face deep in the sofa cushion.

I ring the taxi and, thank God, it comes quickly. Stacey grabs her handbag. She turns to me before she leaves. "See if he comes back … tell him I'll kill him. I mean it."

She doesn't thank me. I decide to get a nap in the

armchair. I don't actually have to be awake.

★ ★ ★

I wake up in bright light but I know from the heaviness of my eyes that it's still the middle of the night. I haven't a clue where I am but the sound that woke me is familiar – the scraping and missing of a key in a lock.

Good. I can go and finish the night in my own bed.

But the person who stumbles through the door isn't Stacey. It's Cian. He's totally loaded. Drink, by the smell of him. He sways in the doorway. It takes him a long time to focus on me. It's just like the first time I saw him.

"What the fuck?" His voice is slurred.

"What the fuck is right." I keep my voice down in case Courtney wakes up. "Thought you were babysitting?"

"I had some business to see to."

"Business! Look at the state of you."

"I was trying to get some money together – *you* know why. Nobody'd help me!" His voice rises to a self-pitying yelp. "You wouldn't! What was I meant to do?"

"Well, your Madison pulled a kettle of boiling water over herself. She's in hospital. It's very serious."

I don't know why I say that. I think I want to shock him. It works. The colour bleeds out of his face and for a second I think he might pass out. I remember the shock Mum got three years ago when she found the bloodstains after Barry McCann had thrown me down some steps. She always says that was the turning point for her – when she knew she had to do something about the drink. So maybe this will be the turning point for Cian. I lay it on thick. "She looked terrible."

Cian's breath comes in jagged gasps. "Ah shit. Ah shit. Did my ma – what did my ma say?"

"She said she was going to kill you."

Cian sits down hard in the middle of the floor and hugs himself. Sudddenly he's crying as hard as Courtney was. He bends over and rocks himself like somebody mental. For a second I feel sorry for him. He's only a kid, and I know what it feels like to be responsible for a horrible accident. Part of me wants to tell him that, and tell him to make sure he apologizes sooner rather than later and doesn't let the guilt gnaw at him for weeks. Make him realize that when something like this happens it's a chance. You messed up but you can make things better.

But that's not the kind of thing I could ever say. And Cian's not the kind of person who'd listen.

And it's nearly two o'clock on a Monday morning and I have to be up for work in five hours. And I just want to go home, away from this pink house which has nothing to do with me and well away from this strange, desperate kid. So I leave him crying in the middle of the pink living room.

8.

Cam's campaign to keep me working like a slave continues the next day.

"This is around the time of year the BHS inspector usually comes," she says when I groan at being told to wash all the grooming brushes. "We need to be ready."

I don't have much time to think about Cian, except to wonder if his ma has killed him yet.

I'm far more bothered by Folly. The vague thoughts I had last night of taking off somewhere, turning up in some horsey area and looking for work, are taking hold of my imagination – you have to have something to think about when you're filling wheelbarrows with horse shit. But I'm kidding myself about taking her with me. The whole point would be to take off on my own with nothing holding me back. The thought of just plodding through all winter, the endless rounds of mucking out and carrying haylage to wet fields, and the long cycles through biting winds with no shows to brighten it up, is so depressing. Spirit's going brilliantly and the beautiful and perfect Promise is obviously going to do the job she was bought for, so Cam and Lara will be going out jumping every week. I can go with them but it will be to watch. To be the groom. Not really part of it.

I look around the yard I've always loved. At the whitewashed stone buildings with their red-painted doors, and the green hills behind that have always made me feel so free and safe. Why isn't it enough any more? I dump the umpteenth wheelbarrow on to the muck heap and check my phone. Just about knocking-off time, so I'd better go down and get Folly in. I lean on the gate and look at her. She's not grazing for once; just standing looking up the field, as if she can see something that nobody else can. I have one foot on the gate ready to climb over when I realize that Lara's above us in the school, cantering perfect circles on her perfect horse. I can't bear the thought of her watching while Folly gives me the run-around again. I don't need to catch her. I can see she's fine from here.

What's she looking at? Does she see me? Does she hate me? Does she wish I'd just left her there in that death barn?

I'm being stupid. I grab my bike and cycle home.

★ ★ ★

Mum's all bizz about the situation over the street. She starts talking about it before I've even sat down.

"One of the burns is quite deep," she says. "She may need a skin graft."

Emmet McCann's da stubbed out a cigarette on the

back of my hand when I was fourteen. That was quite deep too. Mum didn't notice.

"Oh," I say. I yawn. At least not having a girlfriend or any friends means I can go to bed straight after dinner – that's if Mum intends to make any dinner.

"So they're keeping her in to see how she goes. She's running a temperature too. Only Stacey thinks they're only using that as an excuse because they won't let her go home until social services have been to check up on her."

That gets my interest. "What's it got to do with social services?"

"Och, probably nothing. She's just panicking."

"What about Cian?"

Mum purses up her mouth. "She's not speaking to him. She says she can't trust herself. Oh, he was all apologies last night – I went in with her, it was near three, and he was sitting there blurting and sad and looking for sympathy, but she just said she couldn't listen to him."

"I think he *is* sorry."

"You're not taking his side, are you? Leaving a six-year-old to look after a three-year-old!"

"Yeah, but would you leave *him* to babysit? He's high as a kite half the time. Seriously, Mum, the kid's got real problems. What did Stacey expect? It's partly her own fault."

"Och, Declan, that's not fair."

Maybe it's not. I don't know; I don't really care. I'm fed up with the subject. I'm fed up with *every* subject. And tomorrow is just going to be more of the same. Only worse.

SHEENA WILKINSON

* * *

I *have* to catch Folly today; it's time to stop being so feeble. She needs her hooves picked out, and if I bring her in and give her a feed and a groom then maybe I can try getting back whatever bit of trust she used to have in me. After all, she is *my* horse. It's only a couple of weeks since it gave me a thrill to say that, instead of a prickly chill. I take a carrot and hide the headcollar around my back. The ponies are too busy grazing at the bottom of the field to take any notice of me. Folly's in her favourite place under the tree. I walk over slowly, remembering for the first time in ages the time I spent with her at Doris's, before I messed up. She walks towards me. I think she smells the carrot. She stretches out her head to it and lifts her top lip. I slip the headcollar around from behind my back, but quick as a flash she lunges at me with her teeth, then strikes out with a front hoof. I catch it on the knee.

It's over so quickly that Folly's down the other end of the field with the ponies before I realize what's happened.

It could be worse. The bite on my arm hasn't broken the skin – luckily I have my coat on. It's just a deep purplish nip. The kick hurts more. I roll up the leg of my jeans and explore my kneecap. It's turning pink, and it's raw to the touch, but everything moves the way it's meant to.

The carrot and headcollar are lying on the ground. I pick up the headcollar and leave the carrot. I head back up the field towards the gate, headcollar over my shoulder, ignoring the swelling in my throat and the

pain in my knee. I try to whistle.

"Hiya!" It's Sally, on her way up from the bottom field with Nudge. She glances at the headcollar. "Have you just turned Folly out? I haven't seen her for ages – or you. Is your head OK again? You look a bit pale."

"I'm fine, thanks."

"How's Folly getting on?"

"Fine." I can't admit to Sally that Folly hates me, that I've done something to her that I can't remember and she won't forget, that under my clothes bruises are darkening as proof of this hatred.

Could do with a bullet, that thing.

★ ★ ★

"Declan," says Mum. "Run over to Stacey's with this, love, would you? I don't want to miss the start of *EastEnders*."

I sigh but take the Tesco's bag.

"It's just a few wee things I got her when I was doing the groceries. Sure God love her."

It's not so long since Mum couldn't even manage to do her own shopping, let alone anybody else's.

I ring the bell on Stacey's door and nearly die when it's opened by Seaneen. She looks mortified too. Her cheeks flame and she swallows before she speaks; I can see her throat move.

"Oh," she says. "Hello." She stands with her hand on her belly.

"Um." I hold out the bag. My voice comes out funny. "Mum sent this."

Courtney prances up the hall. She's dressed for clubbing. "Declan!" she shrieks. "Me and Seaneen's watching *Hannah Montana*. Do you want to watch it with us?"

Seaneen looks away.

"Uh, no, I have to go, Courtney. Sorry."

"Awwww!" She hangs on to Seaneen's sweater and looks up at her. "Declan's my friend. He minded me."

"That's nice," says Seaneen. She looks at me properly for the first time. Her eyes are huge. "Stacey's at the hospital," she says. "She asked me to babysit. Courtney, go on in and keep watching – you can tell me what I've missed when I get back."

"Awww." Courtney pouts but she trots off obediently.

"Where's Cian?" I ask.

Seaneen jerks her head upwards. "In his room. She doesn't trust him to babysit. For obvious reasons."

"So do you still feel sorry for him?"

Seaneen wrinkles her nose in a way that makes the freckles join together. "Ah, you know – a bit. I saw him earlier coming out of the bathroom. He looked awful. Like everything was too much." She lowers her voice. "Stacey's scared of social services getting involved – with Madison getting hurt like that – and she blames him. Did you hear he stole her phone and sold it?"

"To pay off Emmet?" I remember the "business" he said he was doing the other night.

"I dunno. Because Cathal said, when I was in the shop today, that Emmet's still looking for him. Anyway." She chews her lip. "I better go and see what Courtney's up to."

She has the door closed before I can even say

goodbye.

For a second I think about Cian up in his room. And I nearly knock the door again and say I'm going to go up and talk to him.

Seaneen would know what to say. Maybe me and Seaneen together could help him. But there is no me and Seaneen.

* * *

I reach under my bed for my wad of notes in its new hiding place. It's still not much more than two hundred pounds. That's the trouble with having a horse. There's a million things eating up my wages – feed, grooming brushes, fly repellent, not to mention all the creams and sprays and stuff I had to buy when her skin was still all scabby. And in the winter she'll need haylage, extra feed and rugs. I put the notes into piles, wishing the fivers were tens and the tens twenties. Or fifties would be better. The winter is going to take every penny I earn just to keep Folly alive. All for a horse that hates me.

But what about Seaneen, hardly able to look at me, her hand sitting over her belly in that annoying way? I told her I'd help support the kid. Let's face it, I'm going to have to fork out anyway – Granzilla will see to that – so I might as well do it willingly. I count out five twenties and set them in a pile. It looks like nothing.

And if I go away? Not that I'm really going, but if I did … just say I tried my luck in Middleham? That's going to take money.

And what about Cian? Should I give him some?

Would it do any good?

No. Even if he did give it to Emmet without drinking it first it'd only be a matter of time before the same thing happened again.

I sweep all the notes together again and put them back under the bed.

9.

Courtney sits on our kitchen countertop swinging her legs. In her school uniform she doesn't look as much of a mini-prostitute as usual, though she has her hair tied up on one side in some sort of purple and yellow feathery thing, and her fingernails are bright pink.

Mum is doing something very weird: she's baking. At least that's what it looks like. She's mixing something up in a bowl, and the kitchen's warm with the greasy smell of the heating oven.

"What are you doing?"

"We're making cupcakes," Courtney shouts. "And I'm allowed to decorate them, and they're going to be *pink*. With silver balls."

"It's only a packet mix," Mum says, but she's flushed with pride or maybe from the heat.

"Where's Stacey?"

"Hospital."

"I thought the kid was getting home."

"She's still running a temperature. They're a bit worried about her. Only a *wee* bit worried," she says in a louder voice, but Courtney is mixing some kind of pink gunk in a bowl and doesn't look up. "So Courtney's staying for her dinner."

"We're getting pizza," Courtney says. She looks up from her mixing. "My brother's runned away."

"What?"

Mum shakes her head. "Och, he hasn't really, Courtney." She turns to me. "He skipped school. As if Stacey hasn't enough to worry about. He'll be back when he's hungry."

"Is he allowed a cupcake?" Courtney asks.

"If he's good."

Courtney frowns at her bowl. "I'll keep him one," she says.

★ ★ ★

Cian doesn't come back when he's hungry. When I get in from work the next day both of Stacey's kids are sitting in our living room watching *The Simpsons* and eating chips. It's starting to feel like a daycare. I go into the kitchen for some peace and to see if there's any cupcakes left, and there's Stacey at the table drinking coffee with Mum.

"Social services are going to come sniffing around, I know they are." She takes out a cigarette and lights it.

"But Stacey, they'll see the girls are fine," Mum says, passing her over an ashtray. "Sure you have the two of them lovely, and your house is like a wee palace."

"But if they come and *he's* not there they'll say I

can't cope."

"Well, you can't, can you?" I say.

Mum gives me the dirtiest look you ever saw. "Declan!"

Stacey sniffs. "You don't know what it's like!" She wags her cigarette at me. "You young fellas – have you thought about what that wee girl of yours is going to do?"

"That's nothing to do with –"

"Declan, it's none of your business," Mum says.

"But it's OK for her to –"

"Stacey's just worried, aren't you, Stace?"

I sigh and lean against the door. There's no sign of any dinner. "Any cupcakes left?"

"In the cupboard."

"So, what do the police say?" I ask, taking two lop-sided cupcakes out of the tin in the cupboard.

Stacey hesitates and looks at Mum. "He's only trying to scare me," she says. "He's done it before. Used to stay out overnight. He'll be with one of his mates."

"He hasn't got any mates. Not around here."

"He'll have gone back to Portadown, to his old mates. The ones we moved here to get away from." She nods at the table.

"Have you phoned him? Have you phoned these mates?"

"What on? Sure the wee bastard sold my phone!"

"Declan," Mum says. "I think you should –"

"I'd better go," Stacey says. "Madison shouldn't be out for too long." She gets up, leaving her coffee half-drunk. Mum follows her out. I root around for something more to eat.

Mum comes back into the kitchen and starts on me. "Who do you think you are, Declan, talking to my friend like that?"

"Mum! The kid's fifteen, he's been away for – what, two days? And she hasn't even phoned the police."

But Mum, who used to do a good line herself in disappearing for days, won't hear a word against her new best friend. "I know. But she's scared to – sure that's the first thing's going to get social services sniffing around, isn't it?"

"Maybe she could do with social services sniffing around!"

"Declan, it's nothing to do with you."

"It was something to do with me the other night when I had to mind her kid 'cause she was out banging some guy."

A couple of weeks ago I'd have asked Seaneen if she thought *we* should do something. But I know exactly what she'd say.

Phoning the police – it's not really my kind of thing. From somewhere comes the memory of me telling Seaneen that hospitals weren't really *me*. And I know I need to get over myself.

I go for a walk around the estate. All the streets are dark and wet. Kids hang around outside the shops, hoods up, but none of them is Cian. A silver jeep stops to let me cross the road. It isn't Emmet McCann. But it helps me make up my mind.

I turn down the alleyway behind the shops, lean against the wall, and take out my phone.

* * *

I walk around the school with the wheelbarrow and the scoop. As I bend to lift the plops of dung left behind by other people's horses, I realize that I haven't ridden for ages. Not once since I came back to work has Cam asked me to exercise a horse or take Spirit around the farm trail or anything. I've become some kind of maid.

The fixed-up bit of fence stands out, new and raw against the weathered wood rails, laughing at me – as if it remembers something I can't. I ignore it and take a break, leaning on the handle of the wheelbarrow. My phone buzzes in my pocket and I take it out, glad of the distraction. *Police been around. Checked out C's old friends in P'down. No word. Getting worried.*

About time.

Down below me Sally stops at the gate of the ponies' field, and the three Welshies come bustling up to see what the big deal is and if there's any treats going. Folly stands aloof, her white head held high. I watch. She walks a few steps forward then stops. Then she seems to make up her mind and barges her way into the middle of the herd. Sally holds out a piece of whatever she's got and Folly snuffs it up. Nothing strange about that: she's always been greedy. But even when it's clear Sally has nothing left, when she dangles her bag upside down and flicks out the last few bits, and the ponies drift away to graze, Folly stays. She lowers her neck and Sally strokes it. Folly lips at Sally's hand even though Sally has nothing for her. I bend down and scoop the last lump of dung up. It's only because Sally had treats and wasn't carrying a headcollar. Or maybe Folly's just in a good mood today.

She isn't. When I go down to get her later, she gives me the usual run-around and swings her arse around in her most threatening way. I manage to catch her but we're both bad-tempered and tired by the time I'm leading her into her stable. She hangs back at the door. "Go on." I slap her rump and she barges in.

I lean over the door watching her eat. It's the only thing she seems to like these days, apart from being left alone in the field. When she's finished she starts chewing on the top of the half-door. I shout at her and she cowers and I feel terrible. Next minute she's biting it again anyway.

"She's going to teach Promise bad habits," Cam says, coming out of the stable next door.

"I'm sure Promise is too perfect to pick up bad habits," I say. I place the palm of my hand against Folly's neck. Her skin shudders, and I can feel her, tense and unhappy under my touch.

"She hates me," I tell Cam.

"Stop feeling sorry for yourself," Cam says. "You knew she wouldn't be easy. If you're not up to the challenge, get rid of her, but stop moping around the yard. You're putting people off."

"Thanks."

Cam leans over the door. Folly runs back when she sees her and takes up position in the far corner. "See?" I say. "She hates you too."

"Declan, that's rubbish. She's just nervous. You're stressing her out. She's picking up on your stress."

"*I'm* not stressed."

"Declan." Cam gives me one of her looks and leans

against the door in a way that makes me cop on to the fact that she wants to have A Chat. And suddenly it's no longer about Folly, which is uncomfortable enough; it's about me, which is worse. "Well, you're certainly … preoccupied," Cam goes on. "Oh come on, Declan, you know what I mean. You've lost your – I don't know – enthusiasm?"

I pick at a skelf of wood on the door of the stable. Hard to be enthusiastic about shovelling shit and washing brushes.

"Is it just Folly? Or the baby?"

"The baby? It's not the *baby*."

"You don't need to sound so defensive. And there's no point pretending the baby isn't happening. You can't keep running away from things."

"But it's *not*. Happening. I mean – I don't mean like Fiona's. Seaneen dumped me."

"Ah. Is that why …?"

"I don't mind. She'd rather do it on her own anyway."

Cam stares at me as if I'm mental. "She *wants* to do it on her own?"

"Yeah. She knows I'm not interested. I *tried* to be, but …" I scratch the back of my neck. "It's OK, Cam. I'm still going to give her money. And the thing is, Seaneen *likes* babies. She knows how to look after them. She's very" – I search for the right word – "competent."

"*You* like horses. *You're* very competent. Doesn't mean you're coping with Folly on your own, does it?"

"It's not the same. Seaneen has *loads* of help. Her ma and all. God, even *my* ma, I think. I'd be about as much help as – as *Seaneen* would be with Folly." I give a wee laugh to show Cam how ridiculous this would be. "Anyway." I want to kill this subject stone dead. "I'm *not* worried about the baby. Just about Folly."

"Hmm. Whatever you say." Cam looks at her watch. "Gosh, I must go. Pippa'll think I'm not coming."

I put Folly's headcollar on again and take her out of the stable. Promise looks over her door and nickers as we walk past, a few strands of haylage falling from her soft black mouth. Folly's head goes straight to the ground and she snaffles it up.

As soon as I turn Folly out she races down to her pony friends and they go on one of their mad charges around the field for no reason, tails out like banners. Just running for fun.

Cam's wrong. I'm not running away from the baby. I never have. Seaneen's running *with* the baby, away from me.

And I could run too.

Just go. Anywhere. Middleham. Why not? I can write to Cam when I get there, apologize, say I tried to tell her I was fed up but she wouldn't listen.

Cycling home I have one of those debates with myself.
So you'd just abandon Folly? Like the last person who had her?

No. It wouldn't be like that at all. I could send Cam the money for her keep.

Cam charges eighty pounds a week for full livery. Where are you going to get that? As well as support a baby? You going to go through your whole life taking things on and then dumping them?

Cam would sell her. Like Libby.

But nobody will buy *a horse like Folly. Only*

254

Grounded

McCluskey and the cat-food factory.

This is a stupid conversation. I'm not really going. It's just a fantasy because I feel so grounded and stuck.

But it's what Seaneen wants, *remember?*

No. It would just be running away.

And then another voice echoes in my head. *I don't walk. I hide.* And out of the fog that's clouded my brain since I got the knock on the head come two boys walking up the road, one of them turning around to look back up the hill.

Walking, running away, hiding – whatever you call it, it's the same thing.

And I know where Cian is.

VI. FINDING

I.

I don't want to go back there. The closer I get, the slower the wheels go around and the more I think I'm kidding myself anyway. I could phone the police or Stacey or Mum. It doesn't have to be me who goes in and finds him.

Only what if I'm wrong? I'm going to look pretty stupid when the police burst in and find the place empty, or if I go and see Stacey and Cian's at home on his own sofa eating chips.

But I can't pretend it's out of my way. Now that I've had the idea I can't just cycle past without checking. If it hadn't been for me, Cian wouldn't even have known the place existed.

Nearly there. Here's the truck yard.

There's something else too. If he is there, if he's been hiding out for the last three days, it's because he's scared. He's in trouble with everybody. And I know what that feels like. Maybe I can talk to him, make him see that he needs to face up to stuff, not hide from it. He's got off to a bad start here, but if someone helped him get McCann off his back and helped him to stop taking drugs, maybe even got him interested in something – the boxing club, or football, or ... I don't know, just *something* – then he'd be OK. And I know for everything I've said about him being nothing to do with me and nothing like me, that it's not really true.

I think these positive thoughts to push away the memories of the barn. But no matter how hard I try I can't stop thinking of the dead mare and the foal and, worst of all somehow, even though she's still alive, Folly, my own ghost horse, tucked in the corner by the wooden pallets, her thin cries cutting through the night. How many times did I cycle past and not hear those calls? If I'd rescued her before I did, would she have been less traumatized? Would I be less wary about coming back here if I could be confident Folly's story was going to have a happier ending?

But I *did* rescue her. I did my best.

And look at her now. She hates you, and you're going to run away and leave her, aren't you?

I'm at the gate now. It's still tied with different colours of baler twine. It doesn't look like it's been disturbed.

Yeah, but he could have climbed over.

I throw the bike into the hedge, making sure it's hidden. The last thing I need is for some joker to come past and nick it and leave me to walk home. I'm going to look stupid enough when there's nobody here.

The field is rutted and scrubby, wetter than it was in June. The same beds and old tires – at least I suppose they're the same – slump beside the hedge, like monsters in the dusk. The house looms up quicker than I expect it, its smashed windows like broken teeth.

I'll try it first. The house isn't the barn, and chances are it's where he'll be if he's here at all. After all, both buildings are derelict and crappy, but surely a house would be a better hideout than a barn?

I sneak around the house and look in some of the windows but it's too dark to see in. The back door's boarded up with old bits of wood. It's obvious that nobody's been through it in years. The front door's closed but the lock's broken. When I push, it resists, because it's so swollen with damp, but it opens.

Inside the chill hits me like opening a freezer. Stairs rise straight up from the small front hall. There's a door at each side of the hall, both open. I look into the first room. It smells of mice. I wish I'd a flashlight or something. I use my phone to make a feeble light, just enough to show that the room is empty.

I don't know if I should shout. Do I want to scare him off? Not that he'd get too far. He'd have to run past me to get out. Anyway, it's not me he's scared of. He might even be glad to hear a familiar voice. If I'd thought in advance I could have brought some food, shown him I wanted to help, not just turn him in. And it's not like he's done anything *criminal*. If we get McCann off his back, all the rest of it can be sorted. Maybe he could even stay with us for a bit, give Stacey a break, give Mum someone to fuss over.

"Cian?" My voice echoes in the empty room. "Cian? It's Declan."

Nothing. The house feels even emptier when the echo dies.

I go back into the hall and try the door on the right. This room has a bigger window and the moon lets me see a pile of beer cans in front of the fireplace. The stench of old piss makes me screw up my nose. I remember the policeman saying kids had been using the place as a drinking den and toilet.

I don't want to go upstairs. I know this is a wild goose chase. But I might as well do the thing right. And when I go home I'll tell Stacey what Cian said about hiding. Mum said the police had drawn a blank with his mates in Portadown, but what about his hiding places there? Where was it he'd said? An old house? I hadn't believed him but I think I do now.

"Cian?" I shout again. "Are you up there? It's OK. I want to help you."

My voice sounds ridiculous in the empty house. I feel like I'm in a really bad film. The naive teenager in the haunted house. Where the next frame has the gang leader standing at the top of the stairs with a gun, laughing.

Only there is no gang leader, just an even more naive teenager who needs his head seen to. Or maybe nobody.

Anyway, I've come this far. My eyes are getting used to the dark, and there'll be moonlight in the bedroom windows to help me see. The worst danger is probably from the rotten wood of the stairs. I test the first few. It's so damp my feet sink into the carpet like it's moss. A couple of them creak but I get to the top safely. The biscuity smell of mice is stronger here, and when I open the first door there's a scuffle. My toes clench inside my boots. Two years of hanging around stables has made me pretty cool about mice but I don't fancy them running over my feet. Anyway, he isn't here. Nobody could stay for three days somewhere so crawling with mice.

OK, it was a stupid idea, but at least I tried.

Outside feels warm and quite light compared to the gloom of the house. But the looming, corrugated-iron barn makes me shiver. I've thought about it so many times in the last few months, even though I've tried so hard not to.

I don't *have* to go inside.

You've come this far. What if he's hiding there and you miss him?

I *can't* go in.

Don't be daft. Maybe if you did ... it can't be as bad as you remember. Nothing could be as bad as the dead horse and the dying foal, and your poor, angry, ghostly Folly.

Ghosts is right. What if they're haunting the place?

No. The place is haunting you. You and *Folly. If you go in now, just look at the barn, maybe it will help you understand her.*

It's not about Cian now; it's all about Folly.

The rope that tied up the barn door is gone, and it slides open easily.

The barn is even darker than the house because there are no windows. No wonder Folly's eyes are so sensitive. But as I slide the double doors further apart the moon shines in behind me and starts to show me the scene I've been flashing back to all these months.

Only different. The same reek of death – but is that my imagination because I know what happened here? The straw's been roughly cleared out – I suppose the police or environmental health or somebody cleared it out when they came back for the mare's body. It's just an empty barn now. In the corner where Folly stood the wall's all battered, as if she stood there and kicked it. In the other corner is the pile of wooden pallets.

I force myself to look. And remember. And it doesn't make me feel any better at all. It makes me ashamed that Folly came from here and I wouldn't let myself think about what that meant, about how traumatized she must be. It was too horrible to think about where she'd come from, so I cared too much about where I wanted her to go and what I wanted her to be.

Look. Stay. I know you want to jump on your bike and cycle home and never think about this place again but you must see it for what it was.

I make myself walk right in.

I force myself to go over and look at the wooden pallets, as if seeing Folly's teeth marks on them will make some kind of difference.

Something bigger than a mouse scuttles over my foot and I jump and shiver. And that sense of being in a film takes over again. Only it's turning into a horror film.

And then something – a sense of movement, of something swinging – makes me look up.

And see Cian. Because he was here all along. I just didn't notice because he's high above me, hanging from the beam.

2.

It's not real. It's a game – I always knew he was a nutter.

And this has happened to me before – when I went in that morning three years ago and found Mum lying in bed with a bottle of pills beside her. I was sure she was dead but she wasn't. And Cian can't be. He's fifteen. He can't be dead.

But I'm kidding myself. The way his body's hanging and especially the way his head lolls, swollen and purple, with his eyes staring and popping – of course he's dead. Dead but not *real*. It's still like a film. It's not the kind of thing that happens in real life.

I fumble in my pocket for my phone. That's when I realize how much I'm shaking. My fingers slip on the screen but I manage to hit the nine three times and tell them what's happened and where.

And saying it – *I've found a body. A boy has hanged himself. I know who he is* – makes it real.

When we found the horses I could hardly bear to stay inside in the barn, but now I feel I can't leave Cian alone. I feel as if I should touch him, even though I can't bear to, but he's so high up – he must have climbed up the pallets – that all I can reach is his foot. But I can't bring myself to touch it. His trainers are laced up properly. It seems incredible that he can be hanging there, dead, and his trainers stay on.

It's just a body; it's not really him.

But it *is* him. The face is distorted but it's Cian's face and his red hair falls over his forehead in the same way it did when he was alive. I wish I could cut him down – there's something grotesque about him dangling there – but I wouldn't know where to start, and anyway, I know I shouldn't mess with anything. It would be different if there was any chance of resuscitation, if it had just happened, but even though I'm not an expert on corpses I can see there's no chance of that.

I need to phone Mum; she could tell Stacey, before the police get there. I can't remember now what I said to the police. I didn't know his surname but I told them where he lived. They'll have gone around there. And then come here? Or maybe a different lot will come here?

Thinking about procedure, wondering what happens, keeps me just about sane while I'm waiting. I phone Mum but it rings and rings and then goes to voicemail. I listen to her voice and then to the sound of my own breathing, and there isn't anything I can say so I hang up.

And then everybody arrives – police, ambulance – and it's not just me and Cian any more.

A blonde policewoman leads me away from Cian and asks me questions. I feel as if I've been in the barn for hours but when I check my watch it's only been ten minutes since I phoned. She keeps asking if I'm OK.

"*I'm* OK, I'm not the one that's … Does his mum know?" I ask. "Did I give you the right address? I can never remember what number it is but it's straight across the street from number thirteen." I don't know why I'm babbling so much.

"Yes, another car has gone there. Don't worry, you've done a great job."

I haven't *done* anything except make a phone call.

"Do you know how long … when he … how dead he is?" This hasn't come out right but she knows what I mean.

"Not offhand, no. But a day or so, probably."

"If I'd thought – I only remembered today that he might have come here. I came as soon as I could. But if I'd remembered sooner …" My hand flies up to cover my mouth. I don't want to look behind me at what they're doing to the body but at the same time I can't not look. He's on the ground now, his head still at that weird angle.

The sound of an engine breaks into the night and another police car comes into the yard. Stacey gets out and a policewoman half-carries her past me. Stacey looks tiny. She isn't crying, but she's whimpering the way Madison was when she hurt herself. She doesn't seem to see me. "Come on," the woman keeps saying to her, "I'll be with you. I won't leave you."

A moment later there's a scream and then Stacey loses it completely, wailing over and over and over, "Oh, my baby, my baby, my baby!"

My stomach lurches and I have to dash to the doorway and breathe the fresh air, but the wild shouts follow me. I hug myself to try and stop the shivering. Behind me in the barn are professional people doing what they do and yet nothing seems to be really happening.

My policewoman comes out and finds me again. "Poor woman's demented. Not surprising. Nobody wants to believe their child could die, and especially not like that."

"He'd been missing," I tell her. "They were looking for him, but … he's only fifteen. He was in trouble with his mum and school and – well, I think he owed somebody money. I'm sorry, I'm talking too much, aren't I?"

"That's OK."

"How long does all that" – I gesture towards the barn –"take?"

"It depends. He's been pronounced dead. We have to wait for the mortuary to come and take the body away. There's procedure. It all takes time."

"I want to go home."

"You can, as soon as we've taken down some details."

Suddenly Stacey appears in front of me. Her face is wild with shock. "How did you know?" she screams. "How did you know he was here?" She starts beating at me with her fists.

"I didn't! I only – tonight, I suddenly thought of it. I knew it was empty. He once told me he … he liked hiding out in places. I came the minute I thought of it." *You* didn't even phone the police, I think, but I don't say it. Someone takes her away. The blonde policewoman tells me not to worry, it's not my fault, people just strike out at the nearest person and I mustn't take it personally.

I feel tireder than I ever have in my life and, even though I'm surrounded by people, absolutely alone.

I don't want this kind, patronizing middle-aged woman who doesn't know me telling me what I'm feeling.

I'm freezing. I hug myself really tightly. I want Seaneen. And at the same time I'm glad she's not here, that she doesn't have that image of Cian's hanging body seared on her brain the way it is on mine.

* * *

Mum comes out of Stacey's house as I'm taking my bike out of the back of the police car. "Oh, love," she says. "What a terrible ..."

I set my bike down on the ground. "I'm OK," I say before she starts into one of her fusses.

Mum folds her arms and looks in the car window. "I'm sitting with the wee girls," she says to the blonde policewoman. "Her other kids. She hasn't really got anybody else. But if there's anything I can do ..."

"Someone will be around to see her tomorrow. And if you could give her this number – it's a support service for people who've been bereaved by suicide. Most people find it very helpful."

Mum takes the card. "You don't believe it could happen to someone you know, do you?" she says and the policewoman shakes her head.

I stand in the street for a moment while Mum finishes talking to the policewoman. As soon as she does she comes over and tries to hug me, a bit clumsily since I've got one hand on the seat of my bike. "That must have been a terrible thing for you to find," she says.

"I'm tired, Mum, I just want to go to bed."

"I have to stay at Stacey's. The girls were in bed

when the police came – they don't even know. I can't leave them."

"I know. I'll be fine."

"You can't go in on your own! Not after a shock like that. Come on into Stacey's and let me make you a cup of tea."

"No." I can't go in there. I turn and go into my own house. I'm too tired to go around the back with the bike. I just prop it up against the front wall. If anybody steals it, too bad.

I sit in the living room and try to warm up but the trembling inside won't stop. I make tea but as soon as it hits the back of my throat I gag. I turn on the TV but all I can see is Cian hanging.

And I know that's all I'm going to see all night, and for God knows how long.

3.

Usual round of Saturday brats. Somebody gets bucked off and howls. Get over yourself, I think, opening the gate of the school for the end of the eleven o'clock ride. The shivering hasn't stopped and all I've had to eat all morning is paracetamol.

Cam sighs as she passes me. "Gosh," she says in a low voice. "They don't get any better. Some of them really should give up." She laughs. "Only I hope they don't. Go after them and make sure they run their stirrups up properly."

I catch up with the line of ponies making their way to yard. The ponies shake their heads and look bored. Their riders squeal and pull at their reins.

"Stop that," I say to Casper. "Would you like somebody pulling at your mouth that way?"

Unfortunately I say it just as we're going past Casper's mum. Her fish face gulps in horror. "Look, I have to tell him the same thing every week," I say. "If he's that stupid he shouldn't be here. He's too fat for our ponies anyway."

I busy myself checking on the ponies, and ignore the sight of Fish Face striding off to the barn, clearly looking for Cam.

I take the wheelbarrow into the school to clean up any poos before the next lesson. From the school I can see that Folly's fine. I should go and check her properly – I'll get half an hour for lunch when I've done this so I can do it then. Lara rides into the school on Promise, the mare shining like ebony in the autumn sun.

"There's a ride at half twelve," I say.

"So? I'm only going to warm her up and then we're going on the farm trail. She's fantastic at the cross country jumps. But then, she did cost seven thousand."

"Well, *you* wouldn't be fit to ride anything that didn't, would you, Lara?" I can see her working out what that's supposed to mean.

I empty the wheelbarrow on to the dung heap. It seems to take a long, long time.

"Declan!" Cam bears down on me, her face pink with rage, clashing with her red hair. It makes me think of Cian, his red hair, only his face was purple. How can a face go purple? Was it blood, or …

"…can't believe you'd be so bad-mannered! To a customer! I know he's annoying but as I keep saying, that's what pays your wages. Lara's just complained that you've been rude to her – *and* you've put Magic's saddle on Bella – no wonder she bucked! What the hell is wrong with you?"

I shake my head.

"I know you've been in a funny mood recently but this – do you actually *want* this job?"

I look into the wheelbarrow. It's smeared with traces of wet dung.

"Declan. Would you look at me?"

I look up at her and then down at the wheelbarrow. "Sorry," I say and then the wheelbarrow disappears in a blur of tears. I look at my hands on the handles and they're shaking uncontrollably. I can hear the shouts of the brats saying goodbye to each other, and the ponies shifting their hooves in their stables.

"Declan? Are you ill?"

I find some kind of a voice. "No. I – something happened. I found – there was this boy …"

She pulls my hands off the wheelbarrow handles since I don't seem to be able to do it myself. "Come into the house."

"You have a lesson."

"Not just yet."

She makes me come into her kitchen and sit down. She makes me a cup of coffee. I shake my head. "I won't be able to drink it," I say.

"Yes, you will. Now tell me what happened."

So I do. Her face stiffens with horror. "Oh good God. And you – this was a friend of yours?"

"Not a friend. I didn't even like him. But – if I'd found him sooner …"

The tears pour down my face and I'm too tired to wipe them away. I've never cried in front of Cam. She pats my arm from time to time, awkwardly, and says, "I'll ask Pippa to take you home. You can't be around horses in this state, never mind customers."

"No! I can't go home. It's all everybody's going to be talking about. Please Cam, don't send me home. I promise I won't be rude to anybody else."

"You're not fit for work. Did you get any sleep last night?"

I shake my head.

"If you won't go home, at least go and rest in the living room."

"But it's Saturday. You're really busy."

"I'll be OK. I'd like to keep the customers I have." She smiles to show that she's trying to make a joke. "Go on. Take your coffee."

I don't remember being in Cam's living room before. It's shabby and cozy, and as soon as I see the big squashy sofa all thoughts of going back into the yard leave me. The door opens and Spick and Span skitter in, their tiny claws scraping the wooden floor. "Thought you'd like the company," Cam calls in. "I'll see you later."

I know I won't sleep, and I don't even want to close my eyes because that's when I see the hanging body worst of all, but I curl up on the sofa anyway, turn on the horse channel and watch some showjumping from America. Spick and Span bicker to get in the crook of my legs and in the end they both squeeze in and I start to warm up for the first time since last night.

When I open my eyes the room's dusky and the dogs have gone. My head feels thick and my legs are cramped from lying on the sofa.

"Declan?" Cam comes in and sets a tray on the coffee table. Two cups of tea and a plate of toast. Cam sits down with a sigh and stretches out her long legs. Her usually clean jodhpurs are streaked with dirt.

"Oh God – did you have to do everything yourself?"

"Lara helped. Sally's feeding now."

"You didn't tell them?"

"I said you weren't well."

"I'm OK. I just keep remembering …"

"I know." She twirls her mug in her hand. "It's not the same thing, but … I had to identify my parents' bodies when they were killed."

I shudder. "That's far worse."

"Different. And that was just a terrible accident. What you saw – I can't even imagine that."

"It was the shock," I say. "And it's the kind of thing – I mean you see it on TV, don't you, but when it's real … He looked so *ugly*. And so – so dead. And he did it himself. That's the worst thing." I sip my tea. Try to focus on the warmth of the mug in my hands.

"Why do you think he did it?"

"I don't know. Half the time I saw him he was high on something. Drink, glue, drugs. I think he'd have taken anything."

"Which probably didn't do his mental state any good."

"He had all this crap going on – but it could have got sorted out. I wanted to tell him, it gets better – stuff – if you face up to it." I feel stupid saying this. "And one time – he had these marks on his arms. And I thought it was his mum's boyfriend, but now I wonder if he was hurting himself." I chew on a piece of toast though it feels and tastes like sawdust. For once I don't seem to be able to stop the words spewing out. "I just – I knew he was in trouble. But *that* – it's so permanent. Sorry. You don't need to hear all this."

"Don't be daft. It's better to talk about it. He probably didn't think about it being permanent. Just about wanting everything to stop."

"Yeah. There was something kind of desperate about him. Like there was something missing. Like Folly. Oh God, I'm just talking shit. I'm sorry." I look into my cup.

"Look, Declan, I know you won't be able to get the picture out of your head for a while. But it will go away eventually. I'll keep you busy here, give you plenty to think about."

"If I still have a job?"

"Don't be stupid. Now eat that toast and I'll give you a lift home. I've already put your bike in the jeep."

★ ★ ★

After this I can hold it together at work. It helps that Cam knows. She doesn't make any comment when I'm late the next day because I have to go and give a statement to the police, and she lets me take Spirit out on the farm trail. She makes me go with Lara, but at least I'm on horseback again, and Spirit and Promise go really well together, cantering easily up the long ride.

But for some reason I can't go near Folly. I'm scared she'll smell the barn off me or something – I know that's stupid, but I keep getting to the gate of the field and not being able to go any further.

Mum minds the girls a lot. They've been told their brother had an accident and died. They cry sometimes. I wonder how soon before they'll hear the true story in the street. It's all everybody's talking about, even people who didn't know Cian – even people who didn't like him. Stacey's in bits. Her doctor gives her some kind of zombie pills to get her through the first few days. Mum makes her an appointment at the suicide charity. The local paper reports on TRAGIC SUICIDE TEEN.

I keep waking up in the night. Usually from dreams about the barn, but once I have a nice dream that Seaneen's here, and not pregnant or anything, and waking from that's even worse than waking from the bad ones.

There'll be an inquest – not for ages, but that doesn't stop there being a funeral. Mum offered to stay at home with the kids but Stacey said she'd never get through it without Mum, and then Mairéad says she'll take them to the zoo with Saoirse and Tiarna for the day.

It's a lovely clear autumn day. We get to the chapel early, but it's already filling up, even though people don't really know the family. For family, it's just Stacey. There isn't anybody else. "She grew up in care, you know," Mum says. "She's had five foster families." None of the five foster families comes to the funeral as far as I can see. Neither does Darren. But all the neighbours come. It's as if they're saying, if we come to the funeral of *this* kid, it can't happen to *our* kids.

The coffin is already at the altar when we go in. It's draped in a Liverpool flag. I never even knew he liked football. I can't help wondering if he really did or if somebody thought it was the right thing to put on a teenager's coffin.

Mum goes on up to the front with Stacey. She holds her hand, but they don't look like lesbians. You can get away with that sort of thing at a funeral. I don't want to go up there – I don't want it to look as if I'm claiming he was my best friend just because I found him. I sit near the back on my own. Last time I was in here was for Seaneen's granny's month's mind. Seaneen cried and held my hand.

A cluster of teachers from school come in. The headmaster and deputy and Mr. Dermott. Dermie nods when he sees me looking around. I nod back but I'm glad he's at the other side; I don't think I could talk to him.

"Hello." I look around at the voice. It's Vicky, her boyfriend Rory, and Colette. "What are you doing here?" I whisper. "You never knew him."

"Don't be stupid," Vicky says. "We've come for *you*."

That's nice, but it somehow makes me feel even lonelier. I let on to be praying so I don't have to make conversation.

Then I feel somebody slide in at my other side and I move up to make room. "Declan."

I open my eyes. "Seaneen." She looks enormous and tired.

"Isn't it terrible?"

"Yeah."

"I wish ..."

"Yeah."

I'm so aware of her beside me. She takes off her jacket and sets it down between us. She sees Vicky and Colette and leans across me to whisper hello. Her curls brush my cheeks. Her perfume's the same. Her eyes are swollen. She sits back down and rests her hand on her bump. She gives it a wee rub. It's the gesture I always found so annoying, but now I think it's kind of protective. And for the first time I think, that's my son in there. Not just a baby who's come along and wrecked my plans, but a human being. He won't always be a baby. He'll grow up. Like Cian. Like Folly. Not like Flame. Flame never had a chance. Cian – I don't know when it was too late for Cian.

I want to say all this to Seaneen. I turn to her but I can't speak. Her fingernails are bitten. I want to take her hand so much I have to flick through a missal to keep my own hands busy.

The music changes note and the priest walks in. "I thought youse were all at the zoo," I whisper to Seaneen. It's the only thing I can think of to say.

She bites her lip and shakes her head, and then the funeral starts.

4.

"Give my love to your mum," Colette says, hugging me. "I'm sorry she wouldn't come with us, but I understand she wants to support her friend."

"She'll be glad you came, though."

"Sure you don't want a lift on up the road?" The four of us have just spent the last hour having lunch in a café on the Falls Road. I tried to find Seaneen after the funeral, but Colette just grabbed me and said she was taking me out for lunch. Vicky and Rory talked about their trip and Vicky showed me some photos of Flight jumping at the National Championships, which should hurt but somehow didn't. He looked happy and successful.

"No, I'd like the exercise. Thanks."

They all pile into Colette's Golf and I wave them off.

It's a long enough walk home, but I'm glad of it. The only way I sleep, these nights, is to tire myself out. I feel strange, walking up the Falls Road in a suit. I probably look as if I've been in court. I loosen my tie.

Grounded

When I walk past my old school the kids are getting out, hanging around the gates, texting, going to the shop. It was nice of Dermie to come to the funeral. He can only have known Cian a few weeks. Or maybe he just got told to come, part of the job. No. The head and Mr. Payne, yeah, they're just doing their duty, but not Dermie. If it hadn't been for him, I'd never have gone to college; I'd never have been brave enough to ask Cam for another chance after I messed up by joyriding Flight. Dermie believed in me. Mum didn't, not then – she didn't even believe in herself – but Dermie did, and Colette.

And Seaneen. Those days when we'd sneak into my empty house when Mum was in rehab, we weren't only having sex. We talked about everything. She's the only person who's ever been able to get me to say much. Maybe that's why I miss her so much.

And maybe she doesn't miss me. But I wish I could tell her what I thought in the chapel this morning – that I see now that the baby's a real person. And I want to do more than just send money for him. That I don't know anything about being a dad but I do know that a kid needs as many people as possible to keep it grounded and safe, to help it believe in itself.

When I get to the estate I go straight around to Seaneen's street instead of turning into Tirconnell Parade. I've never been so anxious to get to her, not even at first when we couldn't keep our hands off each other. With any luck Granzilla will still be at the zoo. I look up at Seaneen's window. The curtains are shut and the light's on, which is a good sign.

But Granzilla opens the door. She looks as if she can't quite believe the sight of me in a suit instead of covered in mud and sweat, but it doesn't seem to make her like me any more.

"Yes?" she says as if I've come around the doors selling dodgy DVDs.

"Is Seaneen in?"

"Yes."

"Oh. Great." I hadn't expected it to be so easy.

"Is that all you wanted to know?" She makes to close the door.

"What?" Snarky bitch. "I mean, can I speak to her? Please?"

Granzilla shakes her head. "She doesn't want to see you."

"How do you know?"

She comes out and pulls the door closed behind her. She folds her arms. "She doesn't want to see you."

"Mairéad, give me five minutes. I only want to *talk* to her."

"She never wants to see you again."

"Since when?" I go to push past her but she blocks me.

"If you don't leave my house, I'm going to call the police."

"Ah, for Christ's sake, Mairéad." I've lost all sense of pride, so I throw back my head and yell up at the window, "Seaneen! Seaneen!"

The curtains don't even twitch.

Mairéad gives me a triumphant look. "Right? That's your answer. Now leave my house and my daughter alone. She'll contact you through the Child Support Agency and that's all."

And she goes back in and shuts the door in my face.

5.

I last for two minutes in my own house. Mum's left a note saying she's over the street. "I'm sorry not to be there for you more," she's scribbled. "I'll make it up to you."

I pull the curtains. It's nearly dark outside. In about a month it will be time to put the clocks back and then it really will be winter. One of the winter showjumping leagues starts tonight – Cam and Lara will be away at that, trying to get some points. Did I really think I'd be joining them on Folly? It seems so trivial now.

But thinking about Folly makes me ache to go and see her. I've lost Seaneen – and the baby – which I never thought I'd mind about as much as I do, and Folly's all there is now.

Even though I've messed it up with her and she hates me.

I run upstairs and pull off my suit and throw on my old yard clothes. It's stupid to be setting out at this time, but I'm in one of those moods, the kind of mood I tried to explain to Cian. I grab my bike, throw my leg over it and then remember to stop and put the lights on. Then I start cycling.

I can't cycle past the barn so I go the long way and it takes forever.

As I turn into Cam's road I know what I'm hoping for – that she won't have gone jumping, that she'll be there to talk to me. Or even somebody else. Maybe Sally will be there. It doesn't matter, just *somebody* to help me push away this loneliness.

But the yard's in darkness. The truck's not there and the house is dark. Pippa must have gone too, to support Cam. The barn is locked, but I have my keys. There aren't many horses in. Spirit and Promise's stables are empty of course. Joy looks up briefly from her haylage munching, then loses interest. Nudge comes over for a rub on the nose.

The sight and smell of them is comforting, because they're horses, but it's not enough.

I go back out, locking the door behind me. I try not to think about Cian letting himself into that other barn. Taking the rope from the door. He must have felt there was nobody.

I make my way across the yard, past the school and down the path to the fields. I trip over a stone, bang into the fence. There are a few nickers and snorts of surprise as the horses hear the gate unclick. It sounds louder in the dark.

I suppose those shadows at the bottom of the field must be Folly and the Welshies. I think of how stupid it would be to go down there in the dark and get kicked. She won't come near me anyway because I haven't brought any treats.

I call her, just in case there's going to be a miracle, but nothing happens.

I stand under the tree. The moon, which was full the night I found Cian, is still pretty big and it hangs low in the sky. Once my eyes get used to it I can see fairly well. Folly is standing with Mary, or possibly Midge, and they're grooming each other. They look like one animal, a strange two-arsed horse.

So this is it. I've ruined everything. I've lost Seaneen; I've lost the chance to be a proper father to the baby; I've lost Folly because I rushed her and abused the tiny bit of trust she had in me.

I put my hand on the trunk of the tree and feel how rough it is. One of the branches is covered in teeth marks from Folly's assaults on it. I think again of the wooden pallets in the barn, and then it's only a moment to the hanging body of Cian.

Stop it, stop it, you can't keep torturing yourself.

But if I'd listened more. If I'd taken him more seriously. Maybe even if I'd given him that money.

The tears that wouldn't come at the funeral are pushing up the back of my throat now and I hate myself for them because it's only self-pity, but I can't stop them. I rub my sleeve against my face but I just end up with a wet sleeve and a stinging face because it's a rough woolly jumper. The horse shapes at the bottom of the field have gone, melted away in the dark like the ghosts I once thought Folly was.

At the start of the summer I thought I was so clever, winning that trophy, getting that job – and what am I left with? Nothing. Just a mess.

"Declan."

I must be imagining the voice. There couldn't be anybody here at this time of night. Even if Cam came back from the show early she wouldn't come down to the field in the dark.

Then I feel a hand on my shoulder and I jump. I swing around.

"This is the first place I thought of," Seaneen says. I bury my head in her neck and hug her hard. She can't be real. I'd have heard her. But she feels real, and the tears on her face are wet, and her hair tickles my cheek in a very real way, and the bump pressing against me is solid and warm.

"How did you …?"

"Don't talk." She hugs me harder until we both pull away. I reach out and blot her tears with my finger. She does the same for me.

"How did you know I was here?" I ask.

"Where else were you going to be?"

"Your mum said you didn't want to see me. I came to your house but she said –"

"I know. I … I lay there and I heard you calling me and I wanted to get up and look out. I was going to, and then – I don't know, Declan. I didn't want it to be just because of … the funeral and all. Because ever since it happened I've wanted you …"

"Me too." Then I realize that's not the whole truth. "No – not just 'cause of Cian. I never wanted to lose you."

She chews her lip.

"Seaneen – about the baby …" I put my hand on her belly. It's hard but soft at the same time. I know if I leave my hand there long enough there'll be a movement. "I never ... you were right, I *was* running away. I thought because I stayed – because I *said* I was sticking by you – that I was doing the right thing, but I was only pretending. I never saw it – him – as real. Not a person, just a – well, a problem."

Her eyes are dark green in the moonlight. "He will be a problem," she says. "He'll be all kinds of problems. But that's not *all* he'll be."

"I want him to have two parents. I know I might be crap, but I want to try."

"You wanted to leave me. Go abroad."

"Not any more. Everything's different now."

She leans into me and for a moment I feel her breath soft on my cheek. "I don't want this just to be a knee-jerk reaction," she says.

"To Cian?"

She nods. "I can't stop thinking about him."

"I know. And you can't say that something good could come out of him killing himself. That'd be sick. But ..."

"So would it be better if *nothing* good came out of it?" she asks.

"It would be better if it hadn't happened."

"I know." We don't say anything for ages. Then Seaneen says, "I don't want to be a mum at nineteen. I'm *terrified*. What if he grows up like Cian, thinking life isn't worth living? What if *I* can't give him what he needs to be strong?" Fresh tears are running down her face but her voice is fierce.

"I know. That's what I feel. But I thought you ... I thought you secretly wanted a baby."

She shakes her head. "Not yet. But" – she shrugs –

"I'm going to have one, so ..."

"Will you let me help you? I don't mean just the money, or minding him sometimes – I mean, us, together, properly."

"Is that really what you want?"

"Yes. You're the one who dumped me, remember."

"I only said the words. You'd dumped me a long time ago."

"The baby. Not you."

"It doesn't work that way, Dec."

I nod. "I know. I've felt so crap. Not just Cian; before that. I missed you so much. I love you, Seaneen. And" – I feel stupid saying this, but I know I have to – "I'll do my best for the baby too."

She moves in and hugs me again, pulling me really close. We stay like that for a long time, until I think of something I have to say. "Seaneen – I couldn't live with your mum. I know she'll want to help you and everything, but ..."

"I know. Don't worry, that's not an option. And I couldn't live with Theresa – all that smoke."

"We'll get somewhere of our own."

"And now I've passed my test," Seaneen says with something like a smirk, "I don't need to be *that* near my mum." She laughs at my expression and suddenly looks like the Seaneen I've always loved – carefree and cheeky. "How do you think I got up here?"

Before I can answer I feel a dig in my back. "Ow, what was ..."

I turn around. It's Folly. Up close in the moonlight she shimmers like a silver horse. She backed off when I cried out but now she comes closer again, stretching out her neck and sniffing me.

"I haven't got anything for you," I whisper.

"Didn't you save her life?" Seaneen says. "That should be enough for her."

"No, that should have been enough for *me*," I tell her. I reach out my hand and rub it down Folly's neck. She nuzzles at me.

I look at Seaneen and realize she has no idea what a breakthrough this is. I also realize she is standing beside Folly.

"Are you OK, with Folly up close like this?"

Seaneen nods. She pets Folly and Folly lets her. "Yeah, I was just feeling insecure that day. Hormones or something. I've chilled out again."

"So's Folly. We've had – well, a bit of a rough time." I tell her all about how stupid I've been. "I tried to make her into something she's not. I ignored all the signs she was giving me. I thought … I thought I was going to have to have her put down, she seemed so vicious and angry." I bite my lip.

"She doesn't look vicious and angry now."

"I think because I just gave her time tonight."

"What does Doris say about it?"

"Doris? I haven't asked her."

"You can be awful stupid, Declan. And stubborn. Sure she's the obvious person to help you. Even I know that, and I'm supposed to know nothing about horses."

I kiss her. Her face is still damp with tears, but her mouth is as warm and soft as it always has been. Folly gets bored and starts to graze. She moves away, but slowly.

"If this was a film," Seaneen says, "she'd let us both climb on her now and ride into the sunset."

"Except it's dark."

"OK, into the moon, then, if you're going to be like that." She wrinkles her nose.

"This is enough for now." I slip my hand into hers and we walk back up the field, turning around every so often to watch Folly grazing in the moonlight.

THE END